The Knight
Against the Odds

Kate Sherwood

Copyright 2019 by Kate Sherwood

Published by Kate Sherwood

Cover Art by Aaron Anderson

Print ISBN #978-1-988752-21-1
ebook ISBN# 978-1-988752-22-8

Second Edition Issued 2019

CHAPTER ONE

ADAM CHALLONER wasn't a big fan of public speaking. He wasn't phobic about it, exactly, but it sure wasn't something he looked forward to. And now, with most of the continent huddled around their comms waiting to hear his words, with the room full of anxious partisans betting their lives on his ability to lead the way....

He looked across the desk, past the camera operators and the bright lights, past the holoprompter, the director, the crowd of familiar and unfamiliar faces, and he saw Remy. The man was standing just inside the doorway, off to the side, and he should have been unnoticeable. He was clearly *trying* to be unnoticeable, as if he was afraid someone was going to come along, realize that he shouldn't be there, and kick him out. But there was no way, ever, that Adam would be able to overlook Remy. Adam smiled, and Remy actually turned and looked behind himself before tentatively returning the expression. Adam gestured with his hand. *Come closer.*

Remy frowned in disbelief, pointed his chin at the crowd of observers, and shook his head emphatically. Adam had seen Remy stride with total confidence through rooms full of VIPs while he was wearing nothing but body paint and a few strategically placed feathers, and he was being shy *now*? It made no sense. Adam caught himself. It almost certainly made sense, to Remy. Adam just needed to figure out what Remy was thinking, and then he could do something about it.

"We're ready for you, Mr. Challoner," the director's assistant said with an encouraging, vaguely flirtatious smile.

Adam tried to drag his mind back to the business at hand. He couldn't be thinking about Remy all the time, not with so many people depending on him. He forced himself to look at the holoprompter, read over the first few words, and then nodded to the director. "Okay," he said. "Let's go."

"Quiet, please," the assistant said, and the room fell into silence. The red lights flashed on the multiple cameras, letting Adam know that they were recording his three-dimensional image for future holo displays. But most of the people he was speaking to would be watching on flat-screened comms, and he directed his attention to them, through the main camera in front of him.

"Fellow citizens of North America," he began, "I'm Acting President Adam Challoner. I apologize for the recent interruptions to your comm usage, and for any disruptions in your communities." Adam had seen the tapes, had seen some of the events in person. *Disruptions* was a weak, empty word to describe the riots and chaos that had erupted all over the continent.

But the team had been unanimous and clear. He was a leader, not a news broadcaster; he was delivering a message, not a report. So he was talking about disruptions, not pandemonium. "And fellow citizens of the Earth, our neighbors and friends, I apologize to you, as well. Our reorganization has affected your trade, your travel plans, and maybe even your sense of security." He paused, trying to remember what his advisors had told him about looking confident. "But I can assure you, it has all been worth it. At this point, former President Barrett has been formally removed from power, and the Congress and Senate have been temporarily dissolved. By removing the weak and corrupt, we have made room for the strong and honorable." The words sounded good, Adam knew, but he wasn't sure they *felt* quite right.

But he had no time to think about it right then. "More importantly," he said in his most serious voice, "we have seized the financial and physical assets of all North Americans, and are in the process of redistributing them more fairly. Citizens will notice a credit of twenty dollars a day being deposited to their government accounts. For some of you, this is dramatically less than you're used to living on; for the majority, it will be a significant improvement."

Adam paused to let the truth of that statement sink in. Then he continued with a slight smile. "This is the amount that we are absolutely confident we can sustain, long-term. We certainly hope to be able to provide more, as property is redistributed, but for now, we've been sure to give you enough to survive on. Further, the accounts of all landlords, mortgage holders, and other creditors have been frozen, so you are only responsible for your daily expenses." And now the part he didn't want to say, but couldn't find a way to avoid. "All real estate, all personal property valued at more than one thousand dollars, including all vehicles and aircraft, are now, *temporarily*, the property of the state. We will work to redistribute these items as quickly as we can, and we have already taken steps to establish a board to hear claims. In the meantime, though, these things are state property. Any theft, any looting, any vandalism or other deliberate damage, will be considered as a crime against the state, and violators will be subject to the full penalties allowed by law." God, it felt wrong, threatening the people he was trying to protect. He looked at the holoprompter, and then looked away. It wasn't the plan, but he needed to speak his own truth.

"We can't have anarchy. There's a government in place, and we're working hard and fast to sort things out. You haven't voted for me; you haven't voted for any of us. But we are committed to holding elections as soon as we can. And it wasn't like you'd voted for the previous government, either." Well, that hadn't really come out as well as he'd hoped. He tried to recover. "I know everyone feels unsettled, and I understand the temptation to take what you can, now, because you don't know if you'll ever have the chance again. But I'm asking you, as a fellow citizen, as someone who's risking everything he has to make this work: please. Work with us. Be part of this. I know it's hard to understand, hard to see the big picture, but I've got a pretty good view from where I'm standing, and trust me—it's beautiful. And it *will* work."

He felt strong enough to look back and find Remy. He was still in the shadows, but he was leaning forward, totally intent, and his energy and desperate belief beamed across the room straight into Adam's soul. Adam nodded at the camera. "It will work," he repeated, and now he smiled, for real. "It already *is* working. We have full control of the communication and economic infrastructure. We have full control of the military bases, and almost all military personnel. We are in the process of opening up diplomatic relations with foreign nations. We *are* the new government, and we will *remain* the government until we have things stabilized to the point that we are able to hold free, democratic, uncorrupted elections."

He looked over at the director, who frowned back at him. Apparently he didn't like Adam's modifications of the carefully planned script. Adam ran over the main points in his mind; he was pretty sure he'd covered everything important. "These are exciting, frightening times. The light of freedom, after too long in the dark, can be blinding. Please, give yourselves time to see the truth, and to understand that by working together we can create a new, just society."

And then, time for a little business. "We'll be keeping this channel for official government communications. Please check here to see what's open, what's closed, and what's expected of you as citizens. Please feel free to leave feedback. I give you my personal assurance that there will be no repercussions if you choose to criticize any aspect of what we're doing." He knew they wouldn't believe him, but at least he'd made the effort. "And please enjoy the entertainment programming that we're bringing back online as quickly as possible. Thank you for your time. Good night."

He kept his sincere face on until the red lights blinked off, then collapsed back into his chair. Morgan Winters, a lawyer before the revolution and now one of the top strategists on the council, was the first to approach. "Went a bit off the script there," Morgan said. His tone was carefully neutral, as was his smooth, handsome face.

"Yeah. I did." Adam wasn't sure he wanted to fight about this, but he wasn't sure he wanted to apologize about it, either.

"That shouldn't happen again," Morgan said, and this time, his voice was stern. "You were chosen to represent a *group* of people, all of whom expect to have a voice in the decisions made by your office. We decided to go with that script, not with your off-the-cuff remarks."

Adam was pretty sure Morgan was right, but his hackles still rose. "I'm the one talking. I didn't change any information, or say anything that wasn't supposed to be said. I just used my own words, to make it sound more natural, more like something I would say."

"But you're not speaking for yourself. You're speaking for all of us."

"You're right." Adam let Morgan celebrate his victory for a moment before saying, "I should have talked to you all about it beforehand. I should have told you I didn't like the words, and given the team a chance to come up with something we could all agree on." He tried his charming smile, the one that said he was harmless and possibly a little goofy. "I honestly didn't plan to change the words. They just came out that way." He stood up, then reached out and clapped Morgan on the shoulder. "We're all figuring this out as we go, Morgan. I think we're doing a good job, but you're right, there's room for improvement. I'll work on it."

And that was about as far as he was prepared to go. He was tired, and all he wanted was his bed, and Remy. But he had work to do: reports to receive, consultations to be part of, decisions to make. He hadn't been lying when he'd told the world that things were going well, but he hadn't really told them the whole truth, either. The situation was still fragile. The new government was far from stable, still feeling its way, and they couldn't afford to take any chances.

So Adam had a lot of work to do before he could finally allow Remy to lure him off for a few hours of rest, a short, blissful visit that would leave Adam far more invigorated than simple sleep ever would. Not that sleep wouldn't make up the lion's share of their time together. Adam still refused to touch Remy sexually. He still insisted that he wouldn't become just one more of the countless assholes who had used Remy's body without paying any attention to Remy's desires, or the lack thereof. But just sleep, with Remy, was more perfect and intimate than any sex Adam could recall.

He was head over heels, deeper in love than he had ever even dreamed of being; the timing was terrible, but he just couldn't make himself care. He looked over toward Remy, still standing by the doorway, and they exchanged tired smiles. Remy peered around the room almost furtively, then made his way toward Adam. He was close enough to touch when an aide bustled up and edged in front of him.

"Excuse me, Mr. Challoner," the young man said, "but there are visitors for you, downstairs. Two women." He lifted a small holograph machine and held it in front of Adam, clicking a button to create a three-dimensional image of the women in question. "They claim to be your wife and daughter?"

Adam stared at the holo, then back at the aide. "They're *here*?"

"Downstairs."

Adam wanted to roar in frustration. He had made sure his family was safely in Europe before all this began. But now, somehow, they were here. And Remy was hearing about them, like this.

"We're separated," Adam said quickly, but Remy's expression didn't change, and the aide's just became confused.

"Okay," the young man said uncertainly. "Would you like to see them, or...?"

Adam fought to make sense of it. "Did they say why they're here?"

"No, sir, they didn't seem to think they had to."

Of course they wouldn't. "Shit. Yeah, okay, can you show them into my office?"

"Of course, sir," the aide said, and he headed for the door.

"Remy," Adam started, and then he had no idea what to say next.

"Family complications," Remy said easily. "You haven't eaten yet. Should I ask the kitchen to send in dinner for three?"

"For four, if you'd like to join us," Adam said. He was a coward for making an invitation he knew Remy wouldn't accept. But this whole thing was a surreal nightmare; he was making dining arrangements while his wife and daughter had wandered into a war zone.

But Remy seemed to be taking it all in stride. "I'm sure you'll have a better visit with just family. I'll speak to the kitchen. Any dietary restrictions?"

"Kara—my daughter—she's vegetarian." Was he really having this conversation? "But you don't have to do that, Remy. You're not a waiter...."

"I'm happy to help," Remy said graciously.

Damn. Adam was still getting to know Remy, but he felt like he'd come a long way. He'd thought he was starting to understand him, and believed that he was able to see through the calm, controlled mask that Remy wore so often. But in this case, he honestly couldn't tell whether the man was upset or not. It seemed likely, but there was no sign of it. "If you don't mind," Adam said lamely. "I guess I do need to eat."

"Of course," Remy said, but when he smiled, it didn't reach his eyes. He gave a slight nod of his head, almost a bow, and backed up two steps before turning to go. A perfect servant, deferential and always ready to help. A perfect whore, not expecting to be part of Adam's life just because he shared Adam's bed. Adam wanted to go after him, to grab his arm and pull him into a quiet alcove. Then, Adam could explain about the wife and daughter he'd never mentioned and tell Remy how important he was— but Remy was already gone, and Adam had other challenges. He needed things to slow down, and stop happening all at once. He wondered how long he could spend on a desert island with just Remy before he started wanting a change. He bet it would be a long, long time.

But this wasn't a desert island, and there were a lot of people other than Remy who needed Adam's time. Starting with his estranged wife and nineteen-year-old daughter. What the hell were they doing there? Adam needed to get this sorted out, and then he needed to get Antonia and Kara back to Europe, and out of harm's way. That was his first priority; sorting things out with Remy could wait.

"You look tired, darling." Antonia's Italian accent was as subtle and musical as it had always been, but Adam's blood no longer surged toward her when he heard it.

"I'm in the middle of a *revolution*, Antonia. What the hell are you two doing here? How did you even get into the country?"

"Daddy," Kara said, her voice gentle as she stepped toward him and worked into his embrace. "It's good to see you."

Adam let himself savor a quick, sincere hug before he stepped back and held her at arm's length with a gentle shake. "But what the hell are you doing here? This is dangerous, Kara."

"We're here to help," Kara said. Her hair was as dark as both of her parents', her skin as pale, but her eyes were her own, moss green and sad-looking whenever she wasn't smiling. Fortunately, she smiled most of the time. "You should have told us what you were involved in. We could have helped sooner!"

"Damn it, Kara, this isn't a game. It's not a fun story to tell your friends at school!" But Kara wasn't the one Adam was really angry at, and he turned to Antonia. "What the hell are you doing, bringing her here? You're supposed to be taking care of her, not dragging her into war zones." He didn't want to frighten his daughter, but he was pretty damn sure he wanted to scare his wife. "If this doesn't work, we're facing execution. We'll be *lucky* if we die quickly, because if they take us alive, we'll be tortured to death. Do you honestly not understand that?"

"Yes, Adam, I understand." As always, Antonia got colder as Adam got hotter. "And I tried to persuade your nineteen-year-old daughter, who is able to make her own travel arrangements, not to come. But she was stubborn, as I'm sure you understand. She insisted on being here, and I came along to try to keep her safe."

"To keep her safe? What the hell are you going to do, Toni? How are you going to protect her here?"

"Any way I can, Adam. Just as I know you will." Antonia's quiet dignity made Adam feel like a child having a tantrum.

So he turned away from her. He looked at his beautiful, impulsive daughter and said, "You can't be here. I don't know how you traveled with the airports closed, but however you managed it, you can manage it in reverse. It's not safe here." He saw her chin rising, the gesture of stubborn defiance she'd been perfecting since she was a toddler, and he took a quick step forward and caught both of her hands in his. "Things are going well, Kara. We have a chance of actually pulling this off. A good chance. But everything's in a careful balance, and I don't want to upset that. I don't want to be distracted, worrying about you and your mother, when I should be spending all my attention on this."

"I can help. I speak six languages—that could be useful. *Mom* can help even more—you know that. She's got her PhD in economics, Daddy. You need an economist."

"This movement wasn't something we put together in a basement somewhere, you know. I came late to the party but people have been planning this for *years*. Smart people." People who would have been better leaders than Adam, probably, but who, for one reason or another, hadn't been suitable. "We *have* economists. We have translators." He wanted to keep going, wanted to point out that they had security guards and military police who would be happy to politely but firmly escort unwanted visitors out of the country. But everything would be much easier if he could persuade Kara to leave of her own accord.

The comm by the door buzzed. Too early for dinner, surely; Remy was good at making things happen, but he'd barely have had time to get to the kitchen. "Enter," Adam said, and the door slid open to reveal Morgan's smiling face.

"I heard we have some guests of honor," Morgan said with a charming half bow. "Mrs. Challoner? Ms. Challoner? I'm Morgan Winters, Chief Political Officer of the Provisional Government. It's a pleasure to meet you both."

He extended his hand as he crossed the room, and Antonia took it. "Dr. Antonia De Luca," she corrected. "In Europe, we don't view women as possessions of men." But her smile was smooth and easy, and she brought Kara forward for a handshake without hesitation. "But we gave Kara her father's surname. The hyphenate was a little much."

Morgan barely slowed down. "Of course. My apologies. With so many similarities between our nations, I forget the little differences." His smile was still just as charming as Antonia's. "Not that I think our naming conventions necessarily mean that North Americans 'view women as possessions of men'."

"Of course not. The naming is just one indicator." Antonia rested her hand almost possessively on Adam's arm and tilted her head in his direction. "I certainly hope that one of the first goals of your new government will involve addressing the status of women in this country."

"It's on the list, Toni," Adam said. He'd heard Antonia's lectures on the topic many times before and absolutely believed she was right, but things weren't as simple in reality as they were in theoretical conversations. Adam needed to get back in control of this conversation. "Morgan, I'm glad you're here. I'm hoping that Antonia and Kara will be joining me for dinner, and then I'm hoping we'll be arranging safe travel for them back to Europe. Can you look into that for me?"

"Leaving so soon?" Morgan's disappointment seemed genuine, if a little overdone. "That's truly unfortunate. The family image, the stability it conveys... that could be truly beneficial for us. Right now, the people *want* to trust you, but they don't feel that they know you. A First Lady and a presidential family would go a long way toward humanizing your persona."

"'Humanizing my persona'?" Adam didn't like the sound of that. "Interesting idea, but my wife has a doctorate in economics and my daughter speaks six languages. I'm sure they aren't interested in being used as mere symbols, feminine window dressing for a male display." He refused to let himself look at Toni, as tempted as he was.

"But things here are in a careful balance, and you don't want to upset it," Kara said quickly. "You want to make sure people trust you, so you can keep doing all your important work." She smiled. "We can talk about that over dinner, but I think Mom and I could *definitely* contribute. You don't need a translator or an economist, but apparently you need a family." She held her arms out as if presenting herself for admiration. "Ta-da! Here we are!"

"No," Adam said. He couldn't even begin to count the ways that this was a terrible idea. "No," he said again.

"Will you join us for dinner, Mr. Winters?" Kara asked with a charming smile. "I'd really like to hear more of your ideas."

"Well, I don't want to intrude on a family reunion. But I *do* have some suggestions on how we can make this work for us."

"You won't be intruding at all," Kara assured him, and she linked her arm through his before looking at her father. "You can make arrangements, right? There's room for one more?"

It was absurd. Adam thought he had a chance of controlling a whole damned country? He couldn't even make his own family do the smart thing. "For dinner, fine. But you can't stay here, Kara. It's not safe."

"Let's discuss it over dinner," she said. Her smile was confident.

Damn it. He'd spent his whole life protecting her from cruelty and teaching her that anything was possible. Now, she was loose in a world that was full of evil and impossibilities, and she was too naïve to understand it. He wanted to preserve her innocence, but not at the expense of her safety. He looked over at Toni, who looked warily back at him, then nodded. Truce. They were both parents, and they'd both do whatever they could to protect their daughter. Adam thought of the reports that were starting to be uncovered, the true depths of the sadistic horrors perpetrated during the previous regime, and his stomach tightened as he thought of any of that getting anywhere close to his baby girl. Innocence be damned; he'd do whatever it took to get her out of the country.

Chapter Two

"It was *very* exciting," Kara said, her eyes wide as if she were reliving the event rather than just remembering it. "We flew so low we could see people's faces as we passed them. Not that we saw many people, of course. The pilot was excellent—he chose a very remote path for us."

"Is this a possible security concern?" Adam looked at Morgan. "Why didn't our systems pick up on that?"

"I'll look into it," Morgan said. "But I know that we're having some trouble sorting through the different surveillance systems. In the cities, with the population density, there are distinct networks for private surveillance, public surveillance, and military surveillance. In the more remote areas, I believe that all three ran on the same network. Shutting down the private surveillance tools may have interfered with the military sensors, as well. It's one more argument for putting the private surveillance back online."

"No," Adam said firmly. "The people will never trust us if they see that we don't trust them. The cameras need to stay off."

"The red lights need to stay off," Morgan amended. "We can't *advertise* that we're watching people, can't use the cameras as threats to keep them in line. But I'm sure our brilliant engineers could find a way to activate the cameras without turning the red lights on."

"To what end? 'Cause I'm sure our brilliant engineers can *also* find a way to get the military sensors online without reactivating any cameras." Adam tried to keep his voice level. "The cameras are a huge part of what we're fighting *against*. Totalitarian control, constant surveillance... there's no point to any of this if we're just as bad as the people we replaced."

"That's a little dramatic, Adam," Morgan said, and then he turned toward Kara and Antonia. "I didn't meet Adam until after the revolution. Our identities were closely guarded secrets in order to protect everyone in case of capture. And when I finally *did* meet him, I was amazed by how mild-mannered and unambitious he is. You can't imagine Adam being a dictator, can you, ladies?"

Kara snorted. "Actually, yes, I *can*. Let me tell you a few stories about growing up in his household!" Her smile was warm, her eyes dancing, and Adam felt a surge of love so strong it almost made him ill. She was *his*, damn it. His joy, but also his burden. He'd stayed in an unsatisfying marriage for years longer than he should have, lived a good chunk of his life in Europe because it was a better place for Kara to grow up, done everything he could to protect her, and he would *not* allow all that to be for nothing.

He took a steadying sip of wine and made his voice serious. "Get ready for a little more dictatorship, Kara, because I *need* you to get out of the country. We'll find a safe way for you to travel, but you can't stay here."

Kara shook her head emphatically. "If it's safe enough for you, and for the hundreds of millions of people who live here, why on Earth would *I* need to run?"

"It's *not* safe enough for the people who live here! But they don't have a choice. You do."

"That's right, *my* choice. Just like you've made *your* choice."

"This is my country, Kara. I know you don't think of it that way, but I grew up here. I live here now. These are my people, and I've neglected that responsibility for too long."

"So, what, this is some patriarchal *noblesse oblige* trip you're on?

No one else can take care of the poor, stupid peasants, it has to be you."

"More like *humanité oblige*. It's not something I have to do because I'm special, it's something I have to do because I'm *not*. I'm just the same as everyone else, and it makes no sense that I should be able to walk away when they can't."

"But why doesn't that argument apply to me too?" Kara wasn't fighting, really. She was asking a genuine question. Fortunately, it was one for which Adam had a genuine answer.

"Because you're European. You're mother insisted on you being raised there, but she didn't have to fight me very hard. She wanted to keep you away from nonsense like this. You aren't running away, you're just going home."

Kara nodded slowly, and for one short, glorious moment Adam was sure that she was convinced. But then she smiled almost sadly and said, "But being European doesn't remove me from humanity. So if being a member of the human race gives you an obligation, it gives me one, as well."

"I agree," Toni said.

Adam swiveled his head toward her. "You *what*?" He tried not to let the feelings of betrayal into his voice, but he didn't shy away from expressing his amazement.

"I agree." As always, Antonia was calm. "We *do* have an obligation to help. But, Kara, we can do that just as well, if not better, at home. We can lobby our government to support the movement, and we can make sure that people understand what's happening, and how important it is."

"It would be a great way for you to use your gift for languages," Adam agreed quickly.

But Kara didn't seem convinced. "So I stay over there, clean and safe, and I expect people to believe what I say? Why? I mean, when they see who my father is, they'll think I'm just a shill. If I stay here, and work, it'll be like Morgan said; I can help people here trust Dad, make him look more stable. Here, I have an advantage, a way to be useful. In Europe, I'd be just another spoiled rich girl spouting off about something she doesn't really understand."

Adam really wanted to punch Morgan in the face. The man was smiling at Kara, and when he turned to look at Adam, his oily sincerity was on full power. "I really believe we can keep them safe, Adam. We'll have an evacuation plan in place, of course, and they could be the first ones to leave if the situation warrants it. But them being here, them being *seen* to be here, will go a long way to making the people feel confident in you, and, of course, in their own safety. If the leader has brought his lovely wife and daughter over from Europe, then obviously the leader feels that the country is safe. It's a slight increase in risk for Antonia and Kara, but a dramatic decrease in risk for everyone else."

Adam needed people to stop talking to him. He needed a quiet, dark room, with Remy's arms wrapped around him, Remy's soothing voice murmuring inconsequential things in his ear. "Remy," Adam said thoughtfully.

Morgan frowned at him. "What about him?"

Adam ignored the caution in Morgan's voice and reached for his comm unit. One button, a short wait, and then Remy's face was on the screen. Adam gave himself a moment to savor the beauty displayed, then said, "Remy, would you be able to come by my office? I'd like some people to meet you, if you don't mind."

"Now?" Remy sounded confused. "I mean, of course I can...." But his hesitation made it clear that he thought Adam had lost his mind.

Adam didn't let himself stop to think about what he was about to ask Remy to do. It was unfair, maybe even cruel, but Remy was strong, and Kara needed to be protected. Still, it would probably be best to give a little warning. "My daughter is insisting on being part of this movement. I'd like her to hear a firsthand account of what our former government has done to people who dared to defy their authority."

Remy's expression didn't change, but there was a tiny pause before he said, "Yes, sir. I'll be right in."

The slight hesitation in someone normally so smooth, the formality that Adam had worked so hard to move beyond—Remy wasn't pleased. Adam felt the familiar, anxious churning in his stomach, but tried to ignore it. This was for Kara. His baby girl, his treasure, his best accomplishment and proudest legacy. Remy would understand.

"Remy is one of the few survivors of the Colony Seventeen massacre," Adam said quietly.

Kara frowned at him. "I know about Colony Seventeen, Dad. We learned about it in school. I'm sure they've censored things here, but in Europe, we heard all about it."

"Did you hear that the colonists sent diplomatic envoys to the European colonies, as well as to the European Union itself? Did you hear about the pleas for aid and refuge that fell on deaf ears?" Adam shook his head at her shocked expression. "No? Because Europe isn't quite as golden as we've made it seem. And you need to understand that. If you go back now, before you get involved here, they'll protect you. But if you get involved in this and make yourself an enemy of the old North American government, and that government ends up back in power, Europe may not give you shelter. Morgan can talk all he wants to about setting up escape routes, but they won't do you much good if there's nowhere for you to escape *to*."

The comm panel by the door buzzed, and Adam gave Kara a long look before saying, "Enter." The door slid open and Remy walked inside. He seemed relaxed, but wouldn't meet Adam's gaze. Damn it. But Adam would have to deal with that later.

"Thanks for joining us, Remy. Antonia, this is Remy Stone. He was instrumental in getting us access to the network for our takeover." Adam didn't think it was cowardly that he didn't explain exactly how Remy had done that. If Remy wanted people to know he'd been a whore and had planted transmitters on his clients' mobile comms, Remy could tell them. But it wasn't something Adam was going to bring up in a short introduction. Besides, he had more important information to convey. "Remy, this is my wife, Antonia. We haven't been together for several years, but we've never divorced, either. I never mentioned her to you because it never really came up, but she and Kara are my family." That was probably a little awkward, but it was honest. And it cleared the way for Adam to get to the real reason for Remy's presence.

"And this is Kara, my daughter." Kara wasn't all that much younger than Remy, Adam realized as he saw them look at each other. But Remy had been through so much and Kara had been so protected that Adam felt as if they were several generations apart. "She's determined to be a part of the revolution, and I'm determined to get her back to safety." Adam really wished Remy would look at him. It was hard to do this without eye contact. "I know it's a painful memory, but I need her to understand how ugly things could get, here, if things don't work out."

Remy still wouldn't look at Adam, but his gaze was level in Kara's direction and there was no hesitation before he spoke. "I could tell you about Colony Seventeen, but it really won't help you understand. Colony Seventeen will be like a parent scolding a naughty child compared to what they'll do here, if they get back in power. The colony was on a distant planet; the rebellion there was only a threat to money, and to pride. Here? People have lost their homes, their fortunes, their sense of security and invulnerability. Making people afraid is an excellent way to make them absolutely savage, and if this movement doesn't work, the people who come back to power will have been terrified, outraged, and demoralized." His level, emotionless voice made his words all the more chilling. "Their revenge will be absolute."

For the first time, Kara looked shaken. She stepped forward, then stopped herself, then took another tentative half step, her gaze never leaving Remy's face. "So why did you do it?" she asked quietly. "Why are *you* taking the chance?"

Remy looked away quickly, still not in Adam's direction, and when he looked back, his expression was fierce. "Because *I've* been terrified, outraged, and demoralized, and I want absolute revenge." His face softened and his voice was quieter when he added, "And because I have nothing to lose. Not like you."

Kara looked at Adam, then, and he could see his younger self in her eyes. The indecision, the instinct to do good without the knowledge of how to go about it. But in Kara, he saw strength he'd been missing, and he wasn't surprised when she shook her head and smiled at him. "So that's why we need to be sure that it works," she said softly. "That's why you need to make your position as secure as possible, and make sure that people trust you. If having a wife and daughter around make it more likely that the movement will succeed...." She stopped, and then turned to her mother. "I'm sorry. I didn't mean to speak for you. I don't know if a wife is necessary, if there's a daughter. Maybe you could go back, and I can stay."

"*Cara mia*," Antonia said reproachfully. "How could I leave? How could I survive, if I lost both of you?"

"So it's not just *your* life you're playing with," Adam tried. He was pretty sure the battle was lost, but he couldn't give up, not without making every damned effort. "Your decision here affects your mother, as well."

"My mother makes her own choices," Kara said, and she lifted her chin. "As do I. I'm staying." Kara stepped over to Adam and took both his hands in hers. "I know you want me safe, Daddy. I understand, and I know I've been lucky to have that for my whole life. But I'm an adult now, and I have to do what I think is right, not what you think is safe." Her smile was sweet. "I want to be with you. I want to be part of this."

"And if I have security remove you from the country?" He was pretty sure he already knew the answer.

She let go of his hands. "I'll sneak back in, just like I did this time. I'll be in more danger that way than if you just leave me here."

Adam felt helpless. Useless. He wanted Remy's touch, his comfort, but Remy wouldn't even look at him. Damn it. Adam needed to be a man, not a weak little boy. But he had no idea what being a man *meant*, not in this situation. "I can't agree with this," he said. "I need to think things over. And I have other issues that need my attention."

"Of course," Kara said with the easy generosity of someone who knew she had won. "We can get out of your hair. Is there someone we can speak to about accommodations? Even if we're only here temporarily, we'll need somewhere to sleep."

Adam knew the answer everyone was waiting for. It was the only one that made sense, even if he wasn't sure what implications it would have. "There are extra bedrooms in my suite. And it's in this building, so it should be safe."

"Sounds great," Kara said. She stepped forward and stood on her tiptoes to reach Adam's cheek with her lips. "Thank you."

He shook his head. "I'm not giving up, Kara. Just thinking it through."

"I know." But she didn't seem too concerned.

They said their good nights, and Morgan guided the ladies from the room. Remy stayed behind, as Adam had hoped he would. Neither of them responded to Morgan's subtle frown of disapproval.

"I'm sorry," Adam said as soon as the door was shut. "For dragging you back into it all. For bringing up painful memories."

"I don't think you're sorry," Remy said. He sounded genuinely confused. "You did what was necessary. You shouldn't be sorry for that."

"So why won't you look at me? If you're not angry, why are you still way over there?" Adam tried to sound playful. If he gave an actual suggestion, Remy would obey, regardless of his own preferences. The habits of a lifetime made it hard to have a conversation sometimes.

"I was speaking to Dar earlier." It seemed like a topic change, but Adam doubted that it really was.

"He's still in the city?"

"He's doing good work. Getting people organized." Remy turned his head in Adam's direction, at least, but his gaze was directed somewhere below Adam's eyes. "I asked if he needed help, and he said yes."

"Okay." Adam still wasn't seeing the relevance, but at least this was something concrete, something he could solve without moral ambiguity. "What does he need? More resources, more people?"

"Both, probably. And someone he can trust, someone to take care of little things so he can focus on the larger issues."

Adam's tired brain finally caught up. "Oh. He wants your help?"

"He didn't suggest it. I did."

"Is that what you want to do?" Adam couldn't have this conversation. Couldn't contemplate the possibility of losing Remy when he needed him so much. But Remy wasn't his slave. The man had his own goals, his own needs, and Adam wasn't doing a damned thing to meet them. He didn't have the first idea of how to even start giving Remy what he needed.

"I think I could be useful there."

"You're useful here too." Adam fought to keep the pleading tone out of his voice.

"Not really. I sit around, mostly. Bring you food. That's about all." Remy was still looking at Adam's chin, or maybe his neck. "Your family is here now. They can take care of you."

Jesus. Had he been treating Remy like a servant? Had he made Remy think his only role was fetching Adam's snacks? "I've enjoyed being taken care of by you." Well, that wasn't what he meant at all. "I mean, I've found you... comforting. I've looked forward to spending time with you." It all sounded so cold and clinical. But if Adam expressed himself more forcefully, he'd be pressuring Remy into a role that Remy probably didn't want. Just because Adam wasn't taking advantage of Remy's physical affections didn't mean he had any sort of right to Remy's emotions.

"But your family's here now." Remy sounded as if he was getting a little exasperated by Adam's cluelessness.

"Yes. Okay. And you want to find a more active role. That makes sense. Fair enough." Adam struggled to find a way for this to work. "You'll still be here when you're not working, though? I mean, you're not *leaving*."

"I'd still be in the city, I guess. But I don't think I'd need to be in this building, would I?"

Adam was being dumped. Remy was breaking up with him. Whatever they'd been, it was over. Whatever tiny, tentative steps they'd been making hadn't been enough. Adam had wanted Kara to feel safe, and he'd made her overconfident. He'd wanted Remy to find his balance in a new world, and now Remy was using his stability to walk away. "When?" Adam whispered.

Remy barely paused before saying, "Dar's sorting out a shipment of first-aid supplies right now. He's downstairs. I thought I could go with him when he leaves."

It was unacceptable. Literally. Adam couldn't make himself believe that this was happening. Remy was his. And that was okay, because he was Remy's, as well. But Remy had never really agreed to the exchange. Even if he'd gone along with Adam's fantasy, it didn't mean a damn thing. Remy had been nine years old when he'd signed the contract that had made him a sex slave; he hadn't been in a position to see any alternatives or understand what he was signing. And any agreements he made with Adam in the eight short days since he'd been freed would be just as morally nonbinding as the original. Remy had been no more able to make an informed, truly consensual partnership with Adam than he had been with Baryman. Adam couldn't argue with this, couldn't be one more person to imprison Remy. "Will you come back?"

Finally, Remy looked Adam in the eyes. "In a second, if you need me. If I can help. With anything. With the government, or with you, or with telling stories about Colony Seventeen to spoiled rich girls. I owe you everything. Anything."

Adam closed his eyes. Remy *owed* him. That was all it had ever been, Remy's misplaced sense of gratitude and servitude. He fought to keep his voice level as he opened his eyes. "Thank you. But you've done more than enough. There's no debt here." And therefore, no reason for Remy to stay.

"I should go," Remy said as if he'd heard Adam's thought. "Dar said he'd wait, but they're on a tight schedule."

"Okay," Adam made himself say. "Keep in touch, though? Let me know how things are going, and if you need anything. If Dar needs any help."

"Sure," Remy agreed. He frowned at Adam, as if looking for words that wouldn't come, then smiled brightly. "Thanks for everything," he said, and he turned and strode from the room.

Adam watched him leave, and gripped the edge of the table in front of him, keeping himself from following, convincing, begging. Enslaving. Remy was free. Adam had to let him go.

CHAPTER THREE

ADAM threw himself into his duties. He'd been working hard before Remy left, but now he barely rested. It didn't make sense, really. Remy had been with him such a short time; how had Adam become so dependent on the warm strength of Remy's arms in order to fall asleep? How had he grown so accustomed to looking across crowded rooms to find Remy's beautiful face, waiting patiently in case Adam needed him for something? And how the hell had he let himself ignore the fact that Remy had still been acting like Adam's slave, still sublimating all of his own needs into the simple act of being what Adam wanted?

It was these questions that came to Adam when he closed his eyes and tried to sleep. These questions that kept him awake. After five days with only brief, restless naps, Antonia walked into his office and said to the staff surrounding him, "My husband and I need to have a conversation. Could you please excuse us?"

The people left the room. "If I'd known it was that easy to get rid of them, I would have done it days ago," Adam said, but Antonia didn't even pretend to be amused.

"I've never seen you like this, Adam. You need to take care of yourself."

"You've never seen me like this? You've never seen me in charge of a provisional government scrambling to meet the needs of half a billion people, fighting for legitimacy on the world stage, and dealing with the constant threat of counterattack from those we deposed? No, I guess you *haven't* seen me like this. And I sincerely hope it's a once-in-a-lifetime situation."

"That's what I thought it was at first," Antonia said calmly. "I thought it was the job."

"It's not just a job!" Adam forced himself to lower his voice. "Do you know how I was chosen as leader, Toni? I was the only one that nobody vetoed." He saw her blank expression and shook his head. "I was chosen as leader by the organizers over in Asia—expatriate, mostly, people who loved their country enough to want to save it but not enough to actually come home and risk their necks. They'd been working at it for years. The rest of the council, they'd been working for years too, and they *were* here, risking their lives if the movement was uncovered. I was over in Europe, goofing off." It had taken Adam a while to realize all this, but it made perfect sense now that he'd figured it out. "So I hadn't made any enemies. I hadn't become part of this or that faction, I hadn't argued an unpopular position, I hadn't made any mistakes. I was chosen to be the leader because I was a blank slate, and nobody knew me well enough to object. I don't have the job because I'm uniquely qualified, Antonia. I'm not really qualified at all. I need to work my ass off because I don't know what I'm doing."

"I've been talking to people, you know. It's not as simple as you make it sound. You impressed people. *You're* the one who made the revolution happen, after all. You and Remy." She smiled at him. "And speaking of Remy... I could tell that people were keeping something from me, and I finally found someone willing to tell me what it was." She shook her head in confusion. "Why did you send him away, Adam? You and I haven't been together for almost ten years; I have no claim on your affections."

Adam didn't want to have this conversation, but he didn't know how to escape it. "I didn't send him," he said. "He wanted to leave." Hopefully that would be enough to satisfy her.

"He's devoted to you," she said. "That's what I was told. Why did he want to leave?"

"Toni, please. Does it really matter? I have work to do."

"If I didn't think it mattered, I wouldn't have brought it up. You need people to support you right now, and you're pushing Kara and me away. I thought you were just angry that we were here, and worried about her safety. But that's not it. You're pushing us away because we're not *him*."

"Enough with the melodrama and psychoanalysis. I'm *busy*. I'm in the middle of the most important thing I've ever done. I don't have time to worry about this nonsense."

"The person who told me about him... about Remy. She works in your office—one of the secretaries. She said that he'd take you by the hand and lead you to your bed when he decided you needed to sleep. She said you followed him like a docile little lamb. Is that what you want? You want a shepherd?" She stretched her hand out toward him. "It's time to sleep, Adam. Come to bed."

"I don't need a shepherd, and I don't need to sleep." Adam closed his eyes and pinched the bridge of his nose, trying to hold back the headache that had been pulsing behind his temples for far too long.

"But you need *him*." Antonia didn't sound jealous, just sad. "Why did he leave?"

"Because he's not a whore anymore." Adam supposed he was being petty, but he was tired of Antonia thinking she knew everything. "Because if I'm not paying his pimp for his time, he has no reason to be here. Because he has no actual interest in sex, at least not with me, and he decided that he could do something more constructive with his time if he wasn't wasting so much of it being my platonic bedmate."

Antonia gave herself a moment to think. "So he wasn't 'devoted'? That was the wrong word?"

"He's used to being a slave. He's a very, very good whore. I've seen him declare his love for a disgusting, lecherous old cretin, and

I was damned near convinced he meant it. Whoever your source is, she probably doesn't know a whole lot about high-end whores, and she doesn't know what someone like Remy is capable of."

There was another pause before Antonia asked, "Does he know that you love him?"

Adam thought about objecting to the assumption, but didn't. Instead, he said, "I never told him. Never used the words. But he wouldn't... Toni, he wouldn't really know what it meant. He wouldn't understand the concept the way you or I would use it."

"Because he's an alien?"

"He might as well be."

"So why do you love him? If he's so odd, so unlike us...."

The whole conversation was like working his tongue over a cut lip. It hurt, but he couldn't stop. "He's the bravest person I've ever met. Strong. Funny, and smart. Beautiful, obviously. Determined—well, stubborn, really, once he decides on something. He cares about other people, tries to do what's right. And he stands up to me, when he's not in robo-whore mode. Argues with me, lets me know when I'm full of shit."

"He sounds like a keeper." Antonia smiled. "So why aren't you fighting for him?"

"Fighting *who*?" Adam demanded. "*Him*? Because he's the only one keeping us apart. There's not some big conspiracy. No enemy, for a change. He just doesn't want me, Toni." She opened her mouth to reply, but he held up his hands. "No. It's not a question of me just winning him back, or whatever you're about to suggest. He's been in the sex trade since he was nine years old. He doesn't want anybody. Doesn't want sex, doesn't understand affection." Adam pinched the bridge of his nose again. "That's not quite right," he said, his eyes shut tight. "He understands it intellectually. He knew that I had to do whatever I could to keep Kara safe. But he doesn't feel it, I don't think. Not the same way we do."

"I wish I'd spent more time with him before he left."

"If wishes were horses, we'd be able to keep the population well-fed on horse meat." Adam stood up. "There's nothing to be done, Toni, and I'm handling it. I'm sorry I'm not behaving the way you want me to, but...."

"But I should mind my own business. I should let you wallow in misery, and work yourself to death, without saying or doing a single thing."

"Yes," Adam growled through gritted teeth. "That sounds perfect. Thank you." He returned to his work and, after a long while, Antonia left the room.

She did leave him alone after that, at least for a few days. And he did wallow in his misery, and work himself to exhaustion, if not quite death, and he was satisfied that he could have done nothing else. Remy didn't want him. That was all there was.

He was working quietly at his desk, trying to understand the subtleties of the latest communication from the African diplomats, when a chime rang to indicate that someone was at his door. "Enter," he said, glad of the distraction.

The door slid open to reveal Morgan and several other top strategists. "There's rioting." Morgan strode into the room, almost excited by the news. "Looting. It broke out in Sector Seven, but there are signs that it's spreading. We've shut down civilian comms in the area, and we've got extra security personnel on the way."

"Damn it." Challoner strode to his desk and poked angrily at his comm. This wasn't a surprise, but it was something they'd hoped to avoid. "Does it seem organized? Are there any specific targets?"

"More or less what we expected. They started with some of the larger homes and high-end retail establishments. But they're going after whatever they can find now. Just mindless destruction."

"The security teams have been told to use nonlethal means, right?"

"They're not trained in nonlethal suppression, Adam." Morgan sounded like he'd anticipated this conversation and prepared for it. "We'll *get* them trained, but for now, they have to use the techniques they're used to."

Adam found a live security feed on his comm and looked at the images. "They're just kids," he said. "They don't know what the rules are, anymore, so they're testing. Pushing. They're stupid. They don't deserve to die for being stupid."

"Our security forces don't deserve to die for being stupid, either. And that's what they'd be, if they went into an explosive situation without a well-rehearsed plan. They'll use their traditional techniques this time, and we'll work on getting them trained for a different approach in the future."

"No." Adam was tired, but not that tired. "Where's Ackerman? The security forces are his responsibility. I want to talk to him."

"He's en route to the scene," Morgan said.

"So get him on the comm."

"Adam, I'm sure he's got a lot of things to worry about already...."

Adam stared at Morgan incredulously, then looked over his shoulder to the next aide in line. "Get Don Ackerman on my comm, immediately," he ordered.

"Yes, sir," the aide replied, and he scurried to comply. That was more like it.

Morgan stepped in closer and spoke so quietly that only Adam could hear. "We've spoken about this before, Adam. You have the title, but you represent a group of people. People who were working on this revolution for years before you came along. You're not a dictator."

"A *dictator*? You're accusing me of acting like a dictator because I *don't* want to kill my citizens for a minor breach in order? That's what you're saying?" Adam knew his voice was loud enough for the room to hear, but he didn't think he cared. "I will absolutely consult with the members of the council. But I don't think you've had time to call a meeting, neglect to invite me, and then decide how to handle rioters, as a group. So this comes down to your individual opinion against mine, and, yeah, in that situation, mine's going to win."

"Mr. Ackerman on the comm, sir," the aide said quietly.

"Thank you." Adam held Morgan's gaze a moment longer, then took a deep breath as he reached for the comm tablet. "Don," he said. "I've only had a preliminary briefing. What's your plan?"

"I'm new to this job, Adam. I'm taking advice from the security managers. They say we need to hit hard and fast, send a clear message."

Adam could feel Morgan's self-righteous smirk even without looking in his direction. "Are they talking lethal force, Don? Is that what we're planning to do? Kill a bunch of kids?"

"We've hardly made any changes to the security teams yet. They have a set way of doing things, and they aren't big fans of change. I think we have to use the tools we have, this time. We'll find better solutions to the next problem."

"That's not going to be much consolation for the people who die this time. Or for their families, who will never forgive us. Or their friends and neighbors, who will never trust us."

"They're destroying state property. They're stealing. These are not model citizens, Adam."

"Model or not, they're citizens. They're the people we're supposed to be helping. Jesus, Don, you and I could both have had much easier lives if we'd just kept our eyes shut and gone about our business under the old regime. We took this chance because we want to help people, not kill them!"

"So what do you suggest?" Don sounded about as frustrated as Adam felt. "I'm not disagreeing. I just... what do you suggest?"

That was what it came down to. It was easy for Adam to criticize, easy for him to say what they shouldn't do, but a hell of a lot harder to know what they should. He could feel the desperation creeping in, threatening to overwhelm him. God, he wished Remy were there. Just one look at his calm face would be enough. Maybe he could get hold of him on the comm. Or maybe.... "Turn the cameras back on," he said. "Red lights, to let them know they're being watched and recorded. And override all signals on their comms, so they can't get messages in or out. The only message they should get is someone in charge, warning them to get off the streets. Have the shuttles with the security forces there, but have them hover. Make it clear that they *could* land, but have the person on the comm explaining that we don't want to use lethal force." Damn, this was beginning to sound like a plan. "We need to treat them like citizens, not like criminals."

"They *are* criminals," Morgan interjected.

"They're citizens as well. We need to give them a chance to do the right thing." Adam was pretty sure he was right. "Don? What do you think? A little delay won't hurt much, and if it works, we've found a new tool."

Don's gray-haired head was nodding slowly. He turned and spoke to someone beside him, and Adam tried to look more confident than he felt. Finally, Don turned back to the comm camera. "Okay," he said. "We can give it a try. Who's going to send the message?"

"They know my face," Adam said. "Is that going to be an advantage or a disadvantage?"

"An advantage, I think," Don said. "They're starting to trust you. And a lot of this is probably just kids looking for attention. If they see you noticing them, maybe it'll be enough."

"And we'll have established a precedent that smashing or stealing someone else's property gets you nothing more than a scolding," Morgan said.

"We'll still investigate. We'll look at the footage and see who did the worst of it, and we'll give them a trial, not a spontaneous execution." Adam nodded at Don. "Okay. You get the security shuttles lined up and ready. Morgan, take care of the cameras; get those red lights back on." He waited until Morgan started moving, then turned to the aide who'd gotten Ackerman on the comm. "You any good with a camera?"

"I can do the basics."

"That's all we need." He sat down in his desk chair. "Give me a minute to get organized; while you're waiting, call down and let the tech guys know we need an emergency override of all comm channels in Sector Seven." He stopped. "Actually, make it nationwide. All channels. I won't talk long, but if everyone hears the warning, they should understand if we end up having to go in anyway, right?"

The aide nodded without a lot of confidence. "That sounds right to me. But, you know, I'm not an expert."

"Me neither," Adam said quietly. "But I think this is worth a shot."

"Okay," the aide said, and he moved away to perform his assigned tasks. Adam settled himself in his chair and tried to remember how to look conscientious and trustworthy. "Morgan," he said, calling the man's attention away from his comm. "You were right. About having my family here. I don't like using them, but they'll be effective."

"They will," Morgan agreed cautiously, not sure if Adam's words were a peace offering or a trap.

"Have someone find Antonia, and get a chair for her. Just off to the side, maybe, and we can pull the camera back a little farther than usual so it'll catch her. Close enough for all the other mothers to see that she's worried too."

Morgan paused, then nodded grudgingly. "That sounds good."

"Mr. Challoner!" an aide said, alarm in his voice. He raised wide eyes from a comm panel to look at Adam.

"What?" Adam strode the few steps between them and looked over the man's shoulder down at the screen.

The picture was poor quality, probably from one of the private security cameras that some store owners had installed in the days since the master cameras had gone off-line. It showed the inside of a small store, one that stocked basic groceries if the empty shelves were any indication. There was a group of men standing there... no, two groups, it became clear. The ones with their backs to the camera must be looters, and the others seemed to be trying to defend the place. One of the looters shifted, giving the camera a better view of the other men, and Adam's whole body froze. Remy. Remy and Dar, and some other man, someone Adam had never seen before. They were standing between the looters and the back room, and Dar was talking, but the camera had no sound. Whatever he was saying didn't seem to be having much effect; the looters weren't leaving. In fact, they were steadily moving closer to Remy and Dar.

"We have face-recognition software running on everything that comes in," the aide explained. Now that he was sharing his burden, he seemed calmer. "I don't know who programmed him in, but his face triggered an alarm."

"Where are they? Sector Seven?" Adam tried to jump-start his frozen brain.

"I think so. The system's all messed up, with some cameras off-line, and private citizens adding their own to the network without knowing the registration protocol." The aide seemed to realize that he was giving more details than needed, and restated, "I think they're in Sector Seven."

"The comms in that store...." Adam couldn't stand there and just watch. "Will the comms broadcast? Can we send a message to them?"

"Not directly," the aide said. "I don't think. The comms should play our message, but we're still figuring some things out. They wired their cameras into the system, but we don't have an address, or anything. We can't send *just* to them."

And Remy didn't have a private comm. He'd had an account

through the agency, before, but that was lost. Dar didn't have one, either; he'd been off the grid before the revolution, and the government wasn't issuing new comm addresses until things settled down. Damn it. How had he let Remy out of his sight without coming up with a way to contact him?

Once again, the situation was literally unacceptable. "Let's go!" Adam barked to the room as a whole. "We need to do the broadcast, *now*. We need to end this."

Most of the room hadn't seen the comm images and didn't know what had changed, but they scurried anyway. Adam grabbed the aide's screen and carried it with him over to the desk. Antonia was already there, but her sympathetic expression didn't help. The standoff in the store continued, and Adam wanted to scream at Remy. *Give them what they want! Get out of the way, and come back to me, safely. I'll never let you out of my sight again.*

"Broadcast signal synched," said a voice from the back of the room, and the comm panel with Remy's image went black.

"I can't see them!" Adam tried not to panic, waving the comm at the aide who'd originally supplied it.

"The synch," the aide said. "We had to override all other signals in order to make the broadcast work. Once your message is done, we'll try to get the camera back."

Adam swallowed his instincts. He needed to be calm and controlled. He needed to remember all the pretty words he'd been thinking of before he'd seen Remy's frightened but determined face on the screen. He needed to make this work.

"Fellow North Americans," he said, and Toni's hand found his behind the desk. "Especially those of you in Capital City Sector Seven. We *cannot* have anarchy. The government is working hard to make things better, to fulfill all of our promises and goals. We have kept everyone fed, and have given every citizen means to satisfy their basic needs until order is restored. Medical care is being provided to many who had always thought it was out of reach. We are taking steps to provide universal education.

Universal hope. We are a government that is *devoted* to the well-being of our people." He paused and tried not to imagine the scene in the store with Remy. Were they hearing his voice? Did they care? "We cannot allow anarchy. Looting and rioting are destructive acts, contrary to everything we are working toward. We do not want to adopt the practices of the previous government, but we also cannot allow our cities to be destroyed.

"Security forces are moving into Sector Seven. They will move into any sector where people are tearing down instead of building up. We have turned the surveillance cameras back on, only temporarily, and only in areas where we know crimes are being committed. Our goal is to record footage and bring responsible parties to trial." He leaned forward a little, and willed his message to travel through the comms directly to the ears of the men threatening Remy. "But if we have to, we will deploy the security forces. This is your warning. All citizens in Capital City Sector Seven are ordered off the streets, and out of public places. If you are at home, we will fight to keep you safe. If you are anywhere else, we will consider you a threat, and the security forces will respond accordingly." Surely that was tough enough. Then he thought of Remy, outnumbered and cornered, and added, "There will be zero tolerance for any violence against citizens or against security forces. If you hurt anyone, we will find you, and we will prosecute you to the full extent of the law."

He was pretty sure that was all he had. Prior to the revolution, he'd tried to prepare himself for his new role by studying leadership techniques, and now he dredged up the lessons he'd received on clear communication to the masses and tried to summarize his main points. "Sector Seven is now under full curfew. Get home, immediately, or face the consequences. We want this to end nonviolently, but we will use force if necessary." *And I will use my bare hands to destroy anyone who touches Remy Stone.*

Adam nodded to the man holding the camera and the recording light blinked off. He immediately grabbed the comm panel in front of him, poking frantically, trying to get the images back online. When the screen finally refreshed, the men were gone. The looters, but also Remy, Dar, and their friend. What did that mean? "Is there a way to pan the camera?" Adam demanded, but the aide shook his head. "Damn it." Then Adam's eye caught movement on the screen. There was something on the floor of the back room, the room that Remy had been protecting. Something dark, just peeking out past the doorjamb. It was a foot. Someone was lying on the floor of the room, and there was no reason any healthy person would do that.

"There's someone injured," Adam said. He turned to the aide. "We need to get people in there, now! A medical team, security personnel...."

"We don't even know where the store is," Morgan said. He'd obviously been listening for a while. "And if we send in security right after telling people they had time to get home, it could set things off. It could make the situation much worse."

Adam was pretty sure his head was going to explode. There was no way he could just sit there in his safe, remote office and stare at somebody's foot. He couldn't even decide whether to hope that it was someone else so he could believe that Remy was still upright, or hope that it was Remy, because at least the foot had moved. He stood abruptly. "Get my shuttle ready," he ordered. "I'm going to Sector Seven."

CHAPTER FOUR

THE days when Adam could hop in his own shuttle and pilot himself wherever he wanted to go were gone. Now he had to order a security detail, wait for them to check the shuttle, then wait for them to send scouts out along the flight path, then wait for his detail to escort him through the busy halls of the Capitol Building up to the shuttle deck. It was not what he'd anticipated when he'd made the decision to find Remy himself. The whole time, he clutched the comm with the video image of the store, trying to see any details, any new information. The foot disappeared at one point as its owner was apparently dragged further into the back room, but that was all. At least the injured person wasn't alone. Unless he was dragging himself. Jesus, what if it was Remy, alone and hurt, trying to pull himself somewhere he could find help? And Adam wasn't there for him.

He was just settling into his shuttle seat when his comm activated and showed him the smiling face of Don Ackerman. "Looks like it's working," Ackerman said. "The streets have emptied. We're going to land the security personnel anyway, and they'll be going in prepared for anything, but they agree that things seem to have calmed down."

Adam needed to remember his larger job, even if it meant forgetting about Remy for a moment. But maybe there was a way for him to meet both of his goals. "We have a video of at least one injured citizen. In the backroom of a small grocery store, from the looks of it. There are probably other people out there who need help. Can we set up a first-aid station, and send out teams to find injured people?"

There was a moment as Don consulted with somebody, then he turned back to the comm. "They want to make sure the situation is contained first. Then they'll establish a base camp and send out patrols to look for anyone who needs help. We've got a few fires to deal with, as well."

Adam couldn't argue with that plan. It made sense; it was what they should do. It would serve the citizens he was trying to protect. He felt his head nod jerkily on his neck, agreeing to Don's words. Then he bent a little closer to the comm screen. "I have a friend. Two friends. Remy Stone and Dar Wright. Heroes of the revolution. We have footage of them being threatened by looters inside a small grocery store, and we believe that at least one of them may have been injured." Adam didn't know what to say next.

But maybe he'd said enough, because Don was nodding slowly. "You can't pinpoint the location?" He didn't wait for an answer. "Because the camera system is muddled." He frowned thoughtfully. "Okay. Send images of them down, and we'll have the forces keep a close eye out for them. And we'll have them take note of all grocery stores on their initial patrols, and those'll be the first places we check once we're sure the place is secure. Okay?"

It wasn't enough. But it was all Adam could ask for, and he nodded again. "Yes. Thank you. And I'm going to come down and look around myself."

"What? No, Adam, that's not possible. The forces don't want *me* wandering around out there, and I'm nobody. There's no way it's safe for you."

"I'll take the chance."

"Think it through, Adam. You're one man, searching an entire sector. But if you're down here, we have to reassign twenty or thirty men, who would otherwise be searching, to be your bodyguards. How does that help?"

"I don't need guards."

"Sure, yeah, and when you're murdered or kidnapped, and the whole country panics and riots, we'll have even *fewer* people available to find your friends, and nowhere safe to take them if we *do* find them." Don's voice was a little softer when he added, "You're not a private citizen anymore, Adam. You need to stop thinking like you are."

Adam stared at the screen. He was supposed to just sit there and wait? He was the most powerful person in the country, but he couldn't do something as simple as look for the man he loved?

"We'll find him, Adam. *Them*. Both of them." Don didn't seem embarrassed by his slip, but he apparently wanted it clearly corrected. "Dar Wright, Remy Stone. Send the pictures down, and we'll take care of it." He waited, then said, "Adam?"

"Yes, fine." Adam didn't think he could say much more. "Pictures are on the way." He tapped the screen to cut the transmission off. It was a rude way to end the conversation, but he didn't think he'd be able to force another civil word past his clenched jaw. He jerked his head at the aide sitting a few feet away. The kid had heard the whole conversation, but was trying to look nonchalant. "Get those pictures sent down," Adam growled, and the aide scurried to comply.

Leaving Adam helpless and useless. His luxury shuttle was a traveling fortress, but it felt like it was keeping him in, not keeping trouble out. He slammed his fist into the padded arm of his chair and then thought about punching the wall, as well. Less padding, there, so a better chance of feeling some pain. "We're still not seeing them on the cameras?" he asked the aide.

"Most of the cameras have been disabled, sir."

"We couldn't reactivate them?"

"It would appear that they were mostly damaged on-site, sir. An issue with the hardware, not the software."

"The people smashed them? Before the riot?"

"It would appear so."

It was good to have at least a bit of distraction. "Check and see if that's happened elsewhere. If *everyone* is smashing cameras, it's probably just a natural reaction. People expressing their rage against the former government. But if only these cameras were damaged, that might mean that this riot was more planned than it seems."

"Yes, sir. I'll look into it."

Adam looked at the aide a little more closely. Everything had been so crazy lately that he'd been rushing through his life paying attention to only the big things, with no time for the details. "I'm sorry, I've forgotten your name."

"I'm surprised you ever knew it," the aide said with a quick grin. "I'm Paul Nickson. Mostly just 'Nickson'."

"Thanks for all your help with this, Nickson. I really appreciate it."

Nickson nodded in bashful acknowledgment. His skin was the rich medium brown of the proletariat, no racial purity to be found. He was probably about Remy's size. Remy's age too. They could have been friends, maybe, if Remy had ever let his attention stray from Adam. Now that Adam thought about it, he realized that Nickson was very attentive as well. Many of the aides were. They were excited to be part of something big, eager to be of service in any way they could, and they focused their attention on the leader of the movement. Adam had barely noticed any of them. He supposed it was a sign of his own self-absorption, but it actually made him feel a little better about himself. He wasn't attracted to Remy just because Remy was servile and ego-lifting. And since Adam wasn't having sex with Remy, that wasn't the source of the attraction, either. Whatever fascination Remy held, it was something more than being a handsome young man interested in Adam. There were lots of handsome young men who were interested in Adam. There was only one Remy.

Adam stood up and paced around the shuttle, spent some time

peering out the windows at the ground below, and then paced a little more. The pilot asked if they should head back to the Capitol Building, and Adam wanted to scream at him. Remy was still down there. He might be hurt. He might need Adam. "No," he said. "Find somewhere nearby to set down, if you want, but don't leave the area."

"Got something," Nickson said quietly, staring at his comm screen. "The recognition software just tweaked." He tapped at the screen as Adam rushed to peer over his shoulder. "They've moved past the camera that gave us a view of their faces, but we've got him... here," Nickson said, calling up a grainy image of two men carrying a third, working their way down an alleyway. The men were all facing away, so Adam couldn't see their faces, but he recognized the lines of Remy's body, the way he moved, even though he was currently carrying a heavy load. He wasn't the injured one. Now Adam just needed to keep it that way.

He slammed his hand down onto his own comm screen, calling Don into view practically by force of will. "They're moving," he said. "Two men, carrying a third. Tell your men that they're not a threat. Make sure your men *help* them."

Don nodded, then turned his head and issued a few terse orders. When his face returned to the comm, he was frowning. "Message has gone out. But why are they moving? The order was clear, they're supposed to stay off the streets. This isn't a great move on their part, Adam."

"They must have a reason," Adam replied. He knew it was true. Dar was a risk-taker and not fond of authority, but Remy was smart. And they were both fully aware of the dangers posed by trigger-happy security forces.

"They just left the camera's line of sight," Nickson reported, "and there are no functioning cameras at their current location. But they're in the alley parallel to Seventh Avenue, between C and D Streets."

Finally. "Get there," Adam ordered the pilot. "Don, we've got a location. We're sending it down to you. Have you got forces in the area?"

There was a pause as Don consulted, and then he said, "About six blocks away. They're working in that direction...."

Adam felt the shuttle decelerate as they reached the destination. "Advise them that my shuttle is now on the ground, and we're picking the guys up." Adam wanted to add a whoop of joy or at least a yelp of stress release, but he managed to restrain himself, instead drumming anxiously on the bulkhead as the pilot did his double checks before opening the door. When it finally eased forward, giving Adam a ramp, he ran down it, ignoring the protests of his bodyguards. "Remy!" he yelled. "Dar!"

A head poked cautiously from the alleyway. "Adam?" Dar looked at the shuttle. "This is a handy coincidence."

And then, finally, Adam saw Remy, easing out beside Dar and yelling, "We need a medic. Have you got one?"

That was businesslike. Adam let his guards catch up to him and strode toward the alley at a more dignified pace. "No," he said when he was close enough not to yell. "But we can take him wherever you want." God, he wanted to touch Remy. All Adam's careful self-discipline, his hypersensitivity to not being someone who used Remy's body without consent, it was all gone, washed away by anxiety and need and love. But, no. The love was the reason for the discipline, and when Adam remembered that, he was able to control himself. He allowed himself to reach out and grip Dar's shoulder, then Remy's, the strong, healthy muscle beneath Adam's fingers the proof he needed in order to finally take a deep breath. "Wherever you need," he said, and he looked into the alley to find their friend, a rough bandage wrapped around his head, lying on the ground.

"They hit him with a bat," Remy said as he and Dar moved to pick up their burden. "We were going to try to wait it out until things calmed down, but he started having seizures. We didn't know what that meant, but it didn't seem good."

"Wait, there's a stretcher coming," Adam said. He didn't let himself think about how close the violence had been to Remy. "Let the guys do it. They have training."

Remy and Dar backed off to stand with Adam and watch the bodyguards do their work. Adam tried not to stare at Remy, but he was pretty sure he wasn't doing a very good job of it. It hadn't been that long. It had been horrible, but Remy hadn't even had time to miss him. He needed to get a grip. On himself, not on Remy.

"You'll come with us to the hospital?" he asked. "And then maybe back to the Capitol? Just for the night? I mean, you can't get any work done down here, anyway, not until the curfew is lifted."

"I wouldn't say no to a night in a soft bed," Dar agreed, but he looked like he knew the invitation had only been extended to him peripherally.

"I should probably stay at the hospital," Remy said. "Sergei has no family, and if he wakes up, there should be someone there for him."

Dar smiled softly, looking at Remy, then Adam, then back to Remy. "I can do that," he said. "I've known him longer. You go back with Adam."

Adam mentally apologized for all the times he'd said or thought that Dar was an insensitive pain in the ass. But Remy didn't seem convinced.

"No, you need the rest. You're going to have a big job down here, cleaning up after the curfew is lifted." He turned to Adam. "And they'll need more resources. We hurried to this sector as soon as the rioting started, but we'd already lost most of our stuff. Sergei got hurt trying to protect the one room of medical supplies we have left. We had to leave it unprotected when we moved him. Hopefully it'll be okay, but people are hoarding. They're worried that there won't be enough to go around, and they're trying to protect themselves. Their families."

"They're being assholes," Dar corrected. The three of them fell in behind the stretcher as it was carried back to the shuttle. "But that's to be expected—human nature, and all. So, yeah, we could use more supplies. And maybe a more secure storage location. We've got the central depot, but once we go out into the communities, it gets pretty sketchy."

"Okay, we should look into that," Adam agreed. He was pretty sure he was pushing too far, but he couldn't help himself. "Remy, maybe that's something you could work on from the Capitol. You could look at the maps and figure out the best routes, the best locations."

"Sounds like chess," Remy replied, "and we both know how good I am at chess."

"You've got lots of potential at chess. You just need to practice more."

"People need medicine *now*. They can't wait a few months for me to get better at something. I'm good at the grunt work. Counting, carrying, delivering. That's what I can do."

"Negotiating, bartering, improvising, scrounging," Dar added. "You're pretty damn good at those too." They waited outside the shuttle as the stretcher was secured. "Thanks for lending him to me, Adam. He's a lot of help." His eyes were kind as he said, "I know it's been a sacrifice for you."

"He's not something I can lend or keep," Adam said. "If he were, you'd never have gotten hold of him."

Dar nodded his acknowledgment, and they all climbed aboard the shuttle. Remy found a spot beside the stretcher and reached out to gently smooth a lock of hair away from the patient's face. Adam was shocked by the heat of the rage that washed over him. Who the hell was this Sergei, and why was Remy touching him when he wouldn't touch Adam? It had only been a few days, and logic dictated that it would take longer for any real attachment to form. But Adam had been head over heels for Remy after a shorter period of time. Hell, Adam had been deep in lust from the first sight of Remy, and pretty close to love after only a weekend. Time didn't mean too much, Adam knew, and he watched in horror as Remy wrapped his fingers around Sergei's.

"They're friends," Dar said softly from the seat beside Adam's. "That's all."

Adam tried to believe him. "It looks like more than that."

"Remy's pretty comfortable with physical contact, Adam. You're the one who shies away from it."

"I don't shy away. I just want to be sure it *means* something."

"Well, right now it means Remy's worried about a friend." Dar leaned back in his chair and was silent as the shuttle lifted off the ground and started to move. "We saw the broadcast," he said. "You laying down the law for the looters. It was good... it's what got the bastards out of the store, even if one of them did take a swat at Sergei before they left."

"I'm glad it was effective," Adam said numbly.

"Yeah, it had an effect, all right." Dar glanced over at him, and Adam returned the gaze with a question in his eyes. "Your wife?" Dar prompted. "She looked pretty comfortable there. Looked like an established part of the scene."

Adam frowned. "She's a friend. But for that shot, she was essentially a prop. They're trying to make me look more stable. A family man, concerned for other people's families."

Dar nodded. "It's a good idea. It looked good." He paused as if deciding how much more to say. "Remy's not stupid, and he wants what's best for you. What's best for the country. When all this is over, if you want to run around with a brown-skinned ex-whore, more power to you. But right now, the wife is a good look on you. And Remy knows that."

Adam was so sick of it all, but maybe there was a glimmer of hope in what Dar was saying. "Do you think he'd actually want that? To be with me when all this is over? Or maybe even sooner." Now Adam was getting excited, but he tried to keep it contained.

"He's used to being discreet. I was too open about him before, maybe... I can see that. I wanted him to understand that I wasn't ashamed of him, but maybe it was politically unwise. But he could come back, and he could be—"

"Your piece on the side? Your dirty little secret?" Dar's voice was little more than a hiss. "He's not a whore anymore, Adam. He deserves better than that." He sounded a little calmer when he added, "And the work he's doing... it's good for him. I mean, good for me too, 'cause I wasn't lying about him being good at it. But he's meeting people who don't know what he used to do. He's making friends, being useful, getting some self-confidence. He's being more than a whore, and he knows it."

Adam didn't think he had an answer to that. It was reassuring, really. Adam wanted Remy to be happy. But he wanted Remy to be safe and close, as well. Safe, that was the biggest one. Safe, then happy, then close, those were Adam's priorities. But they didn't seem to be Remy's.

"If you asked him to come back with you... I mean really asked, not suggested that it would be a good place for him to get work done, or whatever... he'd go. In a second." Dar sighed. "But I'm asking you to not ask. For Remy's sake, give him a little space, and let him do this himself."

"It's dangerous," Adam said.

"Yeah. It is, a little. But he's tough, and smart." Dar's grin was back to its normal cockiness. "And he's got *me* looking out for him, so he's practically invulnerable, really."

"You didn't do too much for Sergei, over there," Adam said. It was a cheap shot, he supposed, but why should he be the only one feeling miserable?

Dar didn't answer right away. It was as if it took him a moment to regain his bluster, and for the first time, Adam saw it as a defense, rather than a natural part of the man's personality. "Would have been *way* worse if I hadn't been there," Dar claimed. "Probably a total bloodbath."

Adam nodded. "Yeah. Good work."

The shuttle bumped a little and Adam looked out the window to see the big blue "H" letting everyone know they were at the hospital. The bodyguards moved efficiently, and Adam could see that there were already medical personnel waiting on the roof; the guards or the pilot had obviously had the foresight to call ahead. Adam hung back, staying out of the way and watching Remy. He *did* seem a little different, even after such a short time. He wasn't shrinking away from the bodyguards, wasn't quite as alert to every shifting mood as he normally was. Hell, Adam was the most powerful person in the area, and Remy was pretty much ignoring him, so obviously *that* little bit of conditioning had been dealt with.

"Back to the Capitol, Mr. Challoner?" the pilot asked.

"Not yet," Adam replied. He looked at Remy. "Can we talk, before I go? We can find somewhere quiet."

Remy nodded, and Dar said, "I'll go keep an eye on Sergei. I don't think I want a soft bed, anyway. No point in spoiling myself." He clapped Adam on the shoulder, then thought better of it and leaned in for a quick hug. "You're a good man, Adam," he said softly. "I can only imagine how unpleasant that must be for you." A quick grin, a nod to Remy, and he was gone.

Adam stepped forward cautiously. "Maybe out on the roof?" he suggested. "There's usually somewhere to sit."

"Okay," Remy agreed. The word was casual, but the "sir," while unspoken, was clear. Remy was back in agreeable servant mode. It wasn't going to make this conversation any easier. Then again, Adam couldn't think of anything that would.

CHAPTER FIVE

THE bodyguards kept a discreet distance. They weren't the former president's guards; those men had been removed from their jobs at the same time as the man they protected. The current guards hadn't even been a team before the revolution. They were specially picked from the security teams of various supporters, with a few from the military as well. Adam watched them fan out and secure a space for him to have his conversation, and wondered whether any of them had any idea what the hell he was planning to say. He certainly didn't. "Damn it," he muttered.

"What?" Remy didn't look alarmed, exactly, but his familiar wariness was back. He looked around them as if trying to find something that had displeased his client, then down at himself. "I have blood on me."

"I'm just glad it's not yours." Adam sank down on the bench that was obviously intended for people waiting for shuttles to arrive. He wondered if he was tying up traffic for the hospital, and decided he didn't care. Well, if there was an emergency, obviously he'd care, but if it was just someone wanting to go home after visiting a loved one, they could damn well wait. Adam was visiting his own loved one.

Remy sat cautiously beside him, and waited.

"Remy, I—" Adam stopped. He'd wanted to use the word. He'd wanted to just put it out there, tell Remy that he loved him, and see what happened. But he thought of Dar, saying that

Remy would absolutely return with Adam if that was what he asked. And he thought about some happy day in the future, when he could maybe use the word as a vow of faithfulness instead of a tool of control. "I care about you. A lot. More than I want to, really. I care about you enough that I absolutely want you to be happy, and complete, and... I want you to be *you*, and I'm trying to accept that you need a bit of space to find out who that is in this new world."

He waited for a response, but didn't really expect one. Remy would be processing information, trying to figure out what it meant and how it could be used. He wouldn't respond until he needed to, because a response would commit him to a certain position, and Remy preferred to stay flexible as long as possible. But he did reach out, tentatively, and his fingers were warm and strong as they wrapped around Adam's hand.

"I also want you to be safe, and I think the safest place—" He stopped with a rough laugh. He loved three people in the whole world, if he counted his ex, and he'd already tried this approach, with no success, with all of them. "I think the safest place would be Europe. My accounts here are frozen just like everyone else's, but the trust fund I established for you over there is still open."

"Challoner...."

"I know. You don't want to go to Europe. And I'm assuming that you don't want to go to any of the other safe continents, either. So the second safest place would be the Capitol. And I know you don't want to go there, either. I'm not asking you to do any of these things, Remy." Adam kept his grip on Remy's fingers, but turned on the bench so he was facing the other man. "I just want to say it. I want to make it crystal clear to you what I want. What I feel. I just... I understand that you need to make your own decisions. I respect that, most of the time. But I want to be sure you're making decisions with all the information you need. Okay?"

Remy nodded wordlessly.

"Okay." Adam took a moment to absorb the beauty he was being allowed to stare at. Remy was wearing grubby clothes that covered his lean, lithe body. He had a smear of blood on his shirt, and there was red under his fingernails. His hair was messy, he had a couple days' worth of stubble, and he looked exhausted. He was perfect, and Adam couldn't imagine not being able to look at him anymore.

"I want you happy and safe. There's other things I want too, but they're selfish. The same old 'I don't want to be an asshole' stuff." Remy shook his head in tired disgust at Adam's scruples, but his fingers tightened, and Adam chose to take that as appreciation. "In terms of what I feel... I feel a *lot*, Remy. More than I ever thought I could. And I understand how that could be... how it could be a burden on you. A cage. I don't want you to feel trapped with me. And I know you don't...." Damn it. How could Adam say the next part in a way that would be fair to Remy without tearing out his own heart? "I know you aren't in a place to feel that way about anybody, probably. Certainly not about me. And I know that even if you *do* start feeling that way about somebody, there's no guarantee that I'll be the one you chose. I get all that. I hate it, but I get it."

So that was probably it. Adam had made his position as clear as he could. Remy, of course, had said nothing. "Is there anything you want to ask? Anything you want to say?"

And now Remy shifted away. He disentangled his fingers and looked out at the city skyline. Finally, he said, "Sasha got out of the hospital a couple days ago. He was in there for almost two weeks, and they didn't charge him for it. They said the state was taking care of its people now." Remy looked like he still wasn't sure he could believe that, but he moved on. "We found him a place to live, and he's in contact with the others. They're thinking of starting their own business. Whoring, still, but doing it for themselves. You know, keeping all the money."

Adam felt dizzy. He forced himself not to speak, and was rewarded when Remy said, "I don't want that. I mean, I want it for them, if that's what they really think is best. But I don't want it for me." He looked over at Adam and grinned quickly. "But if you're looking for ways to keep yourself entertained, I can give you their number."

Adam rolled his eyes. "Yeah, I'm all about prostitutes. You know me well."

Remy reached for his hand again, then said, "I don't know what I want. I don't know what I feel. I think what I want is to be someone who wants things, and feels things." He paused, letting himself catch up to the tangle of words. "I want to be real. And at the Capitol, I don't feel real." He frowned. "When it's just you and me, I do. When we sleep. When I kiss you. That's me."

Adam wanted to say something encouraging, or at least grateful, but he didn't think it was a good idea to interrupt.

"I can help people," Remy said. "I'm being useful. With real stuff—food and medicine and things people need, not just sex. I want to keep doing that." He stopped and looked at Adam with a frown. "And I want to do it for real, not as a made-up job in some office somewhere."

So that was that. Or maybe not. "You could do that during the day, and still come home at night."

Remy nodded slowly. "I can. If you want me to."

Remy could do two jobs instead of just one. Remy could work hard during the day and still be Adam's whore at night. Adam stood up abruptly. "No. Of course not. I'm glad you've found something that makes you happy." He kept his face turned away, looking out over the city, until he was sure that his expression was under control. Then he forced a smile onto his face and said, "Okay, then. You or Dar can send us a list of what you need, and we'll look into finding more secure depot locations. And I'm going to look into setting up some security for you guys. We've got troops drilling all day who might as well be out with you—"

"No, that won't work." Remy stood up and moved toward

Adam. "People barely trust us as it is. If we're traveling around with a bunch of soldiers, they won't talk to us—"

"I don't care," Adam growled. "You have to give me *something*, here, Remy. You have to give me some way to keep myself sane...."

They stood quietly for a moment. Then Remy said, "Would the soldiers have to wear uniforms? Would their guns be visible? If they were just guys, wearing regular clothes and helping us to carry stuff, that might work."

Adam nodded gratefully. "Okay. We can work with that. I'll get on it." And then there was nothing more to say. Remy had made his choice, and Adam just had to live with it. He tried to smile, but Remy wasn't fooled.

He stepped around to stand in front of Adam and laced their fingers together again. "I want to want you," Remy said quietly, and he leaned in, his lips finding their home on Adam's neck. The kiss was soft and quick, but Adam's skin felt cold when Remy leaned away. "I want to be the person you want me to be."

"I want you to be *you*," Adam whispered.

"Me too," Remy agreed. And then the professional smile was back on his face and he took a few steps backward toward the door. "So, Dar or I will probably be in touch. We're working on a comm number for him, so soon you'll be able to get in touch with Dar when you need him. We can definitely use more help, and the supplies would be great." He nodded like a businessman ending a meeting. "Thanks for everything." Then he turned and disappeared through the doorway.

Adam was left alone on the windy roof. He searched his memory of the conversation, trying to find something he could use as a foundation for his dreams. Remy didn't want to be a whore anymore. Was that really the best he could find? No. Remy had said he didn't feel real at the Capitol, but he felt real when he was alone with Adam. That was it. That made sense.

Adam couldn't abandon the revolution now, not after all the

work they'd done. He wasn't arrogant enough to consider himself indispensable in terms of the job he was doing, but he was the chosen leader, the public face that the citizens had grown used to. He couldn't walk away from that commitment. But he could damn well hurry things along! The country needed to get stable, and they needed to have elections and choose a new leader and let Adam get on with his damn life.

He strode toward the shuttle with determination and the beginnings of a smile on his lips. Remy wasn't hurt, and he wasn't running away from Adam. They weren't right next to each other, but at least they were on parallel paths. There was hope, and that was enough for the time being.

Adam climbed the ramp onto the shuttle, and the pilot said, "There's a message from Mr. Winters. He'd like you to contact him as soon as possible."

Morgan. No, Adam was going to let himself savor Remy for a little longer before exposing himself to Morgan's poisons. "I'll talk to him when we get back to the Capitol."

He settled into one of the plush leather chairs and closed his eyes. He could dimly hear the sounds of the bodyguards shuffling into their places around him, and he felt the nose of the shuttle rise a little as they took off, but it all felt far away. He was lying in his bed, Remy wrapped around him, neither of them fully asleep or fully awake, just drifting in that magical in-between state where they were still themselves, but where anything could happen. They were warm, and safe, and together. It was a dream, but Adam would damn well make it a reality.

Chapter Six

"We need to do something decisive!" Morgan wasn't a large man, but he had a way of holding his arms and puffing his chest that made him seem a little larger. Larger, and more ridiculous. In the month since the riot, Adam had been disagreeing with Morgan almost constantly and had gotten more familiar with the man's bombastic body language than he'd ever wanted to be.

Adam would have liked to have laughed at him, but he couldn't, not on such a serious topic. "Having trials *is* decisive. Governing by rule of law instead of rule of man—also decisive. Again, Morgan, you're asking us to establish ourselves as a government by behaving the same way the previous government did! That's not what the revolution is about."

"Those are pretty words, Adam. But the people are angry. They're restless, and they're looking for action on this issue."

"They're looking for *revenge*, Morgan. That's not what a government is about. We have laws, and we have courts, rustic as they currently are. Those are the venues for these matters."

"The people—"

"The people have been given bread, and now they want circuses." Desmond Chan shook his head. He was the oldest member of the council, and probably the wisest. When he spoke, people listened, even Morgan. He was one of the men who'd been considered for the leadership role, as Adam understood it, and had only been disqualified because of advanced age and fragile health. Now he seemed strong and energetic as he said, "Adam's right. The people's anger is natural. Their desire for revenge is understandable. It's a good sign, I suppose, that they are finally able to realize how cruelly oppressed they truly were. But injustice is not remedied by further injustice. We need to have fair trials for the former government in order to show how the new government will proceed."

"Most of the former government is already *gone*." Morgan sounded disgusted. "While we were messing around, setting up tribunals and leaving them on house arrest, most of them packed up and took off."

"Thereby abandoning all claims to their North American property," Desmond said calmly. "We knew that was likely to happen." He turned to the man next to him. "Samuel, are we having any luck with the foreign authorities? Are we any closer to reclaiming the assets of our deposed friends that were held abroad?"

"No change," Samuel Turay said. He shrugged. "They're still waiting to see how things go over here, I think. We've been in power for less than two months. If we're in power for over a year, maybe they'll start listening to our requests."

"By that time, the assets will all be too well hidden," Morgan fumed.

"The assets are already long gone, Morgan." Adam was tired of these arguments. "We knew that would happen. If we're able to recover any of the foreign-held wealth, it'll be a bonus. And we're a hell of a lot more likely to get them if we can present evidence and verdicts from legitimate trials, rather than a record of summary executions and torture-derived confessions."

"So they just get away with it?" Tom Mackie's voice was as light and polite as it always was, but he still got all the attention he wanted. He'd been one of the top generals in the armed forces prior to the revolution, and without his cooperation, the movement would have been much bloodier, if it had managed to succeed at all. He was respected for what he'd done, and for the power he still had.

"They've lost their homes, Tom. They've lost most of their fortunes. We didn't give any clues that this was going to happen, so there was no time for them to get much money offshore. Most of them have enough to live on, comfortably by most standards, but not by theirs. I'd like to see them bear more consequences too, but I don't think revenge should be the major principle of our new government." Adam waited for the general's nod of agreement. It didn't come.

Instead, Morgan said, "Well, actually... we've been looking into that. We've found records of all finances transferred from North American to European banks in the month prior to the revolution. We've looked at any transfers of over one hundred thousand dollars." Morgan raised an eyebrow at Adam. "Can you imagine what we've found?"

Adam squinted back. "I have no idea. I'm sure there were quite a few... wealth is transferred all the time, looking for new investments. Is there some pattern you found interesting?"

"A pattern? No, not a pattern. It was an individual transaction that caught my eye." Morgan lifted a comm panel as if offering proof. "When we embarked on this project, we all agreed that we would not shelter ourselves from the impact. We would accept that our fortunes had been made on the backs of the workers just as other fortunes had been, and as such, we agreed that our fortunes should be returned to the community pot. That was the agreement we made."

"I'm aware of that," Adam said. "I'm not aware of you having much of a fortune to contribute, Morgan, but I know that many of the men in this room gave up a lot, myself included."

"*Most* of the men in this room gave up everything," Morgan said. "But one of them transferred a considerable sum to a European account days before the revolution." He looked pointedly at Adam. "Do I need to clarify who that man is?"

Shit. Adam had been too slow. "Me," he said. "But the account wasn't in my name. I was trying to get a friend out of the country... not because of the revolution, just because he was in a bad situation." Remy had refused to leave, of course, but Adam had set up the account just in case. "It's not in my name. I no longer have access to that money."

"Your whore does," Morgan said. "Are we really expected to believe that you'd allow him to use it for himself without sharing with you?"

"Watch your language," Adam warned. "Remy is the one who made this entire revolution possible. He was forced into a life when he was nine that you wouldn't be able to handle as an adult, and he stayed strong enough to fight back and let us win. Don't use that word again."

"No disrespect to your friend, Adam." Tom Mackie gave a charming smile that made him seem like he'd be better placed at a cocktail party than a military command center. "But the transfer *is* problematic."

Adam frowned. "I guess I can see that. But the amount involved... it was less than one percent of my net worth. If I was really trying to hide my money, I'd have sent a little more, wouldn't I?"

"It's enough money to give you a backup plan. An escape route." Morgan was still on the offensive. "The rest of us are 100 percent committed to this. Maybe we feel more concern about a restless population because we don't have the option of walking away if things go wrong here. You can treat this all like it's a game, like you're an honorable knight in some fairy tale, because you don't really have to deal with the consequences if things go wrong."

The room was silent as Adam tried to come up with a response. But he wasn't the one to speak. Instead, a single word, in Desmond Chan's clipped and aristocratic voice: "Bullshit."

All heads turned in his direction. "Pardon?" Morgan finally managed.

"Bullshit," Desmond repeated with the same clear tone. "If things go badly here, we're all dead. All of us. The money doesn't matter, because we won't be around to spend it. We all know that now, and we all knew it in the days before the revolution. This entire issue is an unnecessary distraction."

Morgan wanted to argue. He probably had some comeback all ready, but he'd been expecting Adam to make the argument, not Desmond. Morgan looked over at Mackie, who smiled and said, "Absolutely. What's done is done, and there's no point worrying about it now. We should continue with our discussion of the criminals."

"I think that discussion is over, as well," Adam said as mildly as he could. "As Morgan mentioned, we all agreed to certain things prior to embarking on this project. One of them was that we would immediately set up a legitimate court system to investigate the abuses of the previous government, and to hold trials for the perpetrators. I don't think anything has changed, has it? I don't think there's any reason to override that agreement?"

"Oh, convenient that you recall the agreement when it suits your purposes," Morgan challenged.

"Enough." Mackie's voice was firm. "We're moving on. And, fine, let's continue as planned with the trials, at least for now. But we will need to find some way to convince people that justice is being served."

"We'll need to start by educating them about what 'justice' really means," Desmond mused.

Adam wished he had more time. He'd like to sit down with Desmond over a couple brandies and maybe a game or two of chess, and get some advice. Not on the day-to-day aggravations, but the big things. What did it all mean? Were they doing the right thing? Did any of it really matter?

But there was no time for such discussions. They were both far too busy dealing with minutiae. Case in point, the next item on the agenda. "Reestablishment of shuttle safety standards," he read out loud, and one of the men at the table stood up to deliver his report. Adam sank back in his chair and tried to seem interested.

"You look tired." Antonia's smile was warm and gentle and welcoming. She eased Adam's jacket off his shoulders and guided him to his favorite chair. It wasn't as nice as his room at the country estate, but that estate wasn't his anymore. It was being maintained, and the same people who'd been employed there still were, but they weren't his employees anymore. He could make an application to have the property returned to him, but for the motion to be successful he'd have to prove that the estate had been purchased and maintained with money not earned by underpaying and oppressing the workers. And there was no way Adam could prove that. He'd paid his employees fairly since he'd taken over, but that had been quite recent. His father had paid the going rate, at the estate *and* at the factories and businesses he owned. One year of fair salaries wouldn't be enough to override decades of abuse. The estate was gone.

Adam sipped the brandy that had somehow appeared in his hands and looked over at Antonia. "You weren't this good to me when we were actually together."

"You had no good reason to be tired when we were actually together. If you'd been doing something productive with your time, things might have been different in a variety of ways." She smiled at him in a way that took most of the sting out of her words, then softened them even more by saying, "You were looking for something, weren't you? Looking for an activity that would be worthy of your skills and your energy. And now you've found it."

Adam didn't have much to say to that, and they sat in friendly silence for a while. Then Antonia made a face and said, "I have something to tell you. Something you won't like."

Adam took a calming sip of his brandy before saying, "What's Kara been up to?"

Antonia smiled in rueful acknowledgement. "She's been going into the city. Without guards. She says she's safer without them, incognito, than she would be with them, announcing her presence."

Adam wanted to throw the brandy snifter across the room. He set it down on the side table instead. "Why?" he managed to ask.

"She's making a holo. Well, she's calling it a *film*, going for that artistic edge. Or it may be a series of short films... I don't think she's quite sure on that yet. She wants to use them to gain popular support in Europe. She's shooting footage of people being helped, workers being initially distrustful but then coming around... I don't think it's a bad idea, to be honest."

"You knew she was doing this?" Adam knew the anger came out in his voice, but he also knew Antonia would be the last person to be intimidated by him.

"No, of course not. I knew she was up to something, but I didn't imagine it was anything so dangerous. I just found out this afternoon."

"Where is she now?"

"I don't know." Antonia shook her head at him. "She's an adult, Adam. If we don't give her *some* freedom, *some* trust, she'll be beyond our influence entirely. We talked this afternoon, and I told her how worried I was, and how worried you'd be, and I asked her to take some time to think about it and then come back and talk to me again."

Adam waited, then stuttered, "That's *all*? You're going to *talk* about it some more?"

"Adam, don't make it worse. I know you're worried. I'm worried too. But we can't drive her away, or she'll be in even more danger."

"We could chain her up and throw her in the damned basement."

"I asked her to take guards with her. She said she couldn't, because people still don't trust the security forces and won't talk to her if there are guards present."

It was frustrating to be having the exact same problem with both of the people he loved, but at least it had set him up with some solutions. "The guards can wear street clothes and help her with the cameras. She can call them her assistants." Adam hadn't seen Remy since their time on the hospital roof weeks earlier, but he'd been getting daily reports from the guards, and it sounded like Remy was fairly safe under their protection. Something similar would work for Kara.

But Antonia was frowning at him. "What?" he asked. "That should work, shouldn't it?"

"I think it might," she agreed. Then she shook her head in bewilderment. "When did you get so reasonable? So flexible? I thought we were going to have an hour-long fight about the 'chain her in the basement' option."

"I'm too tired to fight, Toni."

"No. You've changed."

"Give me a break."

"It's not just that you've found your calling. It's because you're in love," she said. "You've never really... no, Adam, don't argue with me now. You and I were good together. We loved each other. Still do, I hope. But we weren't... we weren't like this. Being with me didn't change you."

"Being with you gave me my daughter," Adam said, then he hastened to add, "and a lot of other wonderful things. Memories." He leaned his head against the back of his chair and let his eyes drift shut. "You know what I mean."

"I'm not feeling insecure, Adam. I'm not digging for compliments. I'm just really intrigued. Loving Remy has changed you."

"Or maybe it's being in charge of a continent full of pissed-off people and a cantankerous cabinet that's changed me. My will to fight has been drained right out of me." He opened one eye to see her serene smile.

"No. It's Remy."

"I never knew you were such a romantic," he muttered.

"I never knew *you* were." She reached a hand out and gently ruffled his hair. "How's he doing? Have you heard from him?"

"Do requests for more supplies count? If the little bastard wasn't being watched so closely, I'd swear he was running the black market. He sure seems to be able to find a need and then get it taken care of."

"Probably helps that he has the leader of the nation wrapped around his little finger."

"Okay, that's a bit much," Adam started, but he let himself be mollified by her gentle smile.

"You're sleeping better," she observed. "You go in that bedroom and stay there for hours at a time, some nights. Very impressive."

Adam didn't tell her quite how he was managing that. He didn't think he needed to give her any more ammunition. "Like I said, I'm tired. Tired people need sleep."

"And what do grumpy people need?"

"I wouldn't know." He took the last sip of brandy and heaved himself to his feet. "I'll ask the guards to set something up for Kara. You'll make sure she takes them with her? If she has a problem with it, have her come find me."

"Yes, sir."

He rolled his eyes, then leaned down and kissed the top of her head. "You're a good mother, Toni. A good wife too, in a strange sort of way."

"The way that lets you fall in love with pretty boys half your age?"

"And then teases me mercilessly about it."

"There have to be *some* perks to the job." She smiled up at him. "Good night, Adam. Sleep tight."

So he went to his room, stripped down to his underwear, and just as he had every night since the visit on the hospital, he fell asleep while imagining himself wrapped in Remy's arms. It wasn't as good as the real thing, but it was the best he could do. At least for the time being.

CHAPTER SEVEN

ADAM woke up and struggled to figure out where he was. Hell, he struggled to figure out *who* he was—he'd been deep asleep. Maybe he should add peaceful brandies with his wife to his list of things that helped him rest. The comm on the bedside table buzzed again, and he reached for it. "Yeah?" he mumbled.

Morgan looked as alert as ever. "We have a problem with the colonies. Emergency council meeting in ten minutes."

"Okay." Adam turned the comm screen off and let himself sit there for a moment, gathering strength. Then he surged up and out of the bed. The council room was just one floor down. "Shower, on," he said in his clear, I'm-speaking-to-the-electronics voice. "Make coffee." He stripped out of his underwear and stumbled into the bathroom. A quick rinse before he threw some clothes on, pulled the mug out from the coffeemaker in the kitchen, and headed down the stairs. A problem with the colonies. Excellent.

He was among the first to arrive, which made sense; most of the others lived nearby, but not right upstairs. Morgan was busy on a comm, so Adam found Nickson, the aide who apparently never slept, and sat down beside him. "What's going on?"

Nickson sent a worried look in Morgan's direction, as if unsure whether he was allowed to spread the news. Finally he said, "It's the colonies, sir. They've declared independence."

It took a moment for that to be absorbed. "Independence. All of them?"

"Yes, sir. Apparently they want to form their own federation, of sorts."

"Wait, just *our* colonies, or the European and African and Asian colonies as well?"

"All of them, sir."

"Jesus." Adam leaned back in his chair and tried to wrap his head around that one. When scientists had first found the wormhole that led to a habitable planet, the agreement had been for each of the continental governments to share equally in the new land. South America and Oceania had opted out in exchange for more extensive rights to the Earth's oceans, leaving four continental governments to establish six colonies each. The colonies were never heavily populated, but they didn't need to be. Agriculture was highly mechanized, with only a few people able to control machinery that would cultivate half a million acres of land. The people clustered in small villages and developed subsistence-level skills to take care of everything they would have picked up at a discount store on Earth. They shipped raw materials back through the wormhole in ships so large that they could not withstand gravity and had to be loaded and unloaded in space. Each ship could carry over ten million tons of food: wheat, mostly, but also rice, corn... anything that would store well. Agriculture on Earth had become devoted to specialty crops, luxury items like meat and fresh fruits and vegetables. The colonies were the breadbasket of the Earth, and without their contributions, the people of Earth would starve.

"What have we heard from them?" Adam asked. "Was it a simple declaration, or have they opened up negotiations? Are they asking for diplomatic recognition?"

"*Diplomatic recognition?*" Morgan sounded incredulous. "Who the hell cares what they're asking for? They can't have it! They can have a day or two to come to their senses, and then they can have the full weight of the Earth's combined military forces bringing them to their damned knees!"

"Listen to yourself, Morgan. Then go back and listen to some of the tapes just before the Colony Seventeen Massacre. I think you'll be startled by the similarities." Adam forced himself to stay in his seat; if he stood up, he was pretty sure Morgan would be bumping his chest and trying to start a fight.

"Colony Seventeen was *one* colony. This is *all* of them! Do you not understand what that means?"

"It means we'd have a harder time oppressing them, since they'll be acting together."

"Jesus, Adam, are you really that stupid? Do you not see that without the colonies, we'll have no *food*?"

"Do you think they're going to just release it all into space? Think it through, Morgan." Adam knew the room was filling up. He knew there was an audience now, everyone watching him and Morgan go through the latest iteration of their struggle for power. But this time, the stakes were much higher than they'd ever been before, and Adam tried to dredge up all his persuasiveness. He didn't need to change Morgan's mind, but he needed to convince the majority of the people listening to the discussion. "They have food; we need food. We have technology, medicine, education; we have the factories that make the machines that let them *grow* the food. They need all that. I'm not saying that independence isn't a potential problem, and I'm not saying I'm pleased with this development. But we can't go flying off the handle. We need to talk to the leaders up there and figure out what they want. *If* we can't negotiate a solution, and *if* it actually comes down to being a choice of force or starvation, then and only then should we consider using force. But we're nowhere near that point yet."

"Your pacifism has always been a detriment, Adam. But it's fast turning into a fatal flaw." Morgan's voice was chilling, but Adam refused to let himself be affected.

"Is that all you've got? No counterargument, just an insult?" Adam turned to the men who had assembled around the conference table. "We're still getting information on this, obviously. We still need to learn what's going on, and try to speak to the leaders of the colonial movement. But I'd like to take this opportunity to advocate for a calm, measured approach. The draconian response to the Colony Seventeen rebellion was a black stain on the history of this nation. It was unnecessary and barbaric. We *cannot* repeat that mistake by overreacting to the current situation."

"Our nation... our *planet* is threatened with starvation, and you think the threat of military force is an overreaction?" Morgan shook his head in disgust.

"I agree with Adam," Desmond Chan said. He ignored Morgan's rolled eyes. "This is a crisis, yes. But it is not yet a critical matter. We need to gather more information and proceed with caution. And most importantly, we need to remember the principles that brought us together as a group. We believe in freedom for all, regardless of age, class... or colonial status."

Adam looked down the table and realized that the members of the council had started seating themselves according to their alliances. Adam and Desmond, Sam Turay, and a few others were on one side of the table. Tom Mackie, the other military types, and their allies sat on the opposite side. Don Ackerman and a couple others sat alone, obviously torn between two parties. The council members hadn't met each other until after the revolution, but they'd spent their lifetimes developing different ways of viewing the world, and it hadn't taken them long to find like-minded allies once they were able to be in the same room. Adam made a quick count. The two polarities were reasonably even; it was the middle group that would make the difference. They were the ones who needed to be persuaded.

"The Colony Seventeen Massacre didn't need to happen," Adam said softly. "The government rushed into it. They didn't try to negotiate, didn't look for any solutions other than killing men, women, and children who'd done nothing worse than declare themselves to be free. Thirty-seven days ago, we made that same declaration, on behalf of ourselves and of every citizen of this continent. Are we ready to destroy colonists for making the same decision we made?"

"You're always so full of pretty words and pretty ideas," Morgan said. "But how pretty is it going to be when we run out of food? We can take a firm line with a few thousand colonists now, or we can watch hundreds of millions of people starve to death in a month or two."

"Those are really the only two options you see?" Adam shook his head and spoke to the audience. "*If* those were the only options, I would reluctantly agree with Morgan. But we all know they aren't." It was a gamble, but he was pretty sure he had the votes. Morgan and Mackie did well one on one, and if they had time, they might be able to persuade the undecided. Adam couldn't take that chance. "I'd like to make a formal resolution." He paused and searched for the right words. "I propose: In regards to the recent declarations from the wormhole colonies, the provisional government of the North American continent resolves to use all reasonable tools of negotiation and diplomacy to find a solution that allows our mutually profitable trade with the colonies to continue. Given the absolutely vital nature of the goods received from the colonies, military force *may* be necessary, but it will be considered as a last alternative only." He paused and looked around the table.

"Seconded," Sam Turay said. Adam was glad it was him, rather than Chan. Turay was in charge of external affairs, and he'd be the one who'd have to find a way to make these negotiations work.

"Do we really need a vote?" Tom Mackie smiled. "With such reasonable, and vague, wording, can anyone really vote against the motion?" He shook his head as if Adam was being silly. "The problems, of course, will come when we have to decide when we've exhausted 'all reasonable tools', and when it's time to look at the 'last alternative'. I mean, if this is what we're voting on, of course I vote 'Yea'. But it doesn't really resolve anything, does it, Adam?"

"It's a complicated issue. I think it would be a miracle if we could resolve it after five minutes of discussion and one vote, without any new information from the colonies or the other continents. I was just trying to be sure that we took that time." Adam was starting to feel a little foolish. "The way Morgan was talking, I thought he was going to be sending for the warships before dawn."

"Morgan doesn't send for the warships, Adam. I do. And I hope you know that I would not do so without exhausting every other possible remedy." The general leaned back in his chair and looked at Adam as if he were an eager but not very promising student.

Adam definitely felt like a fool. He was pretty sure the motion had made sense when he made it, back when Morgan was sounding so aggressive. But now, just a few minutes later.... "Well, do we want to table the motion, then?"

"You're moving to table your own motion?" Mackie frowned playfully. "Is that even allowed?"

"I was thinking that *you* might make the motion to table," Adam said. He needed more sleep.

"Oh. No, I don't think so. Let's have the vote. It'll be nice to have something that we all agree on for a change!"

It would have been funny, back when the revolution was just a pipe dream. Sparring, playing, looking for advantages—Adam would have loved it. But now, with everyone operating on too little sleep and too much responsibility, it wasn't funny at all. It felt like he was losing ground, losing control of the whole thing. And if he wasn't in control, then who would be? Or would it just be anarchy?

"Further discussion on the motion?" he asked, following the routine by rote. After a pause, "Okay, then. As usual, we'll go around the table. Say 'Yea' or 'Nay' when we get to you."

With clear directions from both of the factions involved, the vote was unanimous. And empty. "We still need a strategy," Adam said. "A direction for Sam to work in."

"Let's divide things up," Mackie said calmly. "Sam, you contact the other governments; maybe this will be the trigger that gets them talking to us. Morgan, you gather as much information as you can on the colonies: their leadership, their interests, whether there's been any warning of this sort of move. I'll draft up a few plans for military intervention, just in case such a move should become necessary." He smiled. "Adam, you should get some sleep. You look terrible."

He was taking over, and Adam wanted to let him do it. He *did* need some sleep. And it wasn't as if he was power-hungry. He wanted control because he wanted to be sure the right thing was done, not for its own sake. If he could be confident that things were going smoothly, he'd be happy to curl up in bed for as long as he could.

He knew the table had noticed the shift, and they were all watching to see how he would react. God, he was so sick of all this. But he still had his pride. "Great," he said with what he hoped was a smile. "You can all brief me in the morning, and we'll see how things look then. Now, is there any other business we need to attend to? We've all been hauled out of our beds, we might as well make sure there's no other pressing news...."

Morgan looked unhappy, and Adam took a petty satisfaction in that, at least. Then he was ashamed. He and Morgan both had good arguments to make, and they both tended to get caught up in the competition. They seemed to disagree on every point lately, but they were still on the same side, ultimately.

But Adam was too tired to make peace. He'd deal with it all in the morning, unless Morgan had found a new way to piss him off by then. "Okay. Back to bed. I'll see you all tomorrow."

He headed back upstairs and was asleep before his head hit the pillow. He woke after a few hours, decided against another shower, and gave the order for more coffee.

Another day. Another desperate fight to hold things together when they seemed determined to split apart. He sipped at his coffee and stumbled to the kitchen, hoping to find something edible.

Kara was there, sitting at the glass-topped table, eating an orange. She watched him tentatively as he walked past her and peered into the fridge. He pulled out an orange of his own, then headed for the cupboard. He had his cereal poured and mixed with milk before she spoke. "Are you mad?"

He thought about it. "No. Just tired."

"Tired, like, sleepy, or like sick and tired?"

"A little of both, I guess." He sat at the table and took a spoonful of cereal.

"Because of me?" She sounded like a little girl, and somehow that was what made him so angry.

"The colonies declared independence last night, Kara. We have no idea whether we're going to be able to negotiate with them, and if we can't, we'll have to either starve the planet or baptize this new government with a bloodbath that will make Colony Seventeen look like a hangnail. We have civil unrest in our cities for no discernible reason—apparently when people are given freedom, they sometimes use it in the stupidest possible ways. The council that I thought had the best minds in the country on it is falling apart, turning into a partisan nightmare. The other continental governments still refuse to recognize us. The sinister bastards who used to run the country are sunbathing in the south of France, and I'm being accused of corruption because I put some money aside to try to help a friend. A friend who was just as stubborn as my daughter in terms of refusing to find somewhere safe to be. So, am I sick and tired of my daughter throwing herself into dangerous situations and giving me one more thing to worry about? Yeah, I guess I am. But it's not at the top of my list of concerns right now." He took a mouthful of cereal and wished that it was something tough and hard so he could spend a little rage chewing it. Instead, he swallowed, and sighed. "You're going to take the guards with you, right?"

"Yes," she agreed meekly. Then she stood up and left the room.

He was tempted to go after her. He could apologize, or at least offer her a little comfort. He'd signed up for all this, so it wasn't fair to act like he was some sort of victim.

But then she was back, carrying a large comm screen. She set it on the table beside his cereal bowl and said, "Look at this."

She tapped the screen and an image appeared. It was a downtown street, people lining up for something, shuffling impatiently, and Adam realized that most of them were somehow infirm. A few had limps, others just seemed generally weak. There were benches set up, and people were slumped on them in almost comatose states. Adam didn't want to see this.

But then a small group of people appeared, working their way along the line. These people were wearing medical scrubs, carrying comms, and they stopped and spoke to each person in the line.

"It's a free clinic," Kara said softly. "It's the first time some of these people have ever seen a doctor in their lives."

"There's so many of them," Adam muttered. He'd known there was a shortage of trained medical staff, but it hurt to see such a graphic depiction of the problem.

"There didn't used to be," Kara replied. "The first few days of the clinic, nobody showed. They didn't trust the doctors, didn't believe it would really be free. Then a few people, brave or desperate enough to try anything, took a chance. And the word spread." He looked up in time to see her sad smile. "I know it must be frustrating, when each of your victories brings a whole new set of problems along with it. But this...." She tapped the screen. "This is a *victory*, Daddy. These people are getting medical care, and they never would have without what you've done. You and your partisan nightmare of a council."

He stared at the screen, and traced the people's faces with his fingers. "Thank you," he said.

"There's more where this came from," she assured him. "I've got some great scenes. I know I don't know what I'm doing, in terms of making a film, but I've been speaking to some people, some experts, and they're interested in helping out. I'm sending my raw footage to them, and they're going to look at it and see if they can make it something. Something good."

"It's already good, Kara."

"Well, then, they're going to make it *great*." Her smile was pure and innocent, and her eyes danced with enthusiasm.

"You're being careful, though? And you're not going to do anything stupid, like try to ditch the guards?"

"No, I won't. I'm sorry I didn't talk to you about it before. I thought you'd be less reasonable than this."

He didn't think he was up for that fight. "I love you, Kara. I need you to be safe."

"I love you too, Daddy. I'll be careful. I promise."

And that was probably the best he could hope for. He shoveled the remaining cereal into his mouth and pushed his chair back. "I've got to go. I've been out of the office for several hours, so I expect we've had at least one horrible crisis, if not more."

"You'll take care of it," she assured him. "You'll be great."

He gave her a quick kiss on the forehead, then gathered his belongings and reluctantly made his way to the door of the suite. It would be so much easier to stay in there and hide. But he had a job to do, so he waited for the automatic door to open and stepped outside.

"Daddy," Kara called from behind him, "take some fruit with you. You're not eating—"

He didn't understand what was happening at first. As he turned and stepped back into the suite, the doorjamb beside his head exploded into bewildering slivers, and he heard a loud cracking sound from somewhere out in the hall. He stood there, stunned and confused.

"Daddy?" Kara asked from the kitchen, and her voice was enough to kick Adam back into life.

"Close and lock," he yelled at the door, and it responded, although far more slowly than he would have liked. He punched at his comm screen. "Get security to my suite immediately," he ordered as soon as his call was answered. "I think there's a shooter in the hall."

"Daddy!" Kara's eyes were wide. "You're bleeding!"

He didn't stop to investigate her concern. "Is your mother here?"

"She's still in bed."

"Wake her up, and get her...." Where? There was no plan for this, no steps to follow. "Get her into the bathroom and lock the door." He looked around the kitchen, frantically searching for a weapon he could use to defend his family. "Kara, go!" He pushed her a little, and she turned and ran.

He fumbled in the drawers and found the longest, heaviest knife they had. It was nothing, not compared to whatever gun had sent the bullet into the doorjamb, but it was what he had, and he would use it if he had to. He found a spot just inside the door that led to the bedrooms, and waited. He looked at the knife in his hands and thought of the gunman outside. He hoped security was moving fast.

CHAPTER EIGHT

"I WAS pinned down in my apartment for over an hour while you hunted for the bastard, and you couldn't find a trace?" Adam knew it was mostly stress release making him so crabby, but that didn't mean there wasn't *some* reason to be upset. "What about the damn security cameras? You insisted that they be left on inside the Capitol, so... what did they see?"

Don Ackerman shifted uncomfortably. "We're still working on that. There was apparently some... malfunction."

"Malfunction?" Adam tried to control his voice. "Or sabotage? What did the cameras pick up, Don? Anything? And if they didn't catch it, was it incompetence, or are we looking at an inside job?"

"Possibly neither." Ackerman looked at one of his aides, who nodded his agreement. "We're looking at the possibility that a virus was planted in the system. It would be ironic, obviously, but not impossible. We used a virus to take down the previous regime, so we shouldn't be too surprised if someone tried to do something similar to us."

"No, we *shouldn't* be surprised." As always, Desmond Chan's voice was calm. "So why weren't we prepared?"

Ackerman nodded as if his head weighed more than his body. "Excellent question. And I have no answer. I don't know how the gunman got inside the building, I don't know how he got out, and I don't know why our cameras didn't work." He looked earnestly around the table. "This has been a failure on my part. I accept that, and I will offer my resignation if that is deemed necessary. I will follow the will of the council as a group, or, as Adam was the one most personally affected, of him as an individual."

"No, Don." Adam stood up. "We're all figuring things out, here. We're all doing the best we can, and scrambling to patch things together. There's nothing to be gained by putting someone new into your job, and a lot to be lost." He looked around the table. "Does the council agree?"

There were murmurs of assent, and nobody spoke up in opposition, for once. Apparently a near assassination was what it took to get the council working together. Adam wondered how to capitalize on the opportunity, but Morgan spoke up before he could say anything more.

"We need to get to the bottom of this. And we all need to take more security precautions. More guards, for one thing. It was Adam this time, but it could have been any of us. We need to take the warning, and prepare ourselves."

Adam couldn't argue, and didn't even want to. His brush with death had apparently made him a little more philosophical about the disagreements in the council chamber. At least until Desmond quietly said, "Increased security will be problematic if we aren't sure we can trust our security personnel." He raised an apologetic hand in Ackerman's direction and said, "Not you, of course. But we don't know how this shooter got into or out of the building." He paused thoughtfully before saying, "We don't even know for sure that he had to worry about that. If he's someone who works here... that would certainly answer a lot of the questions about access, wouldn't it? And if he works in the building, and is familiar with firearms, it's logical to assume that he may be a member of the security forces." He sighed. "And we shouldn't assume that he's acting alone, either. Which means that if we increase our security details, we could actually be making ourselves *more* vulnerable by inviting an assassin into our inner circle."

There was silence as the members of the council thought about that. Morgan was the first to speak. "So what are we supposed to do? Damned if we do, damned if we don't?"

"We need to find people we can trust," Desmond said. "But I'm not sure how to do that."

"The previous regime did it by subjecting all its security personnel to truth drugs, and by keeping track of their families, blackmailing the guards into loyalty by threatening their loved ones." General Mackie didn't sound as if he were recommending the plan, but he didn't seem to be condemning it, either.

"There's no point to any of this if we fall back on all the same bullshit the previous regime used." Adam knew he'd made the argument before, and he supposed he'd probably have to make it again. But no one stood up to him this time.

"I can set up more thorough screening of the guards," Ackerman offered. "And we'll keep trying to figure out what went wrong with the cameras. If we can trace that glitch, it might lead us directly to the responsible parties."

"*Parties?*" Morgan was quiet and without bluster, for once. "Are we assuming that it's more than one person? Not just a rogue, but an actual conspiracy?"

"I think we have to assume that it's at least possible," Desmond said.

Adam pushed away from the conference table. The adrenaline from the morning was doing strange things to his body, and his mind, but he was clear on one idea, at least. "I want a gun," he said to Ackerman. "Or maybe more than one. And I want to learn how to use it."

"How very proletarian of you," Morgan said dryly, but before anyone could respond, he nodded briskly. "I'd like to learn as well. The wealthy can no longer expect the poor to look after every one of our needs for us. That includes the need for protection."

"It won't solve the problem," Don said.

"It'll give me something to distract me while I wait to die, at least." Adam waited for further objections, then sat back down at the table. "So we'll investigate, and we'll try to find people we trust to help protect us, and those who wish will arm themselves." He looked around at the worried faces in the room. "All right. We have a plan. We also have a lot of governing to do. What was on the agenda for today's meeting, before all the excitement?" He let them take a moment to refocus themselves, and then went on with the meeting. There didn't seem to be anything else to do.

"You should have called us immediately." Dar strode into Adam's office as if he owned the place. "You can trust anyone to sort out food and medicine in the city. You need us to cover your ass."

Adam peered around behind Dar. "'Us'? Are you referring to yourself as a plural now?"

It was Dar's turn to look behind him. "Remy?" he called, then he frowned at Adam. "Jesus, he's hard to keep track of. Slippery, is what I'd call him."

"I'm not all that reassured that either one of you was able to *slip* in here. Security is supposed to be heightened." Adam tried to ignore the way his pulse had quickened at the mention of Remy's name.

"We're known," Dar said as if it meant something. "But, yeah, that's going to be one of the first things I tighten up around here. Just because a face is familiar doesn't mean it's safe, right?" He strode back to the doorway. "Remy!" he bellowed.

A moment later, Dar stepped back and Remy eased past him into the room. His face was a beautiful, emotionless mask, but his eyes were quick, scanning the room as if looking for potential threats. When the hell had Adam's object of obsession become a ninja?

"I don't really understand what you're doing here," Adam said.

"Not that it's not good to see you. Both of you." And he let himself stare at Remy, just for a moment, just long enough to see the way his shirt stretched across work-broadened shoulders, the dark stubble on his jaw, the....

"Hey, Adam?" Dar said lightly, and when Adam looked in his direction, he found himself staring down the barrel of a handgun.

"Jesus, Dar!" Adam didn't think he needed to see any more guns in his lifetime, at least not if they were aimed at him.

"Are you afraid, Adam?" Dar asked, lowering the gun. "Would you be afraid if it were Remy holding it?"

"I'm afraid you're going to sneeze and it'll go off, you lunatic."

"But you know that neither one of us would deliberately hurt you, right?" Dar waited for Adam to catch up. "How many other people can you say the same about?"

"There are trained guards—" Adam started, but Dar cut him off.

"And they'll be good. They'll do all the heavy lifting, I hope. But you can't trust them completely, can you?"

"How do you even know about all this? This hasn't made it onto the comm channels, has it? And that bit about not trusting the guards... where the hell did you come up with that?"

Dar's smile was as smug as always. "I make it my business to know things. You used to like that about me."

"Damn it, Dar, this isn't a game! Somebody tried to shoot me this morning. Right in this building."

"Catch up, Adam. We know that. It's why we're here." Dar spoke as if he were dealing with a confused child. "My contacts in the Capitol told me about all this, I dug a little, called a few people, and I made a plan. You need trusted people to help guard you. You trust us." He looked over at Remy as if asking for an opinion on what exactly was wrong with Adam's brain.

"*If* you trust us," Remy said, and Adam was so caught up in the sound of his voice that it took a moment to understand the words.

"Trust you? Of course I trust you." Adam stepped forward, speaking to Remy now instead of Dar. "But this isn't a job you've been trained for. And it's dangerous. It doesn't make sense to drag you into it."

"I've been trained to watch," Remy said. "I fade into the background when I have to, and I keep an eye on things." He paused as if weighing his words. "Not just for whoring," he finally said. "Mr. Baryman wanted us to gather information, as well. He had files. Huge files on each client, and on people the client met with. Their sexual proclivities were just part of it. We reported on everything. We watched everything."

"Remy's the eyes, I'm the ears, and we're both good with guns," Dar said.

"Guns? Okay, yes, Dar, this makes sense for you. You've...." Adam didn't think he wanted to finish the sentence. Dar had spied, he'd hunted, and he'd killed, all in the name of the revolution. Adam knew this. But Remy... it didn't make sense to think that Remy had been *protected*, exactly, but he'd been passive: the victim of violence, not the perpetrator.

"We've been doing some target practice, Remy and me and some of the other guys, just in case. We've done a few drills so we know what to do if we run into trouble. Remy's almost as good of a shot as I am."

"I'm a better shot than he is," Remy said quietly, and Dar didn't argue. "I can help."

"Not as a human shield, if that's what you're thinking." Adam immediately felt like an idiot for saying it, for even considering the possibility that Remy cared enough about Adam to risk himself. But Remy didn't seem offended.

"Preferably not, no." Remy smiled, and for a moment it distracted Adam from the more pressing concerns. Damn it, he needed to stop acting like a schoolgirl with a crush. Remy didn't seem to notice, though. "I know how to use a gun. I know what to watch for. I know how to call for help. You're right, I'm not an expert. I'm just another set of hands."

"And you've learned all this in the past few weeks? On top of all the other work you've been doing?" Adam wasn't sure he wanted to know just how dangerous things had apparently gotten in the city.

Remy shook his head. "We've just been practicing. I already knew most of it." He looked reluctant, but added, "I had a client with a thing for soldiers. He wanted me to be as authentic as possible. So I was given basic training in those skills."

Adam didn't want to think about that for very long. "There's a world of difference between dressing up in a uniform with a few props and actually engaging in a firefight."

Remy nodded, and his face was a neutral mask again. "Just Dar, then." He turned to the man beside him. "You can stay here, and I can keep working down in the city. I know the routes, now, and most of the people involved."

That wasn't the outcome Adam had been looking for, and he was trying to find a better solution when Dar said, "No. If Adam doesn't want you, I do. I can watch his ass, and you can watch mine. There's no way I trust these security-force bastards, and I don't want to be stuck here on my own."

But Remy shook his head and stepped backward. "You'll be fine. You're Dar Wright. You're bulletproof."

"I may have *slightly* exaggerated my invincibility." Dar reached out and grabbed Remy's shoulder. "I need your help, Remy."

Remy blinked, then nodded. Just like that, it was settled; Dar had asked for a favor, and Remy had given it. Adam watched the whole thing, and had no idea how to feel about any of it.

And he was still confused when Dar turned to him and said, "Everyone knows you and Remy had a thing. It's probably best if we go back to that. It's a good excuse for having him close by, without calling attention to him as a bodyguard." Dar seemed satisfied with his plan. "I can do the more obvious stuff, and we can both keep an eye on the guards. I need to make some calls, figure out who'll take over what down in the city. You two are okay here?" He reached out and patted the side of Remy's jacket. "You've got ammo?" he asked, and Adam realized that Dar had been checking to be sure Remy was carrying a weapon.

"That's just routine for you now? You walk around with weapons and ammo every day?" Adam was having a lot of trouble accepting all this. Before the revolution, it had been a capital offense for a private citizen to carry a weapon; since the revolution, things had relaxed. But they'd gone far enough that both of these men had been allowed into his private office, on the day of an assassination attempt, while carrying guns?

"Things are pretty rough in the city," Dar said. "I want to talk to you about that. There's a lot of hoarding, and the black market from before the revolution? It's a hell of a lot bigger, and a hell of a lot more aggressive. If it's happening here, it's probably happening all over the country. You're going to need to do something about it."

"I'll put it on my list," Adam said. "Have you two actually had trouble? More than that one time, with the riot? I mean, enough that you think you need to be armed?"

"Better safe than sorry," Dar said easily, but he gave Remy a look that suggested that there was more that could have been said. Dar didn't leave time for Adam to push further. "So, I'm going to go take care of things. Remy, you're on. Keep an eye on him."

There was an awkward moment after Dar left the room, and then Remy said, "He likes to be bossy. But obviously you can say no to all of this if it doesn't fit your needs."

"It... it fits very well, Remy. Except that I don't want you in danger."

Remy, predictably, shrugged that off. "I'm mostly just watching, right? Not too dangerous." He walked across the room and looked out the window, and Adam could remember them both standing there, arms wrapped around each other, watching their city wake up not that long ago. It seemed like a lifetime ago.

Remy turned back to him and said, "Will your wife be upset? I mean, obviously I can stay... I don't know, in the hallway or something. Somewhere that won't interfere with your privacy. But will she be upset if people think you and I are involved, or that you're hiring a whore? We could probably figure something else out—Dar thinks fast, but he doesn't always work things through."

"I don't think she'll mind," Adam said. He was preoccupied with thoughts of Remy waiting in the hallway, so close to Adam's bed without being anywhere near close enough. "We'll tell her the whole plan. My daughter too. They're both pretty good at figuring out how to make things look the way they should. And they'll be happy that I'm getting some more protection."

"Okay," Remy agreed. He stood awkwardly, waiting for... something.

Adam took a step closer. "It's really good to see you. You look good. Strong. The work you're doing... were doing... it was important, right?"

But Remy shrugged. "I guess. But Dar's right, we need a better system. He'll have ideas for that."

"I'd be happy to hear your ideas too." Adam tried an encouraging smile, but Remy didn't return it.

"I don't have any ideas." It sounded like a reprimand, although Adam couldn't imagine what rule he'd broken. Remy looked around the room and then nodded toward the chair by the door, the one he'd used so often when he'd been in the office before. "I can sit there? You must have stuff to do."

As if on cue, Morgan appeared at the open office door. "Oh, hello," he said to Remy, and then he looked at Adam as if waiting for an explanation.

Remy nodded a respectful greeting before retreating to his chair, and Adam decided he didn't need to explain a damn thing. "What's up?" he asked.

"Uh...." Morgan managed to get his focus back. "We've heard from the continental government in Asia. The colonial rebellion has got them willing to deal with us, at least. They want to set up a conference call between you and their prime minister. We need to figure out what you're going to say."

"Okay. Yeah, great." It was hard to remember what was important. The shooting, Remy's reappearance... they'd overshadowed Adam's political goals. But establishing diplomatic relations with Asia was absolutely crucial, and it was a task that deserved his full attention. He refused to let himself look toward the door, but he could see Remy from the corner of his eye, sitting still and proper, watching and listening. Guarding. It seemed wrong—Adam wanted to be the protector, not the protected. But at least Remy was in the building, and had a purpose to make him feel useful. Adam could let Remy believe he was there for a reason, but really, it was just good to have him close by. He was a pet, not a guard dog. But Remy didn't have to know that.

CHAPTER NINE

ADAM tried to hold out. He wanted to stay at his desk until Remy came and got him the way he used to, and led him gently upstairs to lie down together. But Remy didn't play his part. He sat there, quiet and alert, seeing everything and saying nothing. Nothing. It was two in the damn morning, and Adam had been working all day, and Remy was showing absolutely no interest in saving him from himself, not anymore.

Finally, Adam stood up. "I need to sleep," he admitted.

Remy nodded easily. "Hang on two minutes, okay? I'll call Dar and he'll check the halls."

"That's not really necessary, is it? I mean, at this time of night...."

Remy ignored Adam and punched a code into the wall comm. When Dar's face appeared, Remy said, "You owe me twenty bucks. He just tried to wiggle out of it."

"Goddamnit, Adam," Dar groaned, his head tilting as he tried to see past Remy. "You couldn't make it twenty-four damn hours after the shooting?"

Adam stepped forward. "I'm not trying to wiggle out of anything. I just said I didn't think you needed to check the halls at this time of night."

"Because assassins like to work nine to five," Remy said, and he reached over to the comm. "Twenty bucks. And check the halls. We'll wait here." He tapped the screen and the picture disappeared.

"You say *Dar* is bossy?" Adam asked. It was hard to be angry, though. This was his favorite side of Remy: confident and slightly abrasive, treating Adam as if they were equals, or even friends.

Remy didn't seem too concerned about Adam's implied criticism. "You don't want to trust your safety to just me, do you? You need big strong Dar to keep you safe."

"That's not what I meant," Adam protested. He tried to remember exactly what he'd said about Remy's defensive capabilities. Had he done something to reveal his pet-not-protector philosophy? "I'm sure you could protect me if you had to. I just don't want you to have to."

"Me neither," Remy said calmly. "So Dar will check the hallways before we go anywhere. And he says he wants to go over some security ideas with you first thing tomorrow. For the whole family, he said, because he doesn't think your wife and daughter would be targets, but he can't be sure. He thinks maybe kidnapping, for them, rather than assassination. That makes sense, right?"

"As a way to persuade me to do something? Absolutely, yes. That would be an effective tool."

"They've agreed to stay in the Capitol for now. Seems safer, because it'd be pretty hard to get them out of the building alive without being seen."

"They've agreed to stay in the Capitol? *Kara* agreed? How'd that happen?"

Remy just shrugged. "Dar," he said, as if that was an answer.

"You two get along well." It was probably an inane thing to say, but Adam wanted to keep Remy talking, and any other topic seemed like a potential minefield. "Old friends are the best friends, aren't they?"

"So where are yours?" Remy asked. Apparently he didn't have the same minefield-phobia that Adam did. "You were away for a long time, but you grew up here. You don't have any old friends to get in touch with?"

"No." Adam was tempted to leave it there, but maybe this was something Remy should hear. "I burned those bridges. I charred them before the revolution, really, when I was the prissy one bitching about how we should reform the system and pay workers a living wage. But *since* the revolution?" He laughed, low and quiet. "No. My old friends are... they're not my friends anymore."

They stood silently for a while, and then Remy asked, "So why'd you do it? The whole council... it's almost all rich people. A few of them were middle class, I guess. You've got a couple professors in there, and Morgan was a lawyer, right? But the rest of you were rich. You gave up a lot. Why?"

"You know why. For me, at least."

Remy only thought a moment before saying, "Because you don't want to be an asshole? Is that it?"

"Is it such a bad reason?"

"Like a modified Hippocratic Oath," Remy said with a gentle smile. "First, don't be an asshole." Adam was pretty sure that the way Remy was looking at him just then was the only reward he would ever need for any sacrifice he'd ever made. "It's pretty clear. Straightforward. Yeah, I like it. Maybe it should be the country's new motto."

It was so easy, so natural. Adam shuffled forward, reached a hand out to find the back of Remy's head, and gently, easily, brought their lips together. The kiss was soft at first, but Remy opened his mouth at the first suggestion from Adam's lips, and their tongues met in a sensuous, sinuous tangle. Adam brought his free hand to Remy's waist, fought to find a path under the fabric of his shirt, and was rewarded by contact with soft, warm skin. This was perfect. It was everything. The kiss deepened, and somewhere in Adam's brain a tiny voice shouted desperately for attention, but he ignored it. He reached further under Remy's shirt to the small of his back and pulled him in tighter and closer.

Adam needed this. He deserved it. Remy was his, and he'd waited too long to claim the only prize he wanted.

The comm buzzed but Adam ignored it. It buzzed again, and Remy pulled his mouth away to say, "Dar. He'll be worried if you don't answer."

Adam could barely remember who the hell Dar was, much less care whether the bastard was worried. But it seemed significant to Remy, so Adam tried to clear his mind a little. As soon as he did, the voice he'd been ignoring got louder and harder to ignore. And Adam didn't like any of the things it was saying.

He forced himself to release his grip, but Remy didn't step away. He stood still, his eyes on Adam, waiting patiently. Obediently. Adam's stomach roiled, and he half turned and stabbed desperately at the comm panel.

"I'm outside," Dar said calmly. "Everything looks good. You ready to go?"

"One minute," Adam croaked, and he deactivated the comm, then forced himself to turn and look at Remy. "You didn't want that," he said.

Remy stared at him for a moment, then snorted. "Are we back to that? Poor, stupid Remy can't make up his own mind about things. He's too damaged to be trusted." Remy shook his head, and then his expression grew sharp as he took a step toward Adam. "You said I looked stronger. You said something about how I was getting muscles from lifting boxes. But that's only part of it, Challoner. You know the real reason I'm putting on weight? It's because I can eat enough now. Baryman starved me to try to keep me thin and boyish. Did you know that?" Remy stepped forward. "Now that you know about that, does it mean that I'm damaged about *food* too? Do you think I can't decide for myself what I should eat? Maybe you should take over, set up a diet for me to make sure I'm getting all the nutrients you think I need?"

"Did you enjoy it, Remy? The kiss?" Adam squinted, trying to see past the other man's defenses. "Tell me the truth, and I'll believe you."

Remy nodded defiantly. "Yeah, I enjoyed it. Maybe not like you want me to, but, yeah, I did."

Not like I want you to. "You mean it didn't excite you. Didn't turn you on."

"There's more to sex than orgasms, you know." The comm buzzed again and Remy raised an eyebrow. "We done here? You ready to go upstairs and see the family?"

"They'll be asleep," Adam said. It wasn't what he wanted to say. He wanted to come up with something more profound, something that would make all of the confusion swirling around him stop and settle into some sort of comprehensible pattern. But he had no idea what words would achieve that, so he turned and headed for the door. "Open," he said, and Dar appeared as the door slid sideways.

"Everything okay?" he asked, but he didn't wait for an answer. "Let's move quick and quiet. I say the word, you flatten against the wall and work your way to the nearest door. There's guards stationed all over the place. If one of them wants you dead bad enough not to care if he gets caught, we're screwed. And if there's more than one of them involved and they're stationed near each other, that's a problem as well." He smiled happily. "Other than that, everything's good."

Dar led the way, Adam behind him, Remy bringing up the rear. It felt wrong. Adam felt excluded, as if he were an inanimate object, something to be dealt with and taken care of rather than a grown man who could take his own chances and make his own decisions. The parallels to Remy were disturbing, more so because Adam couldn't decide whether the current situation had more in common with the way Remy had been treated before the revolution, or with the way Adam was treating him now.

They made it to the door of Adam's suite, and Dar paused ostentatiously. "You should add our voices to the control list," he said with a nod to the security panel. "And review who else is on there. I've got a guy coming in tomorrow to check for hacks and to put a little extra security on it."

"Open," Adam said to the door, and then he raised an eyebrow in Dar's direction. "'Extra security'? Do I even want to know what that means?"

Dar just grinned and headed through the door.

The lights were still on, and it occurred to Adam that Dar *wasn't* on the approved list yet, but had still somehow been coming and going from the suite all day. Someone had been letting him in, obviously. Adam was therefore only slightly surprised to see Kara and Antonia sitting in the living room, eyes bright and curious as the little entourage arrived.

"Is something wrong?" Adam asked. "Why aren't you asleep?"

"Why aren't *you*?" Antonia rose gracefully and crossed the room as she extended both of her hands. "Mr. Stone. It's a pleasure to see you again. I'm not sure if it's proper for me to welcome you to Adam's suite, when I'm just a guest here myself, but... we're so happy you're joining us." She clasped Remy's hands and smiled at him, and he smiled calmly in return.

"Thank you, Dr. De Luca. I'll try not to be a nuisance."

Adam had forgotten that Remy was good at this sort of thing. Better than Adam himself, really, who was left unsure of what exactly his role in this exchange might be. Mercifully, Kara was approaching now, and Adam reached his arm out to wrap around her shoulders. "You remember my daughter Kara?"

"Of course. It's a pleasure to see you again, Miss Challoner." Remy actually bowed a little, just a slight inclination of his head.

"And you," Kara replied. She seemed less effusive than her mother, less pleased with the new situation, and Adam was strangely gratified. This was a momentous occasion. There *should* be some uncertainty, some thought given about what changes Remy's presence would make. It shouldn't be just Adam who was being turned inside out by it all. But Kara was well trained, and she smiled over Remy's shoulder to Dar and then said, "We were just enjoying a prebed brandy. Daddy, you'll have one, I'm sure. Dar? Mr. Stone? Will you join us?"

Dar moved obligingly into the room, but Remy hung back. "Remy is fine, miss. But, no, thank you. If it's not an imposition, I'd like to look around the suite. I don't mean to pry, but I'm here in case something happens, and if it does, I'd like to know where things are."

"There's time for that later, surely," Antonia said with a smile. She reached out again and captured one of Remy's hands. "No brandy, if you don't care for it. We can find something else for you. But, please, sit with us." She tugged almost imperceptibly on Remy's hand, and Adam could see Remy feeling uncertain about whether it was more impolite to resist her invitation or to impose himself on a family party. Dar apparently had no such hesitations and was halfway to the couch. Antonia cast a quick look in Adam's direction and then said quietly to Remy, "You're going to be living with us quite closely, I understand. I think it will be less strange for us all if we know each other a little. Please, come and join us."

The subtle command in the last phrase made Adam's skin crawl. It was effective, of course, and Remy obediently trailed after Antonia, sitting on the couch where she placed him and doing an excellent job of looking relaxed. But was it fair to manipulate Remy like that? And how many times had Adam done the same thing, taking advantage of a lifetime of conditioning to bend Remy to his own wishes? The whole situation was becoming impossible.

But there was no way out of it, so he found a spot on the sofa next to Antonia and thanked Kara when she brought him a snifter of brandy. She served Dar as well, and then raised an eyebrow at Remy. "You're sure on the brandy? Can I get you something else? But, you know your way around already, don't you? You can serve yourself, if you prefer." There was a curious undertone to her voice. It wasn't quite hostility, but it wasn't welcoming, either. Adam wasn't sure what to do about it, but luckily, Remy didn't seem to notice.

"I'm fine, thank you. I don't need anything."

"But you *will* make yourself at home, won't you?" Antonia's voice was warm. "Kara and I have installed ourselves here with no invitation whatsoever, so it would be completely inappropriate if our presence made you feel unwelcome in any way." And there it was, the slightly raised eyebrow that warned Kara not to push whatever she was up to.

"I'm sure Mr. Challoner is happy to have you here," Remy said smoothly. "As I said, I'll try to stay out of the way."

"And Kara and I will try to stay out of *your* way."

"Great," Dar interjected. "Everyone's staying out of everyone's way. But with Kara not going down to the city anymore, at least for a while, she'll need something to keep her busy. Adam, you wanted to learn to shoot. I think Kara should learn as well. You too, Antonia, if you're interested. There's a range in the basement of the security office, two buildings over. We can get there by tunnel. I can arrange for a variety of handguns to be brought in, and you can try a few to see what you're most comfortable with."

"Or," Adam said hopefully, "you could go to Europe. Do you have enough footage to start editing? We could probably find some people to work as camera operators, if you want, and they could send their files to you back home."

"What message would that send, Daddy? If you're afraid for your family, with all the protection you have, why should regular citizens feel safe here?" Kara was looking for a fight, and Adam was just tired enough to give it to her.

"I don't give a good goddamn what message it sends. I care that you're safe. That was a real bullet this morning, and we have no idea who shot it, or why. Does that not make it clear to you? We aren't playing a game here."

"And now that your lover's back in the picture, it's a little awkward to have a wife and daughter cluttering up the landscape."

Kara looked at him coldly. "Isn't that what you really mean?"

"No, damn it, it isn't!" Adam hadn't really considered what Kara knew about his relationship with Remy. What she *thought* she knew, more like it. But it was immaterial to the current conversation. "This is absolutely about your safety. Remy...." Adam struggled to find the right words. "I'm happy for you to get to know Remy. I care about both of you, and I'd like it if you could spend some time together. But not here. Not now. Hell, if you can figure out some way to get him moving, I'd like it if all three of you got your asses across the ocean and sent me daily updates from your group vacation in the Greek islands."

But Kara wasn't ready to be appeased or sidetracked. "I know what he did, before. What he was. You don't think that's a bit pathetic, Daddy? For you to be acting like this? For you to bring a... a...."

"Whore," Remy said quietly. "It's inappropriate for him to bring a whore into your family home."

Adam had recovered from his shock and was about to speak, but Antonia's hand on his thigh made him look at her, and he frowned at her gentle head shake. She wanted him to stay out of it. But why?

"If that's the word you think fits," Kara said, staring at Remy. Adam had never heard her use that snide tone before, and never wanted to hear it again. But Remy still didn't seem upset.

"It fits," he said. And he waited.

Kara didn't seem sure how to react. She turned to Adam, who was barely managing to keep his mouth shut, and then Antonia, who was relaxing into the sofa cushions as if they were all discussing the latest gossip among friends. "Mom, you're okay with this? Having him here?"

"He's a guest of your father's. This is your father's home. I have no reason to believe that Mr. Stone is dangerous. I have no reason to believe that he'll be cruel to either of us. Anything beyond that is none of my business."

"It'd okay with you that your husband is cavorting with a...."

She stopped again, and again Remy quietly said, "Whore."

"The word doesn't bother you?" The anger was still there, but there was a hint of curiosity in Kara's voice as well, and Adam let himself hope that Antonia had been right to let the two of them solve this themselves. It was totally unfair to Remy, of course, but he didn't seem to be too upset. Of course, it was often difficult to be sure exactly what Remy was feeling.

He was certainly calm and collected as he shrugged and said, "The word? No, the word doesn't bother me. It's accurate. What it means... what I was... isn't a pleasant memory. But there's no point in trying to forget it, is there?" And for the first time, his expression was slightly bitter as he looked at Adam. "After all, nobody else is able to."

Kara frowned at him, her natural sweetness clearly at war with her equally natural temper. "It's what you were," she said slowly, as if she were tasting each word before letting it past her lips. "And now? What are you now?"

Remy fixed her with a level gaze. "I have no idea. What are *you*?"

She returned his look. "A lot of different things, I guess. I'm just trying to figure it all out."

"Sounds familiar," Remy said gently.

Kara looked at Adam then, and at her mother. Finally, she turned back to Remy. "You're going to help keep my father safe. Thank you for that." She frowned at him, then added, "I'm sorry. For being rude."

"You don't need to be," Remy said softly. Then he turned to Antonia and said, "I was told that you're an economist. Has Dar been grilling you on ways to solve our black-market problems? It would be great to find a solution that doesn't end up with people in jail."

The topic shift would have been smooth if anyone else in the room had been prepared for it. As it was, Antonia took a moment too long to collect herself, but then managed to get back into things. Remy exchanged a few words and then extracted himself from the conversation, letting Dar and Antonia shift into the spotlight. Kara eventually joined them, a slightly subdued version of her usual self, but Remy just watched them. And Adam watched Remy. Remy must have been aware that he was under surveillance, but he didn't even glance in Adam's direction. When Dar finished his brandy and reluctantly stood up, Remy rose almost simultaneously, nodding politely to the ladies and clearly heading for the door.

"Remy," Adam said. "And Dar," he added. "We haven't figured out sleeping arrangements." He didn't exactly want to sort it out right there and then, but there was no other time.

"The fourth bedroom is made up," Antonia said easily. "It's tiny, of course, but the bed's a good size." She stood up and gestured for Kara to join her. "And we know where we'll be. It's gotten so late!" She leaned over and gave Adam a cool kiss on the cheek, then smiled at Dar and Remy as Kara bent and pressed her lips to the other side of Adam's face.

"Good night, Daddy," Kara said. His little girl was back again, the strident warrior apparently forgotten. She smiled at Dar and added, "I'd like to learn to shoot. Thank you. Can we start that tomorrow?"

"Absolutely," Dar agreed. He turned to Remy. "I slept a bit this afternoon. I'll take first watch. You sleep, and I'll wake you up if I need you."

Remy frowned, but didn't argue. Adam thought about saying no one needed to keep watch at all, but he didn't want to be accused of trying to wiggle out of his protection again, so he stayed quiet and watched the ladies head off in one direction while Dar moved purposefully toward the front door.

"Good night, Challoner," Remy said.

It was too soon. It would always be too soon; Adam didn't want to let Remy out of his sight, ever. "You could sleep with me," he said quickly. "Like before. If you wanted. I miss that. And you'd be right nearby if something happened." That was a little cheap, probably, but apparently Adam's desperation had overridden his moral qualms.

"I can if you want," Remy agreed.

And they were right back to it. "If *you* want," Adam said.

Remy looked down at the floor, and Adam's gut twisted, preparing for the inevitable rejection. But when Remy's face reappeared, it seemed uncertain. "Your wife," he said. "Your daughter. They're here. It's not the same."

"I haven't shared a bed with my wife in over a decade," Adam said firmly. It seemed important that this was absolutely clear. "And my daughter...." He trailed off. What was there to say about Kara? "I'm sorry she was like that. I don't know what she was thinking."

"You don't?" Remy frowned at Adam as if wondering just how stupid he was. "She's trying to protect her parents' relationship from an outside threat. Did you really think she wouldn't have a problem with this?"

"My *practically* platonic relationship with you is in no way a threat to my *totally* platonic relationship with my wife. Kara... well, I guess she doesn't have details about me and you. But she damn well knows about me and her mother."

"She's a kid," Remy said. "What she hopes for and what she knows... if they don't correspond, she's going to go with what she hopes for."

"A kid, huh? You're not that much older than her, you know." It probably wasn't a good idea, but Adam felt like pushing this just a little further. "What do *you* do when what you hope for doesn't match what you know?"

Another look as if Remy thought Adam was clueless. "I stop

hoping," he said flatly. Then he raised an eyebrow. "So, platonic with your wife, practically platonic with me, don't like whores... are you getting laid at *all*, Challoner?"

Another topic change, and Adam let it happen. He grinned in what he hoped was a charming manner and said, "It has been a pretty long dry patch, my friend. So... let me get whatever action I can? Come sleep with me?"

Remy nodded and started to move. Then he stopped. He seemed to brace himself, and then he looked Adam in the eye. "Yes. I'd like that," he said, his voice clear and simple.

Adam wanted to do some sort of victory dance, or maybe whoop at the top of his lungs. Instead, he smiled and let his fingers find Remy's. "Thank you," he said, and he let Remy lead him to the bedroom.

CHAPTER TEN

IT WAS amazing what a difference a good night's sleep made. It wasn't a *long* night's sleep, but Adam still awoke feeling rested and optimistic about his day. He let himself lie there for a few minutes, listening to Remy breathing, feeling the warmth of his lithe body, and it was all he could imagine ever needing. Then his stomach rumbled, and Remy's gentle breaths turned into a snorting laugh.

"Go get some breakfast. But don't leave the apartment without checking with Dar." Remy rolled away from Adam's side and looked up at the ceiling. "He didn't wake me up," he mused after a moment's thought.

"You probably looked too damn sweet and he just couldn't bear to do it."

Another snort. "It's sure never stopped him before." Remy rolled again, this time toward Adam and then halfway over him, their bare chests rubbing as Remy reached for the comm on the bedside table. He tapped the screen and said, "Dar?"

Adam let himself savor the casual intimacy. They were both still wearing underwear; the night before had involved nothing more passionate than Remy nuzzling into Adam's neck and then falling asleep. But now... Adam had woken up with an erection, and it certainly wasn't going away, not with Remy rubbing against him like that. But what about Remy? Maybe it was time for Adam to start thinking about Remy's lack of interest in sex as something to be investigated and solved rather than simply endured. For twenty-three and three-quarter hours of the day, Adam was either too busy or too unconscious to even think about sex, but for fifteen minutes once a day, he'd give himself the luxury. An investigation into morning wood was justified by science, surely; if Remy was hard when he woke up, wouldn't that be proof that his lack of interest was purely psychological? Which was what Adam had been assuming, but it was probably a good idea to confirm the assumption. Was there any way to justify a wandering hand? Probably not, but if Adam shifted just a little, eased his hip over in that direction....

"Dar?" Remy said again, and there was something in his voice that dragged Adam's attention away from thoughts of sex. "Where the hell is he?" Remy frowned at Adam, then rolled again, scooting over off his side of the bed and reaching for the clothes he'd carefully hung on the armchair by the window. Adam hadn't noticed the gun the night before, but now he watched as Remy pulled his shirt on and then strapped the holster over his shoulder. "You stay here," Remy ordered.

For the first time, Adam realized that this was potentially serious. Dangerous. "No," he protested. "*You* stay here. I'll check it out."

Remy was getting really good at giving Adam *don't be stupid* looks. "That kind of defeats the purpose of all this," he pointed out.

"There's no way I'm going to just sit here while you go out there alone. Not if there's a real chance that Dar isn't okay."

"There isn't a real chance," Remy said. His smile was charming and relaxed. "I'm just being stupid. Playing, really. Let me pretend to be a tough guy for a change, okay?"

"That wasn't even one of your better lies," Adam said as he swung his legs over the side of the bed and reached for his pants. "You're either slipping or I'm getting really good at catching you. Either way, you're busted. Wait for me."

"Let's go back to how that defeats the purpose of having bodyguards," Remy said. "You need to remember that this isn't about you. I mean, it is, but not *just* you. You're the man in charge right now, and that makes you important to a lot of people. Something happens to you, the country feels it, hard. Something happens to me...." Remy shrugged casually.

Adam crossed the room in three big steps and gripped both of Remy's shoulders in his hands. "If anything happens to you, *I* feel it. Hard. And other people too. Dar, and...." Adam probably shouldn't have started the list. He was sure there were more names to go on it, but couldn't think of them. "Sasha...," he managed.

But Remy didn't seem to be getting past the first name. "Dar," he repeated, and he looked pointedly toward the hall.

"We'll go together," Adam decided.

"We only have one gun, and you don't know how to shoot."

"Okay, but—"

Adam was interrupted by a buzz from the comm on the bedside table. "Remy?" Dar's voice came from the device. "You buzzed me?"

Remy dodged past Adam and pressed a button to activate the comm's microphone and camera. "Dar, where the hell were you?"

"Bathroom," Dar said nonchalantly.

"You couldn't take the comm with you?" Remy's relief made him sound testy.

"I don't take calls in there, Remy. It's really not something I like to share with others."

"Get used to it," Remy said. "If you're going to do this, you need to take it a bit more seriously."

"Aw, Rem, were you worried about me?"

"I was worried about *me*. If you were dead, I was next in line. *Plus* Challoner was being a pain in the ass again." Remy stopped talking for a moment, then said, "This is stupid. Why am I talking to you on the comm? You're fifteen feet away." He hit the screen to disconnect and turned to Adam. "See? I was being stupid. Playing. Next time, you should let me have my fun."

"You realize that just because you're talking to the comm it doesn't mean I can't hear you, right? Telling Dar you thought he was dead and then turning around and telling me you're just playing? It doesn't really match up."

"But you're assuming I was lying to *you*. Really, I was lying to Dar. He needs a kick in the ass on a daily basis, I've found."

Adam wanted to hug Remy. Kiss him and fuck him too, but right then, he'd have been happy with just a hug. And a slow crawl back into their bed, a sleepy cuddle, and a return to their peaceful cocoon. But Remy was moving again, pulling his jacket on to cover the holstered gun and then heading for the door. "Me and Dar will have to work out shifts, I guess. But for now, you need to get down to your office pretty soon, right? Or are you going to learn to shoot this morning? Dar's better for that than I am, but I can come along to help, I guess, and he can sleep afterward. Are you going to shower?"

Maybe the barrage of questions was a way for Remy to burn off a little nervous energy, or maybe he was just impatient for Adam to get his ass in gear. Remy probably wouldn't appreciate it if he knew how adorable Adam found him when he was being bossy. "I'll shower," Adam said. He was tempted to invite Remy to join him, but resisted. The fine line between an invitation and a command was still hard to find sometimes. "The security team says the only real way into this suite is through the front door, so if you want to go get some breakfast, that's fine. I'll be safe on my own."

"You could slip on the soap," Remy said seriously. "Crack your skull open. You should probably wear a helmet."

"There's one already in there. I wear it every time."

"Okay, then. I'll go get things set up with Dar." Remy smiled, then stepped forward quickly to press a light, chaste kiss to

Adam's lips. "Good morning."

Adam forced his hands to stay at his side and smiled back as calmly as he could. "Good morning. Thank you for being here."

"I'm a patriot, you know. It's an honor to serve my country." He stepped back, then snapped a very professional salute before turning in sharp military style and marching out of the bedroom.

"He *did* get some training," Adam muttered, then he headed for the bathroom. His morning erection had subsided during the Dar drama, but Adam knew it wouldn't be long before it returned, not if he kept thinking about Remy. He might as well be in the shower when it happened.

OVER the next few days, they fell into an easy routine. Remy was with Adam around the clock, with Dar keeping watch at night. They'd both been there anytime Adam left the relative safety of the Capitol, but those expeditions were rare. There was too much to do at the office, and too many dangers in the outside world.

Adam and Kara learned to shoot, and they both took handguns home with them. Adam was forced to admit that Kara's aim was quite a bit better than his, and in return she conceded that she wasn't really sure she'd be able to pull the trigger if there was a human target in her sights.

Adam went to bed in a black mood, thinking about a world where his nineteen-year-old daughter might have to kill in order to protect herself, and Remy held him close and didn't say anything.

On their fourth morning together, Adam woke up to the insistent buzzing of his comm. Remy was a light sleeper, and he was already alert, slipping discreetly off to the side so Adam could use the camera feature on his comm without advertising his sleeping arrangements. Adam hated it that Remy had been so well trained, but was distracted from that line of thought when the comm buzzed again.

"Yes?" Adam said as he activated the comm and saw Morgan's pinched face.

"Rioting," Morgan said simply. "On the west coast."

"It's still the middle of the night over there," Adam protested.

"It started last night, and hasn't subsided."

"Damn it. How bad?"

"Bad. You should get down here."

"Ten minutes," Adam said. Remy was already moving, and Adam knew he was going to get coffee while Adam made himself presentable. It was one of the many injustices of the world that Adam had to shave and preen to look even remotely businesslike while Remy looked beautiful even with stubble and wrinkled clothes. Of course, Remy wasn't going to be in the spotlight— that was Adam's role.

They had a minute to spare when Dar and the security guards escorted Adam into the conference room. Remy found his spot by the door and waited quietly while Adam found a seat next to Don Ackerman, who was busy on his comm.

"The crowd is estimated at over fifty thousand," Morgan reported without preamble. "There's been significant damage to commercial interests: some vandalism, but also widespread looting."

The room was filling with the other members of the council, and Adam frowned. The timing was strange. Everyone lived close by, but he was in the actual building. He'd gotten there quickly, once he'd been notified. So why were the others arriving at the same time as he was? But he didn't have time to worry about that right then.

"What started it?" he asked. "What set them off?"

"Panic." Morgan's voice was clipped. "There was a news

report last night on the world's food supplies, and the continued uncertainty over the colonies. As far as we can tell, a small group broke into a grocery store with the intention of taking all the food they could carry, even though they couldn't afford to buy it. Things spread from there."

"To over fifty thousand?" Surely there had to be more to this, and Adam needed to know what it was.

"I don't think we can discount the impact of the Capital City riot," Morgan said stiffly. "Or, rather, the lack of impact. Still not a single charge laid? People have noticed that. If there's no punishment for rioting, for looting and taking whatever they want...." Morgan left the rest of the sentence unfinished.

Adam didn't really think he had a response. Not a good one. They hadn't laid any charges yet; that was undeniable. There had been trouble with the surveillance footage, trouble identifying participants, trouble collecting evidence or witness statements. "Are the cameras on this time?" he asked.

"They are," Don Ackerman replied. "I had them turned on last night. And security forces have already engaged the crowd. We're working with the new nonlethal techniques, but trying to be more aggressive than last time. We want evidence, and we want to make it clear that this sort of behavior won't be tolerated."

"So what's left?" Adam tried to sound calm and collected. "It sounds like you're taking the lead on this one, Don. I think it would have been good to get the council together for a discussion first, but it's your department. Your call. So why are we all here now? Is there something that needs to be decided?"

"You don't want to be kept informed of all the developments?" Morgan sounded shocked by Adam's callowness.

"I do want that. I would have liked that last night, but last night, apparently you decided not to share. So now... what's new? What's changed?"

"We just wanted to make sure there was something *to* report,"

Ackerman said. "We've been gathering information, trying to figure out how serious this is."

"Okay." There was no point in dwelling on the past. "So it looks like it's serious. What do we need to do? Another public address? That seemed to work pretty well last time."

"I think we should hold off on that," Morgan said. "You're right, it *did* work, at least short term. But I think it sets a dangerous precedent. People should obey the laws because they're the laws, not because somebody broadcasts a message *asking* them to obey the laws. The first riot, we gave them a warning. This riot... I think we should make it clear that warnings aren't something they should expect."

"*They*," Adam said softly. He wanted to look at Remy, but resisted. Instead he shook his head at Morgan. "Us and them. The powerful and the powerless. We can't set up that system again."

"That's a nice philosophy, Adam." Morgan sounded impatient. "Can you figure out a way to apply it to the current situation?"

"Something different than what you've got? No, not really." Adam pushed his chair back and stood up. "I can't disagree with what you're saying. I just... it's not *them*. It's not the same rioters this time as it was last time. They're on different sides of the continent. Talking about it like there's one big group of people out there... I don't like that." He knew he was rambling, and made himself stop.

"Does it make it sound better if I say *we*? *We* can't be rioting and looting. *We* can't expect the security forces to give us warnings and lots of chances to run away before *we* get caught doing illegal and destructive things." Morgan shrugged to show that the precise terminology was unimportant to him.

"'The law, in its majestic equality, forbids the rich and the poor alike to sleep under bridges, to beg in the streets, and to steal bread.' Anatoly France said that a couple hundred years ago."

"And how does that relate to this situation, Adam?" General

Mackie, as always, sounded mildly amused. "We're *all* poor now, remember? Our fortunes were forfeited. We're receiving the same twenty dollars a day that the rest of the country is receiving."

"There's more to it than money, Tom. Do you really believe you or your family are going to starve? If there *is* a food shortage, do you think we won't get some sort of special treatment? We'll justify it by saying that we're doing important work and need to be protected. Right?"

"That's when we'll have the one big group of *them*," Desmond Chan said, speaking for the first time since the meeting began. "One big, hungry, uncontrollable group, if we can't figure out a way to get food from the colonies. We should let Don take care of this incident. We have a bigger problem, and we're running out of time." He looked around the ring of men sitting at the table. "We need to figure out how to feed our people. If we can't do that, none of the rest of this matters."

CHAPTER ELEVEN

THE next few days were chaotic. The riots spread along the west coast, despite the strong response by security forces, and Don Ackerman spent most of his time traveling back and forth from the capital to the scenes of looting. The rest of the country maintained some level of civilization, although reports suggested that hoarding and black-market sales were rampant. But as Desmond Chan had pointed out, none of that was important, really. The unrest was merely a symptom of the larger disease: the country, and the world, had lost its primary source of food, and no one had been able to figure out a way to address the issue.

"They're barely talking to us," Morgan complained. "It's blackmail. They're not negotiating! Refusing to send food unless we give a full and irrevocable recognition of their independence? They're going to starve an entire planet if they don't get their way exactly?" He shook his head. "Bullshit. They have no military." He glanced over to Remy, sitting by the doorway, and made a face that Adam had to interpret as apologetic. Adam had seen Morgan talking to Remy from time to time, treating him with more courtesy than most of the other members of the council. But now Morgan was considering Remy's feelings in matters of state policy?

Well, not considering them too much, apparently, because after the look, Morgan went on to say, "Military intervention doesn't have to mean a massacre. If sufficient force is displayed, the colonists would have to be stupid or suicidal not to give in." Another apologetic grimace, but he continued. "The Colony Seventeen Massacre, in this context, is almost an advantage. With that as a backdrop, our military presence will seem more threatening. They'll believe that we'll do it, because we've done it before."

Adam watched Remy's face. It stayed totally passive, and Adam felt a quick flash of familiar rage, hatred for the people who'd made Remy so good at disguising his emotions.

"We're not at that point yet," Adam said, wishing Remy would look at him. "We still have time. We can negotiate, we can wait them out, we can look for another way. We shouldn't send the military somewhere unless we're prepared for them to act like the warriors they are. And I'm not prepared to see that happen, not until there's absolutely no other way."

"The other continents aren't being quite so careful," Samuel Turay said. He was the one in charge of foreign affairs, so he should certainly know. "I think they're a day or two away from sending an armada. They want it to be united, with all former colonial powers sending a crystal-clear message that this won't be tolerated." He shrugged wryly. "It's got them talking to us, at least. And it would be an excellent opportunity for us to work with them. We could cement relationships, make it clear that we're a legitimate government."

"We'll prove our legitimacy by engaging in aggression against our former citizens?" Adam was tired of this line of argument, but could never find a way to defeat it permanently.

"That's what our current citizens want," Morgan said quietly. He tapped his comm screen and the oversized screen on the wall changed to display a chart. "Overwhelming support for the threat of military action. Strong support for lethal force if needed." And damn it, he looked at Remy *again* before saying, "A disturbing level of support for 'any means necessary'." He waited to let the inhabitants of the room read the chart before saying, "People are afraid. The former government was brutal and dictatorial, but at least the citizens knew what to expect. With us... they don't even trust us to be competent. They want us to prove ourselves to them, and as habitual *victims* of state violence, violence is one of the only communication techniques they understand. For their whole lives, they've been told that might is right; we can't expect them to forget about all that in less than two months."

"Now who's getting philosophical?" Adam tried to keep the question light, and he tried not to stare at Remy. He tried not to wonder just what Remy and Morgan had been talking about, and how well they'd been getting along. Neither he nor the country could afford the distraction. "I don't disagree," he said. "But I think we can hold them off for another few days. For longer than that, if we can." He looked at Turay. "I agree that it would be beneficial for us to work together with the other continental governments. But not on something like this, surely. If we can persuade them to keep trying to negotiate, and to wait until the last minute, then...." Now it was his turn to look apologetically in Remy's direction. He had his mouth open to finish the sentence when the room shook. The dull, distant thudding sound came a moment later.

"What the hell?" General Mackie managed, and then the main doors slid open and the guards streamed in, their weapons drawn and ready.

"Please remain calm," the lead guard said. "We're receiving reports...." He nodded in response to something only he could hear, then said, "There's been an explosion on the first floor. Evacuation protocols are being initiated." He stepped around the table and headed for the small door at the back of the room. "Please follow me."

Adam hadn't even noticed the movement, but somehow Remy was by his side, handgun drawn but held unobtrusively by his thigh. "Dar's on his way," Remy said quietly.

Adam frowned. "You don't think...."

"Sir, if you'll follow me, please," the lead guard said. The calm authority in his voice was hard to resist.

"Just a second," Adam said. The other council members were filing obediently out of the room, heading out the door. "Where are you taking us?"

"There are evacuation shuttles on the roof, sir. It's standard procedure. Please follow me."

Morgan was the only other council member still in the room. He looked back from the door before going through it. "Adam, what's the problem?"

Adam looked at Remy. *Was* there a problem?

"Doesn't this remind you of anything?" Remy asked impatiently. "A distant explosion, with dignitaries evacuated as a precaution? By shuttle?"

Damn it. Once it was said that way, it seemed far too familiar, and Adam could see the awareness growing on Morgan's face as well. Adam turned to the guard. "How often are the shuttles inspected? Have you changed procedures since the Baryman Hotel bombing?" He didn't think it was the right time to point out that he'd been one of the revolutionaries involved in that incident. "Remy's right—if the enemy couldn't reach us in this room, they might attack an easier nearby target in order to trigger our evacuation procedures. It flushes us out into the open, and if they've had time to sabotage the shuttles...."

That was when Dar arrived, his gun held low and ready just like Remy's. Kara and Antonia trailed after him, looking disoriented but not afraid. Dar must have dragged them out of the suite without much explanation. "You're still here," he said, sounding relieved. "This seems really familiar, right?"

"We were just discussing that," Adam said. He let himself pull Kara in for a quick hug. It was good to know that she was safe, at least for the time being, but her presence reminded him of one more responsibility dragging down on him. He felt overwhelmed, involved in things far beyond his experience or expertise. But he was supposed to be the leader, so he turned to the guard. "Get them off the roof. If things heat up here, we'll still have time to evacuate. But our enemy probably knows our procedures, so following the plans too closely makes us vulnerable."

The guard froze, clearly torn between past training and current events. It was Dar, brash and relaxed, who pushed past the careful balance. "That was an order from the continental leader, Lieutenant."

The guard looked at Morgan, then swiveled to stare at Adam before activating the comm attached to his helmet. "Suspend evacuation," he ordered. "Move the subjects to covered locations and hold position until further orders."

"We should get out of this room, though," Dar said. He looked at the guard. "Between here and the roof—is there somewhere we could go? Stash them"—he jerked his head to indicate Morgan, Adam, and the ladies—"and guard the door?"

The guard frowned. "There's an old service hallway that was converted to an evacuation corridor. There are a few doors off of it, but they've been welded shut."

"Let's just hang out in the hallway, then." Dar smiled calmly. "It'll be fun."

"Fun?" Remy grumbled, but he moved to the side, obviously herding the others out through the doorway. The guard preceded them, and they took one flight of stairs up before they ran into the rest of the council coming back down from the roof.

"What the hell is going on?" Samuel Turay asked. He sounded petulant and exhausted. Adam looked at the rest of the men on the stairs and realized how much they'd aged in the past few months. He wondered if he'd deteriorated the same way. Remy was still beautiful, of course, but even he looked tired.

"We're in a holding pattern," Adam said, and he sank down to sit on the stairs. "They're going to check out the situation before we do a full evacuation. No point in getting too far away if the risk is over."

"Is the risk *ever* really over?" Desmond Chan's lips curled as he spoke, but it wasn't a happy smile. He lowered himself carefully to the step above Adam's. "Until we figure out who's doing this...."

"Check the surrounding buildings as well," Dar muttered to the lead guard. "If they couldn't get explosives onto the shuttles, they might try to shoot them down with missiles."

Adam recognized the idea as one that had been discussed and rejected by his team before the revolution. "We never figured out a way to get our hands on a missile launcher," he said quietly.

"We were working from the outside," Dar replied. "No access to the military or security force equipment. I'm not sure that's the case this time."

Another chilling thought. Adam shuffled to the side to make room for Kara, and she nestled in next to him. He wished Remy would come over, maybe sit a step or two below and lean back against Adam's legs, but he knew that wouldn't happen. Remy was polite but distant in public, or even just around Kara and Antonia. There would be no physical contact, no action that would make the connection between Remy and Adam obvious. Remy was discreet, and Adam hated it.

Antonia was still standing, and she cleared her throat a little, calling the attention of the men to her. "We're apparently going to be stuck here for a little longer," she said in her clear, rich voice. "And I don't mean to be opportunistic, but it does seem like a chance for me to speak to all of you. I'd be ashamed of myself if I didn't mention the work Kara and I have been doing with the women of the continent." She glanced at Adam, not asking for permission, but clearly looking for a reaction. He refused to change his expression, and after a moment, she continued. "As a woman, I feel for my sisters who are not able to fully realize their potential. As an *economist*, I'm shocked by the wastefulness of a system that limits opportunities for half of its human resources. For your political reforms to be effective, your economy will have to undergo a massive transformation. For too long you've relied on what was essentially slave labor, but you all know that cannot continue. As your economy transitions, you will have the opportunity to create freedom for *all* of your citizens, not just the male half. And I'd like to urge you to make that a priority as you work to guide the nation through this difficult time."

"Our priority is food," General Mackie said. His traditional good humor was not as evident as it usually was. Now that Adam thought about it, he realized that the man had been getting more and more surly over the past weeks. Just one more casualty of the stress and high workload? Or was there something else going on? The general looked absolutely scornful as he said, "Until we find a way to feed people, we have no other goals."

"I know about the food issue," Antonia said. "And I agree, it should be a priority. But it's my understanding that we're in a waiting game, there, and doing something about women's rights isn't going to make it *less* likely that the colonies will cooperate with us."

Adam sighed. The staircase railing was metal, and it was cool when he rested his forehead against it. He wanted to close his eyes and let himself drift away.

"Do you have concrete suggestions in mind?" Morgan sounded more patient than he ever did when he spoke to Adam. It wasn't clear whether he was being respectful or patronizing.

"Yes, we do. Kara and I have been in communication with women in a variety of fields—women who've fought to educate themselves even in a country that tells them their minds are not of value. We have a list of demands almost ready to present to you—"

"Demands?" The general sounded incredulous. "The country's about to starve to death, and you ladies are going to start making *demands* of us?"

"If the country starves to death, it will do so with or without our list. If it does *not* starve to death... then, yes, *demands*. Half of your population is still being oppressed, and that cannot be allowed."

"Get your woman under control, Adam!" The general was back to his joking tone, speaking as if they should all be amused by Antonia's silliness. "Maybe if you spent more time with her and less with your little boyfriend, she wouldn't have the energy for this nonsense."

"Enough," Adam said. He wished he had the luxury of exploding. In any other situation, he would have been tempted to punch the general in his patronizing, misogynistic face, but they somehow had to keep working together and one of them had to be the bigger man. And the situation was already teetering on the edge of chaos. "We need to stay calm and work together." He wasn't sure just who he was speaking to. All of them, he supposed. "Are we at least agreed on making our own decisions on the colonial situation? We'll continue to wait as long as we can rather than following the others into battle?"

"If the other continents go in alone, what do they plan to do with our colonies? Just ignore them? Or is there a chance that they'll try to take them over?" For once, Desmond Chan didn't seem to already know the answer to the question he was asking, and all heads turned to see how Adam would respond.

"Should we issue a statement?" he asked. He was talking to Sam Turay, mostly, but he'd have been happy to hear a response from any of them as long as it was vaguely on topic and didn't include insults against any of the people Adam loved. "A public one, broadcast to everyone, including the colonies. We could say that we are still negotiating with our colonial properties, and that we still, at this time, claim full sovereignty and ownership of them. We could send a private message to the colonials explaining that we're saying it in order to keep the other armies away? Could we word it in a way that wouldn't piss off the Europeans if it leaked?"

Samuel nodded thoughtfully. "Might work. I'll have a look at it."

"Might improve our standing with our colonies too," Morgan said slowly. "Make it clear that we're still friendly toward them... might make them more inclined to negotiate." He nodded decisively and looked at the others. "I like it."

It was strange to have support from that direction, strange enough to make Adam want to reconsider his words. But Antonia was staring at him now, obviously about ready to start pushing again, so he didn't have time to worry about Morgan. "Toni, can you and Kara get that list finished off and let me have a look at it? You know I'm interested in that, it's just a matter of finding the time."

"We have a rally scheduled for this weekend," Antonia said. "It would be really good if I had some positive news to share. People can't eat hope, but it can keep them from noticing their hunger, at least for a while."

Adam nodded. "Get me a copy of the list. I'll see what we can do."

Antonia squinted at him, then smiled sadly. "You sound like a politician."

"I guess I do."

"How much longer are we going to be stuck in here?" General Mackie asked. "And where the hell is Ackerman, anyway? Shouldn't he be here to tell us what's going on?"

"He's on the coast today," Morgan replied. "They arrested another couple hundred rioters, and he's trying to figure out what to do with all of them."

The lieutenant stepped forward and whispered something to Dar. He tried to look casual, but every face in the hall turned toward him, and he frowned at Adam before shrugging. "No explosives were found on any of the shuttles," he said. "But they have some footage of an unidentified man carrying something that might be a handheld missile launcher into the bank down the street. They've got the place surrounded, now, and are looking for him."

"We'd like to keep you here for another few minutes, just until we've triple-checked the conference room," the lieutenant added. Apparently once Dar had announced the first piece of news, the guard realized the futility of trying to keep things confidential.

"And the bomb downstairs?" Adam asked. "Was anyone hurt?"

"A few workers were injured. They've been taken to the hospital, but their lives aren't believed to be in danger."

"I'm going to have a serious talk with Ackerman," the general said. "This is bullshit. They were going to shoot down our shuttle? If he can't handle his duties, if he can't keep people under control, then my soldiers damn well can!"

Adam didn't remember a similar level of outrage when it had been only *his* life that had been threatened. And he absolutely didn't want to see the military getting any more power than it already had in the new government. "If we can capture the guy with the missile, it'll be a huge benefit. We still don't even know who the enemy is, or what they want. Having someone to question... someone to target... that'll make Don's job a lot easier."

The lieutenant nodded. "Yes, sir, it will."

"So, we've got a while longer," Adam said to the council. "Should we just continue with our meeting?" He found the energy for a soft smile in Remy's direction. "I'd like to be finished at a decent hour today, if we can manage it."

CHAPTER TWELVE

"THE allied armies are headed for the wormhole." Morgan, as always, sounded vaguely accusatory, but Adam was beginning to believe that was just the man's natural tone of voice, at least when talking about political matters. "We've been scolded publicly by the Europeans, the Asians have expressed their disappointment, and Oceania, for some damn reason, offered to send troops in our place. They'd better not be trying to steal our colonies."

"The way things are looking right now, I'd trade the colonies for their share of the oceans here." Adam tried to sound confident and relaxed, but he didn't think he was fooling anyone. "What's the timeline? It takes about eight days to get to the wormhole entrance, right? And then a few hours to travel through it?"

"Those numbers are for freighters and small passenger vessels," General Mackie said. "The military ships will be a bit faster. About six days to get to the wormhole."

"And it takes time for communication to travel back and forth. Are the expeditionary forces authorized to accept surrender? Or do we have to wait for the message to get to Earth, and then send orders back to lift whatever actions the military is taking?"

"I don't have answers to those questions," Mackie said through a tight smile, "because we are not part of this military operation. Standard procedure would be for the troops on the ground to be able to agree to a ceasefire, with a full surrender needing approval from the Earth commanders. But as I said, I don't have specific information for this venture."

"Our forces are ready to go, right? If we decide we need to send them?" Adam knew he shouldn't have asked halfway through the question. The general had gotten downright touchy since the council had decided against joining the allies, and he wouldn't appreciate any questions about his competence.

"We are fully prepared, as always." Mackie raised an eyebrow. "So that's that, for now. Maybe this would be a good time to ask you about your rabble-rousing females. They're at their rally right now, aren't they? I trust that steps have been taken to ensure that *this* event doesn't turn into another damned riot?"

"Security is tight," Ackerman said firmly. "The crowd is large, but well controlled at this time."

"Seems foolish, having the damn event right outside our door." Apparently the general wasn't ready to let this go. "Just because your women are involved, Adam? You don't trust Don to be able to protect them any further away?" Apparently the talk between the general and Ackerman had gone smoothly if Mackie was now criticizing Adam for not trusting the security forces. Or it was just one more shift in the treacherous sands of council politics.

"The rally organizers asked for permission to use the square, and we didn't see any reason to refuse them. And if we can finish up here, I'd like to go out and show my support."

"Your wife was right," Morgan said with a smirk. "You *are* starting to sound like a politician."

"I sound like a father and husband, one who believes in equal rights and freedoms for the women he loves."

"Very nice," Morgan said. "I may borrow that line. Of course, I'd need to get a wife and daughter, first...."

"Good luck with that, with all the women running around 'expressing their independence'." The general made almost every word sound like a mild obscenity.

"Okay, then," Adam started. He stopped speaking when Remy

jerked to his feet. He'd been reading his comm, but now....

"There's a problem at the rally," he said, looking at Adam as if no one else was in the room. "I just got the message." He stepped a little closer. "It sounds like someone on the podium may be injured."

"Someone on the podium," Adam repeated numbly. Antonia. *Kara.* They'd both been so proud of being asked to speak. He was moving before he knew it, running out the door and down the hall, Remy by his side, the startled security agents trailing along in their wake.

"It might be another trap," Remy said as they approached the outer doors. "Someone trying to flush you out into the open."

"It might be Kara," Adam retorted, and he pushed his way through the doors. If someone was trying to get him, at least he'd be a moving target. He sprinted down the wide staircase, across the concrete, toward the square. He could see guards now, their black uniforms gathered like a cloud over the podium, and then he saw little clusters of them hustling away and realized that the dignitaries were being escorted to safety, surrounded by men in body armor. Adam couldn't see past the guards to tell who was inside, who was still able to move, who might have been hurt....

"They're moving everyone to the secondary location," Remy told him. Adam had no idea how Remy knew. He had no idea what the hell Remy read all day long on his comm, or how he'd heard about this before the guards had told Adam. But he didn't care, not if Remy could help him find Kara and Antonia.

"Where?"

"The basement of the Treasury Hall." Remy grabbed Adam's elbow and pulled, redirecting his frenzied trajectory. They ran on.

By the time they reached the building, the guards had set up a cordon around it, but Adam pushed through, and his own guards smoothed over whatever reaction there might have been. Kara. Antonia. Where were they?

"Daddy?"

Kara's voice affected him like an electric shock, jerking his head up as he searched wildly for her. "Kara?" He could hear the desperation in his voice, the fear and need.

"Daddy!" She pushed through the line of guards surrounding her and headed for Adam like a cannonball. He stepped forward to greet her, wrapped her in his arms, kissed her head, and almost wished someone would try to take her from him, just so he could turn all this adrenaline into anger and violence.

"Your mother?"

"She's okay," Kara said, and then there were no more words, just body-shaking sobs as Kara burrowed into his chest just like she had as a newborn.

Adam let himself relax a little. There was still a problem, still something to be figured out and dealt with, but it wasn't the worst. It wasn't the end.

It took a few minutes before Kara's tears subsided, and Adam was glad to have the chance to collect himself. When she finally seemed back under control, he said, "Kara, what happened?"

She looked up at him and opened her mouth, but then the sobs started again. Adam's relief was beginning to fade.

He felt strong, familiar fingers curving over his shoulder and looked at Antonia in confusion. "You're okay?" he asked, but it was clear that she was. "What happened?"

"Dar." Adam realized that Antonia had been crying as well.

"Dar what?" There were so many questions to which Dar's name seemed to be a completely sufficient answer, but Adam really wasn't sure this was one of them.

"He was shot," Antonia said. She took a steadying breath before saying, "He was killed. Instantly." Her face crumbled, and she said, "No pain," as if it was the only fixed point she could find in a world suddenly tipped sideways.

Adam couldn't make sense of it. He managed not to say *but he's bulletproof* out loud, but it was the only thought in his head. Until, finally, he realized the more important thing that he should have been thinking about. "Remy," he said, and he looked around the room, searching for Remy's familiar, lean shape.

"He's with Dar," Antonia said. She shuffled forward and eased herself between Adam and Kara, taking their daughter in her arms and cradling her just as protectively as Adam had. "We're okay," she said. "Go find him."

It felt wrong to leave Kara, but she had her mother. Remy had... God, with Dar gone, he had nobody but Adam, and Adam really wasn't sure he was good enough to be what Remy deserved. The lack of options was fortifying, though, so Adam gave Kara's head one more fervent kiss and then started off in the direction Antonia indicated.

There was a curtain set up, and behind it Adam could see a shape on a stretcher, covered with a sheet that was marred by a slowly spreading red stain. Adam didn't want to go any closer, and he realized that he didn't have to, because the body was alone. Remy was gone.

Adam's eyes searched the room once again, but didn't find what he was looking for. He saw a familiar security guard and fought his way through the crowd. "Have you seen Remy?" he demanded.

The guard nodded his head toward a closed glass door. "He's talking to the captain."

Adam was moving before the guard finished talking. He knocked perfunctorily on the door and then slid it open. Remy was inside, standing with a couple other men, and he looked... he looked fine. His only surviving childhood friend, his comrade at arms, had just been brutally murdered, and Remy looked as if he was planning a tea party. He saw Adam and turned to the captain.

"We'll get them back to the Capitol, then?"

The Captain nodded in reply, and Remy headed toward Adam. "The tunnels have been secured," he said coolly. "We'll take you and the ladies back underground. It's safest."

"Remy," Adam said, and he reached his hand out to grip the man's shoulder.

Remy jerked away so violently that Adam almost lost his balance, but only a breath later his voice was calm as he said, "Neither of them reported any injuries, but your physician has been contacted and will meet you at the suite, in case he's needed."

Remy was walking as he spoke, and Adam fell in behind him, too confused to resist. Antonia saw them coming and pulled Kara a little more upright, then whispered something in her ear. Whatever it was seemed to be effective, because Kara straightened and allowed her mother to guide her over to where Adam and Remy were waiting.

"Back to the suite," Adam said dully.

"We shouldn't leave him alone," Kara protested, her eyes wide.

Remy was staring at the door that Adam assumed led to the tunnels, his gaze so intense that it wouldn't have been totally shocking to see the doorway being dragged toward them somehow. He barely seemed to notice Kara, and it was her mother who said, "They're going to take care of him. They won't leave him alone."

"But they don't *know* him," Kara protested.

"He's dead." Remy's voice was cold and hard. "You're alive, and we're trying to keep it that way. Let's go."

Kara looked like she'd been slapped, but started moving. She followed Remy through the doorway and along the tunnel, Adam and Antonia trailing behind her, uniformed guards flanking them all. They were silent until they were inside the suite with the door closed behind them.

Then Kara turned to Remy, pushed out her jaw and narrowed her eyes. "Do you not care at all? He was supposed to be your best friend! " She looked as if she didn't have any more words, then wailed, "It's *Dar!*"

"I know," Remy replied. He turned to Adam. "The guards outside have been with us for weeks now. If they weren't trustworthy, you'd be dead. I have to go take care of some things. I know you don't like wearing your gun, but it's in the suite, right? If you need it, you can find it?"

"It's in the drawer of the bedside table," Adam said numbly. The heavy gun had felt oppressive when he'd tried to wear it, his mind always too aware that he had a lethal weapon strapped next to his heart. But now he wondered if the weight might not be comforting.

"Go get it, okay? Just for today." Remy didn't wait to hear Adam's response. He was already heading for the door.

Adam didn't react quickly enough. He was still trying to figure it all out. He needed to find a way to accept what had happened, and then to help Kara deal with it. And what the hell was going on with Remy? He struggled to catch up with the younger man, who was walking briskly toward the door. He grabbed Remy's arm, forcing him to stop, and then had no idea what to say.. "Okay," he managed. "Okay. I'll get the gun. And you need to... to take care of some things. But you'll come back here later? Or find me... I might have to go down to the council room again."

"I'm not sure how long my errands will take. And, really, we can trust these guards. Dar and I were talking about it, and we were pretty sure we weren't needed anymore." He hadn't stumbled or even blinked when he said Dar's name. It was beginning to seem that Adam had somehow fallen in love with a robot.

"Don't come back as a bodyguard," Adam said. "Just... come back."

Remy shrugged. "I'll see what I can do, but don't count on me." With that, he turned and headed for the door. Then he stopped and looked back at Adam. "His family. They're all out at your old place, right? You'll talk to them? Fast, before they hear from someone else."

Adam nodded. He dreaded it, but he'd do it. "I'll try to fly out there and do it in person," he decided.

Remy should have nagged Adam about the risk. He should have insisted on coming along, ready to launch himself between Adam and any potential threat. Instead, he just nodded. "Okay." He turned again, took a few steps, and disappeared out the door of the suite.

Adam stared after him. Antonia said, "Everyone handles grief differently. He'll be back when he needs you."

"I hope he doesn't hurry," Kara muttered.

"I'm sure he won't," Adam said flatly. Dar was dead. Kara and Antonia had almost been shot. Remy had shut down. Adam couldn't deal with all of this in his personal life, not while things were falling apart in the government, as well. "I need to arrange a flight," he said. He'd managed to stay away from the old homestead up to that point; he'd loved the place, and it had hurt to give it up, even though he knew it had been the right thing to do. But now he needed to return. He needed to break the bad news to Dar's loved ones, and he needed to find a way to comfort them better than he'd been able to comfort Remy.

"You'll be okay here?" he asked, and Antonia nodded sadly.

"Go. Give them our condolences. Thank them for his sacrifice, and let them know that we'll always be grateful."

"I still don't really understand what happened," Adam said, as much to himself as to them.

"He was murdered!" Kara shrilled. "One second he was standing there beside me, joking and laughing, and the next, his chest just...." She broke into tears again.

"I'm sorry, Kara." He was going to talk to her, as soon as she calmed down, about going back to Europe. Surely this experience would have been enough to convince her. But for now, he rested his hand gently on her shoulder, then pulled it away. "I'll get more details on the way," he told Antonia. "You two will stay in, right? No excursions, no matter what."

Antonia nodded. "Of course. You'll be back later today?"

"Yes." He leaned over and pressed a kiss to the top of Kara's head. "I'm sorry, sweetheart. I cared about him too." It was probably stupid, but he wasn't sure how long it would be before he got back, and he didn't want any more ugliness, so he added, "And he *was* Remy's best friend. His only friend. Try to be gentle with each other, okay?"

She didn't answer, but he hoped Antonia's sad smile meant that she'd repeat the message when Kara was better able to hear it.

"I love you both," Adam said, and he turned and left the suite. He had a responsibility, and he wouldn't let himself shirk it.

CHAPTER THIRTEEN

REMY didn't come back that night. Adam stayed awake as long as he could after returning from the estate, but by three in the morning he finally pushed away from his desk and stumbled over to collapse on the bed. His sleep was fitful, and when the first rays of the sun trembled into the room, he threw the covers off and sat up. He'd hoped that Remy would creep in during the night, but Adam was alone.

He made his way to the kitchen and found Remy sitting at the table, his face impassive, his hands curled around a steaming mug. "Morning," he said, his eyes fixed on his fingers. "I think you're okay with the regular guards if you stay in the building, but I'd like to be with you if you go anywhere else. Does that sound okay?"

"Remy, are you all right? I mean, about Dar." Adam felt like an idiot, but he was pretty sure he'd have felt even worse if he hadn't mentioned it.

"I'm fine. Does that protection arrangement make sense to you?"

"He was a friend of mine too, you know. Obviously I hadn't known him as long...."

"But now that he's out of the game, someone needs to pick up on the work he was doing. I think that should be me. So if you're okay with having the regular guards as protection when you're in the building, I think I can make it work."

"Damn it, Remy, does he not deserve a few tears?"

"He's dead. Tears won't bring him back. If they did, Kara would have resurrected him yesterday." For the first time, Remy looked at Adam. "Are you okay with the changes to the protection schedule?"

There was nothing more to say. Adam had tried, but Remy wasn't... something. Adam hoped he just wasn't ready, as opposed to not being able. "Yes. That's fine." He sat down at the table, and just as he'd suspected, Remy stood up. "Do you need any help with any of it? Dar's projects? I was never absolutely sure what he was working on, to be honest."

"I'm still figuring it out. I'll let you know." Remy walked to the kitchen and put the mug in the sink. "You have my comm code, if you need to go somewhere. You'll contact me?"

"I will. And I'll call you tonight, if I haven't heard from you by then, and I'll try to persuade you to come back here to sleep."

"Dar didn't sleep here."

"You're not Dar. You can take over his job, if you want, but you can't take over his whole life."

Rem didn't answer. He didn't even seem to have heard. "Let me know if you need me," he said, and he headed for the door.

Adam tried to stay quiet and hopeful, but when he heard the door slide shut behind Remy, he groaned out loud. He missed Dar, not only for himself, but because he seemed to be the only person who really understood Remy. Adam definitely could have used some advice right about then. But Dar was gone.

Adam had cried the day before, when he'd broken the news to Dar's mother and daughter, and the woman who'd given him his child. His sorrow was nothing compared to theirs, but it was real. Remy... what the hell was Remy feeling?

For better or worse, Adam didn't have much time to ponder that question. The security team wasn't sure whether Kara or Antonia had been the intended target of the bullet that killed Dar, but it didn't really matter, they decided. Someone was trying to get to Adam, and if they couldn't attack him personally, they'd go after the people he loved. They were all subjected to heightened security measures, and Adam wasn't at all sorry that his wife and daughter seemed to have decided to stay locked in the suite.

"You may as well go to Europe," Adam tried when he went upstairs to check on them at lunch time. "You've been a great help here, but...."

"But it's time to give up? Time to let them know they've won?" Kara had bounced back, and was obviously now finding strength in the tragedy. "Is that what Dar would have wanted?"

Adam thought of Remy's words. *Dar's dead.* The idea was liberating, really. Dar was gone. There was no point in living for him, or trying to memorialize him in their actions. But he wasn't sure Kara was ready for that sort of freedom. "He would have wanted you to be safe. If he couldn't be around to protect you, I'm sure he'd have wanted you to be somewhere that no one wanted to hurt you."

Antonia raised an eyebrow at him. The night before, she'd told Adam about Kara's crush on Dar; apparently the girl had even been using the word "love," although Antonia had said she was reasonably sure nothing had happened between the two of them. She wasn't even sure if Dar had been aware of Kara's feelings. If things had gone differently, Adam might have had to find time to worry about all that, but as it was, he was desperate enough to at least try to use his daughter's affections as a way to manipulate her into getting out of the country.

Unfortunately, Kara didn't seem convinced. "I think he'd have wanted me to stay here and keep fighting. He believed in this."

Adam nodded tiredly. He'd tried, and his conscience wouldn't let him manipulate the situation any further. "Think about it," he said, and then he went back downstairs to the conference room.

The business of government was a blessing, keeping Adam from worrying about much else. Remy didn't come back to the apartment that night, or the next. Adam saw him a few times each day, usually briefly and always from a distance; there had been no real contact. It was tempting to devise some sort of expedition that would require security, just so there'd be an excuse to spend time with Remy, but Adam managed to resist. He wanted Remy to want him, not to be coerced into being with him.

On the fourth day, Adam worked late, as usual, and the office was almost empty when he left. Morgan had headed out just before him, one of the first times Adam could remember the other man abandoning his post; Adam had always wondered whether Morgan slept on one of the couches in the lounge, or whether he somehow didn't sleep at all. But this night, Morgan had apparently unchained himself.

When Adam followed a few minutes later, he wasn't altogether surprised to see Morgan lurking in the stairwell at the far end of the hallway. But he stopped dead in his tracks when he realized that Morgan wasn't alone. What the hell was Remy doing down there?

He must have been coming to look for Adam, and he'd stopped to chat with Morgan. The two of them seemed friendly, although Adam couldn't see what they possibly had in common. It was good that Remy had someone to talk to, Adam told himself. He didn't need to understand everything about Remy, including his choice of acquaintances. Remy was an intelligent adult, Morgan was an intelligent adult....

Adam wanted to kill Morgan Winters. He didn't think he'd actually go so far as to do it, not with his bare hands at least, but if someone else pointed a gun in the bastard's direction, Adam wouldn't do anything to stop the shot.

Jesus. Of course Adam was being a jealous idiot, but this was what Dar and Remy had been saying all along, wasn't it? The person behind the attacks on Adam, the person who had caused Dar's death... it might be someone high up in the government. It might be a fellow council member. It might be Morgan. That would explain the man's interest in getting close to Remy; he knew Remy was a trusted insider, and he'd see how that could be used against Adam. Not that Remy would ever deliberately hurt Adam; bad moods aside, Adam still trusted Remy. But maybe he could be tricked, or manipulated. He was far from naïve, of course, but he was so used to being submissive. He'd been rewarded when he pleased people, punished harshly when he didn't. Did Morgan know enough to use that vulnerability?

Remy looked over and Adam jerked back into the alcove by the door. Then he felt foolish. He wasn't going to hide from this, surely. It didn't make sense to keep it secret. He just needed some time to think.

He stepped out of the alcove and strode briskly toward the suite, the opposite direction from Remy and Morgan. There was an idea churning through his mind, nothing more than a vague possibility, but something that might grow if he could feed it properly. Was there some way to use this? Not to hurt Remy, of course.

Adam kept his head down, avoiding eye contact with the guards in the hallway, ignoring the ones who he knew were trailing along behind him, weapons at the ready. It wasn't a situation that he could tolerate forever. No, not *tolerate*. It wasn't something he could *withstand* forever. He couldn't live like this, under constant surveillance, his family at risk, hated by unknown enemies. He needed to get to the bottom of it all. He would find out who was trying to kill him, and he would stop them. And if Morgan thought he could use Remy against Adam, Morgan had another think coming.

"You were talking to Morgan yesterday."

Remy hadn't spent the night with Adam, but he'd been there in the morning, in the kitchen, waiting quietly. He had a bowl of fruit and yogurt, and he kept his eyes on it as if searching for the perfect blueberry. "Yeah. I saw you, last night. Were you hiding?"

"No," Adam scoffed. He hoped it sounded convincing. "I just didn't want to interrupt. Were you talking about something private? Can I ask what it was?" Adam leaned against the kitchen wall and tried to look casual.

"Private? No. I wanted some information, and he seemed like the person to ask."

"Him? Not me?"

Remy looked up. "I guess I could have asked you about the VR-M system and its relationship to the DAVOS, but... I figured you might be busy." He apparently found the berry he was looking for, along with several of its friends and a generous yogurt blanket, and shoved it all into his mouth.

Adam wasn't sure how to respond. He was pretty sure the DAVOS was Digital Audio Video... something, but he had no idea what the VR-M system was. Remy was right; Adam had absolutely no expertise in that area. And Adam certainly didn't want to discourage snarky Remy from making an appearance; smartass Remy generally seemed to be calm Remy. But Adam didn't trust Morgan, and he didn't want to let this go. "He helped you with that?"

Remy nodded, and when he was done chewing, he said, "He didn't know that much himself. But he told me who to talk to."

"Did he ask for anything in return?" Adam had a feeling that he wasn't being too subtle about all this.

The suspicion was confirmed when Remy nodded again and said, "I have to name my firstborn child Rumpelstiltskin."

"Remy...."

"What?"

Adam took a deep breath. He'd been fooling himself, thinking he could sneak up on this. Remy was used to deception and doublespeak at a level that Adam could only imagine, and certainly never attain. Honesty was his best option. "I'm not sure we can trust Morgan. I'm not sure we can trust any of them on the council. You and Dar, weren't you working on the idea that the person behind all this might be someone high up in the government? There isn't much higher than the council, and Lord knows, if there's anyone on the council who would like me shut up, it's Morgan." Adam was warming to his argument as he went. "And he's involved in every damn thing. I don't know how he does it, but he knows everything, controls everything... he's like the Department of Domestic Intelligence, I swear."

"The DDI tortured people, Challoner. They spied, and blackmailed, and threatened innocent people." Remy shook his head. "Morgan just listens. He pays attention."

The words felt like a slap. "Are you saying I don't?"

"What are you talking about?"

Remy's confusion seemed genuine, and Adam tried to get a grip on himself. "Morgan listens. That's why you like talking to him. But you won't talk to me; I've barely seen you in days. Are you saying I *don't* listen?"

"Jesus, Challoner, you need to get laid."

"What?"

"Seriously." Remy looked like he couldn't decide whether to be disgusted or amused. "I like talking to Morgan because he *gives me useful information.* He knows stuff I need to know. It has nothing to do with you, but you're trying to drag yourself into it because you're thinking with your dick."

Adam wished he had his own bowl of yogurt so he could fill his mouth and have an excuse not to speak. Instead, he pushed away from the wall, found a mug, and set it under the coffee dispenser. "I don't trust him," he tried.

"Nobody's asking you to."

"But *you* trust him."

"Trust? I don't know. He's useful. He knows a lot, and he's willing to help."

"What if he's lying?"

"Challoner." Remy's voice was firm, and it compelled Adam to stop watching the coffee stream into his mug and turn to face Remy instead. "If Morgan lied to me, that would be *great*. Because I'd catch him. And then we'd be able to figure out *why* he lied, what he was trying to protect, and that would help us understand what the hell is going on around here." Remy shrugged. "And if he doesn't lie, that's good too, because I'm getting good information. Either way, we win."

"*We* win?" Adam was getting a bit tired of sounding like an insecure teenager, but the situation was driving him to it. "*We* as in you and me?"

"*We* as in Team Challoner. A team I'm a member of."

"Yeah?" It was nice to hear it, even in a snarky, falsely patient tone. "Who else is on the team, besides you and me?"

Remy raised an eyebrow. "Your wife and daughter. Your allies on the council. The people in Asia or wherever who pushed to have you be the leader." He stood up from the table, empty bowl in hand, and took the two steps to stand in front of Adam. "The people who knew you and cared about you before the revolution. And the citizens who know you now, who go back inside their homes and sit and wait for you to make things better instead of fighting and stealing, because they believe in you." Remy set the bowl on the counter and stepped back. It had probably been a lost opportunity for some physical contact, but right then, Adam was finding Remy's words even more seductive than his body. "You've got a lot of people on your side. A lot of people who want to see you make things better." He shrugged nonchalantly. "And maybe a few crazy assholes who want you dead. But if numbers are all you're worried about, you're fine."

"They're not *all* I'm worried about."

"Good," Remy said firmly. "Be careful." He took another step away.

"Remy?" Adam wasn't sure if it would work, but he knew he wanted to try. "I'm sorry about Dar. And I'm glad you're taking over for him. But I don't like not knowing where you are, or what you're doing."

Remy nodded thoughtfully. He still didn't seem emotionally affected by Dar's name, but he was considering the intellectual aspect of it all. "It's slowing me down, trying to figure out exactly what he was working on. He should have told me, or at least kept better records. I can do that. I'll let you know whenever I find something important."

"No, Remy, I'm not...." The thought made Adam's stomach churn. "I'm not asking you to set up a system so we can carry on if something happens to you. I want to know because whoever this was tried to kill me, and tried to kill my wife or daughter. I'm not... well, okay, yes, maybe I'm *partly* thinking with my dick. But I *am* involved in this, because I'm the target."

"Yeah. Okay."

"So I want the information. And I want to know that you're okay. And I'd like it if you'd share the information with me tonight, before we go to bed." Adam raised his eyebrows enough to allow Remy to treat it like a joke, but hopefully not enough to make it seem that Adam felt that way.

Apparently he got the right balance. "Yeah. Maybe. If I can."

"You can, Remy."

"I'll try." There was a note of finality to the words, and Adam didn't press further.

"Okay. I hope to see you then." He took his coffee with him as he walked a few paces behind Remy toward the exit, and then stood and watched as the door opened and shut, blocking Remy from view. Adam sipped his coffee. If Dar had been there, he'd have been busy making fun of Adam's obsession, but Adam really didn't care.

CHAPTER FOURTEEN

As IT happened, Adam saw Remy well before bedtime. He appeared at Adam's office midmorning, standing in the doorway and looking strangely uncertain. "Do you want to take a walk?" he asked.

It was a strange request, coming from Remy, but Adam was on his feet almost immediately. "Sure. Outside?"

"Kind of." Remy nodded out toward the hallway, and when Adam joined him, they set off.

"Is something up?"

"Nothing big." Remy held the door at the end of the hallway open, and then they were in the stairwell. Instead of heading downstairs, though, Remy started up, and after a few flights the stairs ended at a utilitarian metal door. Remy punched a code into a panel on the wall and the door slid open. Adam squinted in the sudden bright light, and he tried to remember the last time he'd been out in the sun.

"I didn't know there was roof access here," he said, and he stepped cautiously through the door. "I mean... wait. Where's the shuttle pad?"

"Up there. We're on a lower level."

"Oh. Okay." Adam waited, but the answer didn't come to him. "Why?"

Remy was busy playing with some device he'd pulled from his

jacket pocket. Finally satisfied, he looked up and said, "Because I don't think there are bugs here. The sensor isn't finding any, at least."

"Bugs? Are you telling me that the rest of the building is bugged? By who?"

"Good question." Remy shrugged, but his nonchalance seemed forced. "Maybe nobody. It might just be residual wiring leftover from before. Well, yeah, my guys... Dar's guys... they're pretty sure it's old equipment. But they say it's still active. They just can't be sure whether anyone's listening."

"Jesus! That's an issue of national security! Why the hell wasn't this caught?"

"Good question." Remy waited while Adam thought his way to the answer.

"You think it's someone in the security department? We worried about the guards earlier—you think there's a whole group of bad guards? Maybe higher than that, even. Someone in Ackerman's office?"

Remy looked tired. "Yeah. Maybe in his office." He moved restlessly around their small platform. "Look, I need more information than Morgan *or* Dar's guys can give me. I need a real expert. The virus that was planted in the first place, the one that brought down the government--it was developed by a couple guys in the city, right? Do you know how to contact them? They must know a lot about surveillance tech, since that was what the virus attacked. And they'd be able to track interference, I think, just 'cause they'd have known how to keep themselves from getting caught."

Adam nodded slowly. "Yeah. They might be good. I met them once, after the revolution. I know how to get in touch."

"Can you give me the information? They can contact you if they want to check me out."

"Yeah. Okay." Adam pulled out his comm tablet and found the

contact information, then sent it to Remy. Remy was watching his own screen and nodded.

"Okay. So, be careful what you say. In the office, and in your suite... pretty much everywhere, as far as I can tell. Write stuff down, if you have to, but not on your comm. There's an antique writing pad in the suite, with a pen—use it. Or if you want to come up here, the code's 729-329. But don't come up too often, or people will notice and figure out that you know."

"Jesus Christ." Adam had already felt like he was living in a fishbowl. "Wait a second... you're saying the *suite* is bugged? The *bedroom*?"

"I didn't check the bedroom. The other day, when I was there, I checked the main rooms. But, yeah, I'd assume the bedroom, really. People tell a lot of secrets in bed." He paused as if caught by a thought, but whatever it was, he didn't share it with Adam.

And Adam wasn't paying that much attention. "I was going to ask you to come down, tonight. To sleep with me. But I don't know...."

"I would have said 'no', if you'd asked."

Adam froze. It was too sudden, too clear. He needed to fool himself for a bit longer. But apparently Remy had a different plan. "You would have?" he asked. "Not 'maybe,' or 'I'll try'?"

"I would have said 'no', if you wanted to keep going the way we were going." Remy walked to the very edge of the roof and leaned out over the parapet, looking down at the street below. Then he turned around and said, "Dar's dead. You and me? We could die anytime, either one of us. I'm not interested in playing your stupid game anymore. This is me. Right now. If I'm too damaged for you, or if you don't trust me to know what I want, or whatever other bullshit is making you think you have the right to make all the decisions about my sex life? If that's the way it is, fuck you. Or, really, *don't* fuck you, and I'll fuck someone else if I feel like it."

"*Do* you feel like it, Remy?" Adam let his voice rise. "Because if you actually felt like it, if you would actually *enjoy* having sex with me, or doing any damn thing with me? That would literally be a dream come true. I'm not holding off because I'm trying to control you, I'm just trying—"

"Not to be an asshole. I know. And for a while, it was sort of cute. But now? Fuck you, Challoner. This is it. I'm not saying I'm going to come, or even get hard; I have no idea if I would. But *I'll* be the one to decide whether sex on those terms is worth it, not you. I'm not a little kid anymore, and I'm not a whore, either. *I* decide."

"This is the most fucked-up fight I've ever had," Adam said. "I mean, I'm arguing *against* getting something I want more than practically anything else. Does that make sense?"

"Hey, Challoner? You know what a good whore would do right now? He'd come over, and he'd wrap his arms around you, and he'd whisper that you're a good man, and you're trying to do the right thing, and it's beautiful and perfect that you're making the effort." Remy leaned against the low concrete wall behind him. "You know what I'm doing?" He smiled calmly. "I'm telling you to take your bullshit nobility and shove it up your ass. It's patronizing, and it's annoying, and I'm done with it."

"So, what are you saying?" Adam held up his hands quickly and tried to rephrase. "I mean, I get what you're saying. Very clearly. But what does it mean? What do you want?"

"I want you to treat me like an adult. I want you to let me make my own decisions, even if they end up being mistakes. I want you to understand that I'm not a fragile fucking blossom that's going to wither up if there's a little rough weather."

"Fragile? No, Remy, I've never thought you were fragile. You're the strongest person I know."

"Yeah? Prove it."

Adam tried to control himself. He didn't want to lose his head, couldn't afford to mess up. But damn it, he wanted this so much.

"Remy," he said, his voice low and husky, "what are you doing way over there?" He took a half step forward and tried to look appealing.

But apparently it wasn't working. "I'm over here because I don't want to touch you right now, Challoner. So I'm not going to."

It should have stung, but it didn't. "Remy, get over here right now."

"Kiss my ass," Remy said.

Adam felt like his chest was going to explode. He couldn't name the emotion, maybe because it was so many all at the same time. He didn't want to make a big deal of it, though, didn't want to scare Remy off by breaking down into tears of relief and joy. So he leaned against one of the metal stacks and said, "I'd love to, so why don't you *get over here right now*." He didn't try to hide his smile, or the love that he was sure must be glowing out from him like a beacon.

Remy just raised an eyebrow. "When I feel like it, I'll let you know."

Adam had no idea about right or wrong, but he knew he couldn't fight anymore. Remy was strong and smart and could take care of himself. Adam loved him enough to want to protect him, but love wasn't enough. He had to respect Remy, as well. And he did. "Okay," he said quietly. "When you feel like it." He grinned suddenly. "And if, at that time, I feel like it, maybe something will happen. Unless I'm busy."

"Busy, huh?" And damn it, maybe Remy wasn't a whore anymore, but apparently he'd only lost the attitude, not the skills. He cast his face down a little, then looked up at Adam, his expression a perfect mix of innocence and lustful curiosity, and when he moved, he looked like a jungle cat, lithe and smooth and absolutely seductive. Adam could practically feel the way Remy's muscles would bunch and stretch, testing Adam's strength rather than trying to escape. He'd snarl, maybe, show his teeth, but he wouldn't bite, because he'd want it just as much as Adam did. *Need* it just as much. And then, just like that, Remy straightened and his face shifted into casual neutrality with just a hint of amusement. "I don't think you're going to be busy, Challoner."

"No, probably not." At least Adam managed to get that much out without squeaking. He cleared his throat as Remy eased past him, back toward the door. "You're going?"

"I've got hackers to recruit," Remy said. "Assassins to track down, Conspiracies to uncover. No time for chatting."

"But you'll come by tonight, maybe? For whatever. Sleep, or anything else you want. Your call."

Remy smiled fondly at him, and moved in until there was barely a breath between their chests. Remy's lips found Adam's and they were warm and soft, his tongue gentle but firm. The kiss wasn't long, but it took Adam's breath away, and he gasped when Remy pulled back. "I'll come by," Remy said softly. "For whatever."

He left then, and didn't seem to expect Adam to follow. Maybe he realized that it was going to take a little while for Adam to collect himself. As it was, even after several minutes of taking deep breaths of the warm spring air, Adam's head was still spinning. He went back down to the office and knew that at least a few people noticed the goofy smile on his face, but he really didn't care. He was happy, and he knew enough to savor the emotion; he could never tell how long it would last.

THE good mood barely made it through the morning. Adam walked into the midday council meeting feeling like there was a helium balloon in his chest, and it expanded a little when he found Remy sitting by the door, glowing like a beacon among the other aides and assistants. But the helium turned to lead when Adam saw the expressions around the table. "What now?" he asked.

There was an awkward silence before General Mackie said, "We need a change."

"A change? Can you be more specific?"

"A change in leadership." Once the general got warmed up, apparently he was ready to go. "You did your best, I'm sure, but we all know you were a compromise candidate. You didn't even want the job, Adam. And you're not the right man for it. You're too indecisive, and we're going to end up starving to death as a result of it."

"We're back to the colonies issue, then?" Adam tried to keep his voice level.

"We never should have *left* the colonies issue!" Mackie was apparently not making the same effort to sound calm. "A key national asset, an *essential* part of our infrastructure decides to revolt, and we just let it happen? Because we're too fucking cowardly to do something about it?"

"Cowardly? Come on, Tom. Where's the courage in attacking unarmed civilians? Or do you mean something different when you say 'do something about it'?" Because if you have a better plan, I think we'd all love to hear about it."

"Cowardly," Mackie repeated firmly. "You're afraid of being the bad guy. Afraid of making the hard decisions."

It was uncomfortably close to Remy's derision over Adam's fear of being an asshole. Was there some truth to Mackie's accusations? Adam needed time to think, but he knew Mackie wasn't going to give it to him. "You're right about the first part, I guess. I *am* afraid of being the bad guy." Just talking gave Adam more ideas. "I'm petrified of it. Because I can't ever seem to forget that we're dictators. We weren't elected: we seized control. The only hint of legitimacy we have, the only thing that makes us even a little better than the men who came before us, is that we're trying to do things right. And we're planning to hold elections, once we get things settled down." He shook his head. "We should *all* be afraid of becoming no better than the men we replaced.

We should *all* remember that power corrupts, and that absolute power corrupts absolutely. When we gaze into the abyss—"

"Enough! Goddamnit, you do like to make speeches, don't you?" The general turned his attention to the other men at the table. "That's why we accepted him as our so-called leader. He was meant to be a figurehead, someone to look pretty and talk pretty. But the time for pretty words is *over*." Mackie straightened and turned back to Adam. "It's time for action. The united Earth fleet is at the wormhole entrance. The colonies have sent a message advising us that if we bring warships into the wormhole, they will consider it an act of war."

"An act of war!" Sam Turay sounded incredulous. "As if they think they can scare us! As if we don't have every right to send our troops out to visit our colonies whenever the hell we want to."

Adam hadn't realized that he'd lost Turay's support, but he supposed it made sense. The man had worked hard trying to establish diplomatic relations with the other continents, and that had all been destroyed when North America had decided not to join the united forces against the colonies. It made sense, but it was disappointing.

"We need to make our decisions based on what we know is right," Adam tried, "not based on silly bravado from a bunch of scared farmers. They can say whatever they want, it doesn't give us the right to kill them."

"Enough with the fucking straw men!" The general waved an arm in the general direction of the sky, apparently pointing at the colonies. "Nobody's saying we're going to kill them. We won't need to. We show up, we scare them, they behave. That's all."

"So we use intimidation instead of reason?" Adam leaned forward and spoke with quiet intensity. "How is that different from the men before us? How does that make us *better*? We've plunged this country into disorder, we've confiscated people's belongings and made them afraid for their futures. So if we're not a better government than the one before... and if we're not better, and we put the country through all that? Then we're *worse* than they were."

"It's too simplistic, Adam." Morgan's voice was quiet, and almost sympathetic, so Adam knew not to trust him. Still, the rest of the table was listening, so Adam did too. "We need to look at our government as a whole, not as a single decision. We've done good things. Medical care, turning the cameras off, providing basic income to all citizens... we've done the right thing with all that. We've made things better. One decision isn't going to make or break our legacy, or our legitimacy."

"So you admit that this decision would be wrong? Immoral. But you think we've got enough credit to balance off a debit. But I'm saying that I don't *want* us to make the debit. We still have time. Negotiations could still work. We have food supplies for another couple months, at least. We'll be short on some items, but we'll make do." He turned to address the entire table. "I've said it before. If *all* other options are exhausted, if we truly have no choice, I'll support military action. But we're not there yet."

"Yes, we are." Mackie seemed to have regained his self-control. "And the rest of the world knows it. We look like amateurs, fucking around while everyone else is taking care of business."

Mackie paused, obviously waiting for a response, but Adam decided not to give one. He wasn't sure what Mackie's goal was, exactly, but it was probably best to sit back and let him get to the point of it all instead of trying to guess.

And after an uncomfortable moment, it worked. "We want you out," Mackie said. "Obviously you'd still be welcome on the council. But we want new leadership."

"It's unanimous?" It was harder to sound neutral now, harder to keep his ego out of the way.

"Of course not." Desmond Chan sounded disgusted. "Not even close. We need a vote, I suppose, although it's times like this that make it clear we need a constitution. I would assume that it would take more than a simple majority to depose a leader, especially during times of national crisis."

"The council works based on vote count," Mackie countered. "If the majority of us vote to do something, we do it. So if the majority of us vote to have a new leader, we have a new leader."

"And do you have the votes?" Adam asked. His voice was surprisingly calm, given the tumult of emotions racing through his mind. Anger, fear, pride, and a significant dose of relief... he couldn't be sure just which one would end up being dominant. But he'd started this job because he believed in it, and he wouldn't quit now, not without a fight.

"I think I do," Mackie replied.

Adam turned to the council. "So this is it? He's the candidate to replace me? A dictatorship wasn't bad enough, you want a *military* dictatorship." He looked around the table, trying to figure out the votes. It would be close. They'd been operating on a rough system cobbled together at their first meeting as a council, and they had *some* rules in place. As the leader, he got an extra vote if needed to break a tie, and he wondered if he might need it. He was tempted to delay in order to do some lobbying, but he didn't think the others would allow it, and to try and fail would make him look weak. He smiled. "Let's do it, then. Let's vote."

CHAPTER FIFTEEN

"MAY I make an inquiry, first?" Desmond Chan's smile was calm, but there was something about his eyes that caught Adam's attention.

"Of course," he agreed.

"I'd like to know why we're doing this now. We have had disagreements on this council from the start, and I'm sure we'll continue to have them. The only real additional power that our leader has is the extra vote in the event of a tie. Other than that, we all have an equal say in the decisions of this council." Desmond turned his piercing gaze toward General Mackie. "Why is it important to you that you become the leader at this time? Why does it have to be *now*, when the country is already unsettled?"

"Because we've waited long enough. This nonsense needs to stop."

"But surely it's already too late, if you're talking about joining the united Earth forces going to the colonies. They've got a six-day head start. I can't imagine they'll want to wait for us."

For the first time, Mackie looked just a little uncomfortable. "We can discuss all of that after the vote. Are these questions just a delaying tactic?"

Adam was almost afraid to ask the question, or, rather, was almost afraid to hear the answer, but he forced the words past his tense lips. "Where is our fleet, general?"

"Again, that's something that can be discussed after the vote. This is a simple question of leadership, and I don't think it's good for us to confuse the issue with a lot of other questions."

"You think you have enough votes to assume leadership, but you think the vote will be closer on whatever it is you want to do next," Adam guessed. "So you want the extra vote, the tiebreaker, for yourself. But what is it that you're going to vote on? Something to do with the colonies, I imagine."

"The fleet is near the entrance to the wormhole," Sam Turay said quickly. He looked toward the general as if knowing that he would be displeased, but continued anyway. "I've been taking calls from the other nations all morning; they want to know if we changed our minds and are going to join them. I think we should."

Adam stared at the general. "You sent them to the wormhole entrance? Against the express wishes of this council?"

"They're on training maneuvers. That's all. The council didn't say a damned thing about where I can send the fleet on maneuvers. I just kept our options open."

"The other nations know we're there." Adam turned to Sam Turay. "You knew this was happening, and you didn't say anything to us?" Who else would have been aware? Morgan, of course—he knew everything. The others? How many of them had been sitting there for the past six days, withholding vital information from the rest of the council? But that was a fight for a different time. "Jesus, Mackie, you're worried about how we look on the world stage, but you don't have any concerns about making it appear that we can't decide what we're doing? How stable do we look if our governing council says one thing and our military acts in the opposite way?"

"How stable do we look if we're starving to death while the rest of the planet is having a feast?"

There were no answers that wouldn't just be a repetition of arguments they'd already had. Adam was so tired. It would be a relief to be able to walk away from all this, without the guilt of having quit. He'd done his best, worked as hard as he could, but it hadn't been enough. So be it. After the vote, maybe he could finally persuade Remy to get out of the country, and they could all go live on an island somewhere. "So we're voting on more than a change of leadership, then. The members of the council need to be aware that by installing you as leader, it will be significantly more likely that we'll be joining in a military attack against a civilian target." And that was the part that caught at Adam's heart. Yes, he was tired, and it would be a relief to walk away, but he still had a responsibility. A duty. He'd made a mistake, he now realized, when he'd agreed to be part of the shuttle bombing at the Baryman Hotel. He'd listened to people tell him that the bombing was necessary, and ignored his own instinct that said it was wrong. Innocent people had died because Adam hadn't stood up for what he believed in, and he couldn't let it happen again.

Remy was still fighting, even after everything he'd been through, and Adam had to as well. He had to keep trying to make this government do the right thing, to fulfill the dreams of the revolution. It was tiring to think of having to keep fighting for control of this council, but it would be even more exhausting to have to plan another damned coup.

"This is ridiculous," Desmond Chan scoffed. "We've already discussed the colonies and come to a decision on the issue. We need to stand by it. And we need to stand by Adam. We're going to install a new leader because some of us disagree with the previous one? And then when we disagree with the new one, we'll depose him and find someone new? And then again, and again? We'll be a rudderless ship, drifting wherever the current takes us."

"We need to have a temporary constitution in place," Morgan agreed. "We know how we want the country to be run in the long term, but until we can hold elections, we need to have rules for this sort of thing."

"I'll make that a priority of my new government," Mackie said. "For now, let's have our vote. The council understands my position on the colonies, and on every other issue. I don't think anyone can say I haven't made my opinions clear."

Well, that was true enough. Adam couldn't think of anything else to say. "Okay. We'll vote." He forced himself to smile at the council. "As usual, we'll go around the table, and each person will say... well, in this case, I guess 'yay' or 'nay' won't work. Just say the name of the person you want to be the council leader."

The first few weren't a surprise. They'd been loyal supporters of the general and Morgan right from the beginning, and they said Mackie's name with confidence. It hurt to hear Sam Turay say the same thing, but it was expected. It was worrisome, though. If everyone else voted as usual, they'd end up with a tie, and Adam would have to use his tiebreaker vote to win. It was too damned close.

Desmond Chan was the first to say Adam's name, and several others followed his lead. The general voted for himself, of course, and then it was Ackerman's turn. He kept his eyes on the table in front of him, but when he said, "General Mackie," his voice was loud and clear.

Adam felt his stomach tighten. That was it. It was over. He felt betrayed on a personal level; he'd thought Ackerman was a friend and an ally. But he also felt a twist of surprisingly bitter disappointment at losing the job. He hadn't wanted it in the first place, but he still needed to find a way to make the government live up to its potential, and that was going to be a hell of a lot harder now.

The others kept voting, and Adam tried to find a way to accept the defeat. It wasn't all bad, he supposed. He'd stay on the council, at least for a while, and maybe it would be fun to be the one shooting down other people's ideas instead of trying to come up with new solutions all the time. He could still contribute, still find ways to help—

"Adam Challoner," Morgan Winters said, and every eye in the room turned to stare at him.

"What?" The general seemed genuinely confused. "Morgan, if

it's a tie, *he* gets a second vote to break it. You're voting to keep him in power."

"I'm familiar with the rules, General. I wrote them."

"What the hell are you doing?" Mackie's confusion was fading into rage. "Did you make a deal? Did the little whore seduce *you* too?" He pushed his chair back so hard it toppled over, and then stood with his fists braced against the table.

"General!" Adam fought to keep himself still. He would not storm around the table and attack the man. He wouldn't, no matter how tempted he was. "Watch your language." The words weren't extreme, but Adam knew the anger in his voice gave them more weight. He looked over at Remy, who, if anything, looked mildly amused. "If you need to take a break to collect yourself, please do so. Otherwise, let's get back to business."

His hands were shaking, Adam realized, and he clasped them together behind his back. Too much adrenaline, too little action. "I vote for myself, and that brings us to a tie. I cast the tiebreaker for myself. The vote is over. I am still the leader of the council." He looked around the table, waiting for objections, but there were none, so he pressed on. "There has been no significant change in the situation since our last vote on sending troops to the colonies, so I will not ask for a revote on an issue we've already settled. General, please make sure our troops do *not* enter the wormhole. Allowing them to proceed any further would be a direct violation of the will of this council and, as such, would amount to treason." What else, what else? He needed to keep this moving and not give the general a chance to be offended by the mention of treason. "I think we should strike a committee to look at establishing a stronger framework for the business of this council. Desmond's right—we can't change leadership every time somebody wants that extra vote. Our ad hoc system worked for a while, but we need to refine it. Maybe we need to introduce a new member so we have an uneven number of votes, and make a rule that no one can ever abstain? I'm not sure, but we should look at it. Any volunteers for that?"

A few hands were raised, comments were made, and the meeting continued. Everyone was a little unsettled, but they pushed past it. Adam tried not to look at Ackerman; he'd deal with that later. And he'd deal with Morgan Winters too, although that issue was even more confusing than Ackerman. Morgan had seen the chance to depose Adam, and he hadn't taken it. Why the hell not?

"HE's not your enemy," Remy said quietly. Adam knew exactly who he was talking about, even though neither of them had mentioned his name.

They were in their rooftop sanctuary, so Adam let himself speak freely. "Does he know that? Because he's sure seemed like an enemy in the past!"

"He disagreed with you. He still does, probably, and I'm sure he will again. That doesn't make him your enemy, Challoner."

"He's power-hungry—"

"I don't think so."

"Sneaky—"

"I haven't seen that."

"Manipulative—"

"Not really."

"Annoying—"

"Obviously." Remy's smile was sweet, his gentle kiss even sweeter. "I've been working with him. And Dar had some information on him too. Did you know that he was born to a factory worker? He had a sister, but she died of some undiagnosed illness when he was twelve. He had to scramble and fight for his education and his chance at success." Remy gave Adam another kiss, a clear reward for having listened to the tale of Morgan's nobility. "He's a fighter, and he's more focused on the practical side of things than you are. But he wants what's best for the country. And so do you. So in the long run, you're on the same side. And he voted for you this morning because he knows that your voice is needed on the council. He trusts you more than he trusts the general."

"I wonder what kind of conversation those two are having right now."

"Probably not this kind," Remy whispered, and the kiss this time was deeper and damn it, if Remy wasn't enjoying it, he was an even better actor than Adam gave him credit for. But Remy was the one to pull away, leaving Adam leaning after him, wanting more. "I want to take you somewhere," Remy said. "To see someone. It's not far, but it's a bit risky. I don't think we should take security. I think it'll be safer if they don't know where we are."

"What are you up to, Remy?"

"I've been following up on Dar's leads. I talked to the hackers from the revolution. You know what they said when I contacted them? They asked what had taken so long. Dar had already been in touch with them and asked for their help. He'd even given them my name as someone to trust. And they gave me some really good information. I mean, powerful, useful information. It's not *good*, exactly, or at least you won't think so."

"And that's where you want us to go, now? To see them?"

"No." Remy made a strange face, and it took Adam a moment to realize that it was his version of being nervous. The man had spent his life covering up his fear, and now he was being brave enough to expose it to Adam. It seemed like another milestone, but there was no time to celebrate, and Remy's next words washed the joy out of Adam anyway. "I want to go see Mr. Baryman."

"Baryman." Adam tried to make sense of it. "The man who bought you as a child, made you a sex slave, and tortured you for his own amusement. *Baryman*. Why the hell do you want to see him? He's still in jail, right?" Adam had resisted the urge to obsess over taking revenge against the bastard, but that didn't mean he wanted to make a social call.

"Yes, he's still in jail. Of a sort. But he could be valuable."

"He tried to kill you."

"He didn't succeed." Remy shifted around, still facing Adam, but giving himself a bit more room. "He knows things. He's got a good memory, but he has files, as well. He was obsessive about backing them up, and he wouldn't have put them on the main network, I don't think. Not enough privacy. So his files are still out there somewhere." Remy was speaking quickly, as if he'd already thought this through and made all of his decisions.

But Adam wasn't so sure. "What kind of files?"

"Information about wealthy, important people. Our clients. Most of it doesn't matter anymore, because most of those people are either no longer wealthy, or no longer in the country. It'd probably be good to get hold of it all in case any of them pop up and try to cause problems, but right now, the ones I'm worried about are the other men on the council. Most of them had money before the revolution, so he'll have information on them."

"Wait, they were wealthy, so they automatically used Baryman's services? That can't be true, not for all of them. And what kind of information are we talking about here?"

"They don't have to have used his whores themselves, although I expect some of them did."

"Hang on a second—"

"Not me, Challoner. Stop being territorial. I recognize a few of them from parties, but I don't think I ever worked for one of them directly. But it doesn't have to be direct, because a good whore is invisible. People would treat us like we weren't even there. They'd have important, private conversations in front of us... we were just fuck toys, not human beings. You'd say what you wanted in front of your dog, right? Same with us." Remy turned his head a little and grinned fondly at Adam. "I forget how sensitive you are about this stuff. You look like you're going to throw up."

"Jesus, Remy, I hate hearing you talk about yourself like that. I hate it that they made you feel that way, treated you that way...."

"Well, don't hate it too much, because it could end up being a really useful tool. We went back to Baryman's team and reported anything we heard that seemed even vaguely useful, and he kept track, cross-referenced, found patterns. He started out with whores, but he made most of his money out of more respectable business, lots of wheeling and dealing, and he used the information from us all to make the right business moves." Remy shrugged. "He charged a lot for us as whores, but I bet he made more money, in the long run, from using us as spies."

"And you think that some of that information might be useful now? I don't want to blackmail anyone, Remy."

"Of course you don't. You're too pure for that, I know." Remy rolled his eyes. "But he might know other stuff." He sighed as if preparing to say something he didn't want to. "Because the thing is... the information from the hackers? It makes it pretty damn clear that the cameras were deliberately tampered with at various key times. The attempted shooting, the shuttle attack, Dar's death... it wasn't accidental that we didn't get any good footage for any of those events." Another grimace before Remy continued. "I know you've been assuming that Dar's death was an accident. A missed shot. But I don't think so. I don't think your women were the target, I think *Dar* was. The distance wasn't extreme, there wasn't a lot of wind or anything else to interfere with the shot, and it hit Dar right in the middle of his chest. A perfect shot if he was the target, and a really, *really* crappy one if the shooter was aiming for someone else."

"Why would they have wanted Dar dead?"

"Because of what he was finding out. Because he was tracking down whoever's behind all this, and he was getting somewhere."

Adam wasn't sure if it made it better or worse to believe that. In the end, he supposed it didn't matter. Either way, Dar had died because he was trying to protect Adam and his family; either way,

Dar's blood was on Adam's hands. Adam would just have to find a way to deal with that guilt. But he looked at Remy and a new fear churned around him. "But now *you're* learning the same things. You're on the same track, so now you're a target."

"I'd like to resolve it quickly," Remy agreed, "before there are too many chances to take me out of the game. But everyone knew Dar was smart and good at getting things done. I'm still the invisible whore. I think it'll buy me some time."

"I'm not really looking for ways to make that attitude into a good thing, Remy."

"Reality doesn't care what you're looking for." Remy jerked his head toward the door. "The hackers are in our surveillance system now. They're keeping track of who watches what, who's accessing what files, all that stuff. They say they've got good security around their place, and I think we have to believe them. They seem pretty on top of things. They say they can track our comms and shut off the cameras wherever we go, but they don't want to do it too much or it'll be obvious we know. But I can get them to cover our tracks as we leave the building, and then it's only a couple blocks to the place Baryman is being kept." He reached into his jacket and pulled out a hat with an oversized brim. "You can wear this, and as long as we keep moving, I think we'll be okay. Nobody will be looking for us, so nobody will notice us."

"Now? You want to go now?"

"You've got an hour before the afternoon council meeting, right? That should give us enough time."

"Why am I going along on this trip?" Adam didn't want to be a nuisance, but he didn't want to try to make polite conversation with the man who'd almost destroyed Remy, either.

Another new and strange expression from Remy. "He's not going to give us the information out of the goodness of his heart. He's going to want something in return. I can't say for sure what that'll be, but I doubt I have anything he wants. He'll want to make his deal with you."

"I am not giving a goddamn thing to that son of a bitch."

"Yeah, you will." Remy didn't elaborate, just headed for the door. After a moment of silent rebellion, Adam followed him. Damn it.

Chapter Sixteen

The building didn't look like any jail Adam had ever seen. Not that he'd seen many. But this looked more like a slightly shabby hotel. There were no fences, no bars on the windows, and only one bored-looking guard standing inside the glass front doors.

"Minimum security," Remy explained. "The inmates have monitors implanted in their shoulders, and there are restrictions on their movements. That's all."

"He enslaved you, Remy! Who knows how many others? He tortured you, and tried to kill you. He almost killed Sasha. He's in *minimum* security?" Adam should have kept track of this. Just one more detail lost in the chaos of setting up a new government.

"Baryman's under investigation for the attack on Sasha. That's all. The rest of it was perfectly legal." Remy smiled ruefully at Adam's expression. "Legally, he didn't enslave me. He was my guardian, and he looked after me. I signed a contract—the law's definitely on his side for that one. And the terms of the contract were so broad, he could have done pretty much anything he wanted to me, anything that didn't cause permanent damage, and it would be fine." He shot another look at Adam. "Permanent damage, of course, would lessen my value, so that's why it wasn't allowed. But he wouldn't have done it anyway, since he'd have been wrecking his own property." Remy nodded to the guard. "We're here to see Mr. Baryman. Is he available?"

"He expecting you?" the guard asked sullenly.

"Not exactly," Remy responded. "But I think he'll want to see us."

"Names?"

"Remy Stone. He won't know my friend."

"I'm supposed to get names for all visitors."

"But Mr. Baryman has made arrangements with you so that won't be necessary, right?" Remy smiled confidently. He might not have been in contact with Baryman since the revolution, but he obviously still knew how the man worked. "Give him a call, please."

The guard turned to the comm unit on the wall, and Adam couldn't restrain himself any longer. "*Made arrangements*? That means paid off, right? The bastard is living in better conditions than half the population, he's bribed the guard to be his doorman, and you want me to give him *more* than what he's got, after all he did?"

"I want you to get the information you need," Remy said quietly. He shook his head in gentle disapproval. "You can't let it get personal all the time. He's adaptable, like... he's a rat. A parasite. He gets fat on misery, and if you get upset about it, he just gets fatter. You're here to use him, not approve of him."

The guard jerked his thumb toward the elevator. "He'll see you," he grunted. Remy started moving, and the guard said, "Don't you want to know what floor he's on?"

"The top floor," Remy replied. "Baryman's always on the top floor. If there's a penthouse, he'll be in it."

"This is bullshit," Adam grumbled as they stepped into the elevator and Remy pressed the highest button.

"Don't let your pride get in the way," Remy responded. "Someone's trying to kill you. Whoever it is already killed Dar. We need to get this figured out and get you back to concentrating full time on the council, or next time they *will* fire your ass."

"You think they wanted me out because I haven't been doing a good job?" It stung more than Adam wanted to admit.

"A good job of governing? I think you're doing a great job of that. But a good job of being political? Making deals, getting people on your side side, forming alliances?" Remy shook his head. "You suck. And paying more attention to it won't make you a *lot* better, probably. But it'll help."

"Damn, Remy, don't hold back or anything."

Remy grinned. "You're good at the stuff you think is important. But you need somebody to help you out with the other stuff."

"And you think you're that somebody?" Adam really liked the idea of Remy making a place for himself.

But Remy just snorted. "Me? God, just asking that question proves how bad you are at this. Of course not me. Most of the people you should be trying to get along with don't want to be in the same room as me, much less have a conversation." As usual, Remy didn't seem upset by the situation. "I think Morgan Winters is that somebody. And as soon as we're done with this visit, I'm going to start bugging you to sit down and talk with him."

The elevator doors slid open before Adam could marshal a response, and they stepped out into a somewhat shabby foyer almost completely filled with the hulking bodies of two suit-wearing men. Remy nodded to one of them, and for the first time, Adam noticed that Remy's fingers were curled into tight fists. They relaxed reluctantly, then tightened again when the man said, "You're back. You're not the only one."

"I'm just visiting. Mr. Baryman is expecting us—the guard called from downstairs." Remy's voice was as light and controlled as ever, and his fingers were loose at his sides now. Adam wondered whether he'd imagined the earlier tension.

"Go on in," the man said, and he stepped aside to allow them access to the large double doors.

The doors slid open to reveal a sitting room with a large, heavy desk on one side, surrounded by easy chairs. It was almost identical to the setup at Baryman's old office. And Baryman himself didn't look too different, wearing a well-cut suit that couldn't quite manage to disguise his apelike proportions. He peered under Adam's hat and smiled. "I thought it might be you." He looked at Remy. "What took you so long? You should have brought him by before this."

"I was busy. And when you've got the intel of a whole government at your fingertips, it's hard to get too worked up over a few little scraps of gossip."

"You got mouthy," Baryman said with a bit of a sneer. "Don't forget, boy, it's not just the clients I kept records of. I know a few things about you that would make your fancy boyfriend think twice, now, don't I?"

"I have a hard time getting the stubborn bastard to think once, so if you can manage twice, you'd be my hero." Remy crossed the room and sank down into one of the easy chairs. "You know why we're here. We want access to your records. Adam could just order the security teams to search around until they find them, and if he did that, we all know that it would work, eventually." He shrugged casually and leaned back in his chair. Adam remembered the tensed fingers and wondered how much of this was an act. It certainly felt genuine. "But I'd prefer it if the information was available for Adam's private use, at least initially. So, I thought I'd give you a chance to try to sell it before it gets taken away by force."

Baryman moved lightly for someone his size, and he eased into a desk chair that must have been custom-made. He looked over the desk at Remy, then at Adam, and smiled. "Your *private* use. Maybe you don't want everyone to know that you get turned on by being in control. You like sex rough, even, if you can let yourself relax enough to enjoy it."

Adam thought of that intoxicating moment in his guest

bedroom, the one time he'd almost let himself take what Remy had been so insistent about offering. He'd been frenzied, practically, driven nearly mad by Remy's beauty and strength. He'd wanted to take him, possess him in every way. And Remy had gone back to Baryman and made a report about it all. Because he had to, because it was his job and he would have been punished severely for not obeying orders. Adam made himself smile. "You can't really expect me to pay you for telling me about my *own* sex life." He made his way to the chair beside Remy's. "And I'm not overly interested in anyone else's sexual proclivities, either. If you have some information that will help me understand the motivations of some of my fellow council members, I might be interested in that. Maybe."

Baryman rolled his head lazily on his thick neck and looked at Remy. "You're not stupid. You must already have a pretty good idea of who's behind the assassination attempts."

"Yeah. A pretty good idea. We're working on proving it now." Remy looked at Adam, then back across the desk. "It's the obvious answer. But we'd like to know more about *why*. And we'd like to have background information on the other councilors so we can be sure they won't be similarly corrupted."

Adam was lost. The obvious answer? Mackie. They thought the general wasn't satisfied with trying to gain control through legitimate means, but might have been willing to kill to gain power? It was chilling to consider. But maybe it shouldn't be. The man was in the military, after all; soldiers might have codes of honor, but their main function was killing their enemies.

"I could help you with that. I've been slowed down slightly by recent circumstances, but I still have a network. And of course I have my own records from before the... disruption." Baryman turned back to look at Adam. "But I don't work for free."

"What do you want?" Adam asked.

"Freedom. Immunity from prosecution." Baryman shrugged. "For a start. But, really, I'm interested in forming relationships.

Mutually profitable relationships. Once I'm freed of these annoying limitations, I'll start my business again, and information will flow as freely as it ever did. This isn't a one-time deal."

"People are making twenty dollars a day. Nobody's rich anymore. Who the hell do you think your clients are going to be?" Adam wasn't sure if he was impressed or disgusted by the man's tenacity.

"I've heard your speeches. You don't plan to keep the country like this forever. Free enterprise will return, even if you *do* impose some unreasonable restrictions on the market. People will make money. Some of them will make it very quickly. And they'll want to celebrate." Baryman let his gaze wander lasciviously over Remy's body. "They'll want whores. And I have an eye for talent."

Adam had really thought he was going to be able to do it. Remy was right—they needed the information Baryman had. Adam couldn't let his emotions get in the way of making things work. He'd been almost ready to make a deal, until Baryman had made the last few comments. "No," Adam said. Remy scowled, but Adam ignored him, for once.

"No?" Baryman echoed. He kept his polite, jovial veneer but there was a flash of cold steel in his gaze.

"No. I'm not going to form a 'relationship' with you. I'm not going to do a damn thing to make it easier for you to enslave more people."

"So what the fuck are you doing here, then?" Baryman leaned back in his chair and frowned in Remy's direction. "You know how I feel about people wasting my time, David."

Remy flinched. It was only a moment before he had control of himself again, but in that instant, Adam saw the frightened little boy Remy had been, and the desperate man he'd become. He realized how horrific it must have been for Remy to seek this out, to bring himself back into contact with the man who'd terrorized and almost destroyed him. But he'd made the effort, because it would help Adam.

Adam felt rage curl and flutter around him like a cape, and it felt good. "His name is Remy," he growled. Baryman turned back toward him, and Adam stood up. He leaned over the desk and rested his fists on the polished wood surface. "This is the deal, the only one you're going to get. You're going to give me your records. You're going to give me or my associates any information we want. You aren't going to do it for a reward, you're going to do it because if you don't, I will *destroy* you."

Adam waited a moment for that to sink in. "I run the fucking country, and you're a worthless parasite. I don't usually throw my weight around, but do not think, not for a second, that I don't *have* the weight." He leaned back, then, but didn't sit back down. "Your setup here is a few steps down from your old place, but it's still a palace compared to the cell I can find for you. You're worried about going to trial for a few charges from before the revolution? Don't be, because if you cross me, you'll never see the inside of a courtroom. I don't need *trials* for enemies of the goddamn state. You'll rot in your cell forever, and when you finally die, we'll throw you out, nameless and worthless, with the rest of the trash. You're trying to rebuild something? You need to be trying to survive."

There was silence, and Adam kept his gaze locked on Baryman's. Finally, the big man said, "You're about to make a very dangerous enemy."

"If you give me what I want... yeah, you'll be a little dangerous." Adam knew that was true, but he couldn't bring himself to care. "But if you don't give me what I want, there'll be no danger at all. There'll be no *you* at all, just a walking corpse locked in the cold basement of some prison somewhere."

"You're bluffing."

"Try me." Adam held Baryman's gaze, and it was Baryman who looked away first, although only for an instant.

"What exactly do you want?" he asked, and Adam realized that he really had no idea.

Luckily, Remy was there. "We want copies of your records. All of them, decoded as necessary. We'll review them, and we'll come back and ask you questions if we need to."

"You'll cooperate in *every* way," Adam said, more confident with general threats than with details. "You'll prove to me that you're useful where you are." He took a step sideways so he could lay a hand proprietarily on Remy's shoulder. "Your past? The things you've done? They make me want to see you in a lot of pain. I don't have much room for self-indulgence these days, but I think I could find time to watch you suffer. It's in your best interest to prove to me that you're useful where you are, because the second you stop being useful...." He let his fingers tighten possessively in the fabric of Remy's shirt, and he saw Baryman's eyes track the movement. "Remy doesn't seem too interested in you. I guess he's more forgiving than I am."

Baryman sighed as if this was all quite a nuisance for him. "Fine," he said. He stood up and walked with heavy, feline grace to the wall by the windows. He crouched down and pulled back a loose corner of the carpet, then reached underneath the broadloom to find a small silver object that looked like an antique coin. "This is a backup copy," he said. "I have the originals elsewhere. And there may be little bits and pieces of extra information stashed away, as well. I can't get to all of it, not locked up like this."

"Does this have what we're looking for?" Remy asked.

Baryman nodded. "Yeah. It's on there."

Adam still wasn't sure what that meant, but he didn't think he wanted to get his lesson in front of Baryman. He didn't want to do a damn thing in front of Baryman. "Fine. We'll be in touch if we need anything." He waited while Remy stood up and then let his hand slide down to the small of Remy's back. He wasn't quite sure whether the show of possession was for Baryman, Remy, or himself. Maybe all three.

Remy didn't object. He let himself be guided out of the room, past the guards, and onto the elevator. But as soon as the elevator doors slid shut, he moved quickly, spinning around to face Adam.

At least he didn't push himself away, and that gave Adam hope. He leaned in close to speak in Remy's ear, hoping to evade any listening devices Baryman might have set up. "I'm sorry," he whispered. "I know that wasn't the plan...."

He didn't get any further. He felt a moment of near alarm when Remy grabbed the front of his shirt, but then Remy brought his other hand to the back of Adam's head, pulling him forward, and then Remy's mouth was on his, hard and demanding. Once he got over his surprise, Adam wrapped his arms around Remy's eager body and pulled him in tighter. Adam had no idea what was happening, and he absolutely didn't care.

The elevator was old and slow, and Adam was hard by the time they reached the lobby. He drove his hips forward, searching for something to grind against, and his eyes flew open to stare at Remy. He reached down with his hand, fumbled between their bodies, and found Remy's cock, almost as hard as Adam's, straining against the fabric of his pants.

"I want you," Remy whispered. His eyes were wide, not with lust but with something that looked more like amazement. Maybe apprehension.

Adam had no idea what to say, so he kissed Remy again, twining their bodies together as the doorman looked on with mild interest.

Remy pulled away far enough to say, "You need to go to your meeting."

Adam shook his head. "I need to take you to bed. The meeting can wait."

"You need to go to your meeting." Remy smiled shyly. "I can wait."

"We'll fight about it on the way back," Adam decided. He looked down at their groins, firm underwear only partly controlling their erections. "It's going to be a long walk." He knew he was smiling like a lunatic, and he really, really didn't care.

Chapter Seventeen

"Where the hell have you been?" Morgan's tone was as accusatory as ever, but this time, he seemed to be directing his wrath toward Remy. "You can't just take off with him like that!"

"We had to see somebody." Remy didn't seem too concerned, but Morgan's frown was taking care of whatever had been left of Adam's erection after the brisk walk.

"We need to know where he is. At all times."

"Who's 'we', Morgan? 'Cause you and I both know that some of 'you' really *shouldn't* know where he is, not anytime he's not surrounded by guards."

"So don't take him places without guards!"

"Hey!" Adam finally said. "I'm right here. I'm not inanimate—I took *myself* somewhere without guards."

Morgan took a deep breath. "And now you're back. And you're needed upstairs. There's a... a situation. With the united attack force."

"What?" Adam's stomach clenched and he reached for Remy's hand, not sure if he was taking or offering comfort. "Did they attack? Jesus, what did they do?"

"Come upstairs," Morgan said, and his voice gentled when he looked at Remy. "There's been no attack. There's been...." He looked around, as if concerned that they might be overheard. "It's odd," he said. "Come upstairs, and you'll see."

Remy and Adam followed obediently. Adam still wasn't sure what to make of postvote Morgan. Remy trusted him, and that meant a lot. But there was something about him that made Adam's jaw tighten. Still, diplomacy was important. "Thanks for your vote this morning," he said as they jogged up the stairs.

"It wasn't a personal favor," Morgan replied. "I just don't think the general's the right man for the job. I think the military should stay separate from the executive branch."

"Fair enough," Adam said. He was actually relieved to hear that he hadn't misjudged Morgan's attitude as much as he'd thought. "So you still think I'm incompetent, but I'm better than the alternative."

"You're better than *that* alternative," Morgan corrected. They were at the council room door now, and it slid open to reveal all of the council members, and all of the various support staff, staring at the huge screen on the wall. A screen that seemed to be either shut off, or broadcasting an image of....

"Nothing," Morgan said quietly. "Still no sign of them?"

Nickson was the nearest aide, and he shook his head. "No signals from them, no readings on the sensors. No signs of any explosion or other catastrophic event. They're just... they're gone."

"The united fleet?" Adam whispered. "What's this an image of? What are we looking at?"

"It's the rendezvous point on the far side of the wormhole," Morgan explained. "The planet's behind the camera; that's why we can't see it. But this was where the fleet was supposed to be. And there've been no signals from them anywhere else, either."

Adam's gaze found Sam Turay. "Have we heard from the other governments? Maybe they just changed their plans and didn't tell us."

Turay shook his head. "I've been in contact with all of them. They're using our fleet, on this side of the wormhole, as a base for their search efforts. We're relaying signals for them, sending out unmanned probes, cooperating in every way possible. They're genuinely confused and alarmed. They have no idea where their fleet is."

"It entered the wormhole on schedule," Adam said. "And then just didn't come out the other end?"

"Seems like," Morgan confirmed.

"What's the timeline? It takes a couple hours for ships to travel through the wormhole, but only a few minutes for messages traveling at the speed of light. And then another, what, twenty minutes for the message to get to us from our side of the wormhole? Is it possible that there's just been some delay in the messages? The fleet could be sitting right where we expect it to be, right now, and we wouldn't know about it for almost half an hour after they arrived."

"That's all been taken into consideration, Adam." Morgan sounded impatient, and there was finality in his tone when he said, "The united fleet is missing."

"Have we sent a message to the colonies?" Adam suggested.

"To say what?" General Mackie spoke for the first time, and judging by his tone, he wasn't quite over the morning's events. "Asking whether they happen to have seen an attack force that we misplaced?"

"Do you have a better idea?" Adam asked. "None of the ships were from this continent, so as long as they know that, they shouldn't think of *us* as their attackers. Maybe we can play a role, here, and broker some level of cooperation between the colonies and the other nations. It would certainly be helpful to get some information out of them, if they have any."

"But how would it help *them*?" Remy's voice was quiet, but this was, as far as Adam could recall, the first time he'd ever spoken up in the council, and every head turned toward him. "Why would they be interested in doing favors for the people who were coming to invade and enslave them?" He paused as if weighing his words, then visibly made the decision to continue. He raised his head and said, "Have you considered the possibility that the colonies are the ones behind the disappearance? They were acting pretty confident, weren't they? I mean, they must have known that troops would be sent. They must have known they'd be totally outnumbered and unable to defend themselves. So why would they take the chance, unless they also know that they had some way to make sure that the troops never arrived?"

"You know something." The general's voice was quiet, but filled with rage. He stood up, and Adam moved at the same time Morgan did, both of them putting themselves between Mackie and Remy. But the general didn't come any closer. He seemed content to attack with his words. "You were born up there. You've been a sympathizer from the start. You seduced Adam into being soft on the traitors, and now you're practically celebrating the loss of thousands of brave soldiers."

"I'm not celebrating anything. I'm just trying to figure it out."

"And you've got a good point," Morgan said. "We never understood why they were being so bold. But maybe they knew about this. Somehow." He turned to Mackie. "You have scientists in the military, experts on wormholes, interstellar travel, all of it. What are they saying? Is there some way the colonists could have actually made this happen?"

"How the hell could *anyone* make this happen? You think a bunch of farmers figured out how to... to destroy an entire fleet of heavily armed, heavily *defended* military ships, leaving absolutely no trace of an explosion or any other damn thing? Farmers?" The general's expression made it clear he was disgusted with the entire situation, but had a special focus of revulsion for certain idiots in the council chamber.

"So you're thinking act of God?" Remy asked quietly. "It's easier for you to believe that something supernatural intervened, or that this was all some freak accident of the galaxy, than to believe that maybe somehow the colonies knew what was going to happen?"

"'Knew what was going to happen,'" Adam echoed. He looked at Remy, then Morgan. Then back to Remy, because damn it, Adam was *not* going to start bouncing his ideas off Morgan Winters. "The wormhole hasn't had any physical traffic since the colonies declared independence. Not from our end. But maybe they tried to send a ship through, it was lost, and they realized that the wormhole wasn't working. Maybe they didn't *cause* this, but they still knew about it, and that's why they thought they were safe making their declaration."

"If the wormhole shut down unexpectedly, I think they'd be panicking, and looking for help." Remy sounded thoughtful. "They wouldn't declare independence—they'd send a call for rescue or assistance. And I don't know much about physics, but does it make sense that light would still be able to travel through the wormhole just fine, sending our messages back and forth, if something's gone wrong with the structure of the thing?" He shook his head stubbornly. "I think they controlled it. I think they made it happen."

"A bunch of *farmers!*" The general glared at Remy as if he were the one who'd caused the disaster.

Remy maintained his usual demeanor. "Not just farmers," he said calmly. He frowned, thinking about something, and then looked at Adam with excitement. "Celina Holst!" he exclaimed.

"Who?"

"*Dr.* Celina Holst. There was a big deal about her a few years back. She was born and raised in the colonies—Colony Four, I think, but I can't be sure. Then she came to Earth to do more schooling. University of Cairo, maybe? Somewhere in Africa. She made some big discoveries. In astrophysics. I didn't understand what they were, really, but people were excited."

"You follow news from the astrophysics community?" Morgan didn't sound skeptical, exactly, but certainly surprised.

"I follow news from the colonies. There's hardly any, so it doesn't take much time to keep track of it."

"And you think this *woman* somehow found a weapon that is capable of destroying an entire fleet?" The general was back in his seat, his head resting on his hand as he dealt with the stupidity being presented to him.

"It's worth looking into," Adam said. He would have said it was worth looking into a theory involving a race of space-kittens just to aggravate Mackie, but this really did sound like it could be something. "Nickson, look her up and get in contact with her. Low-key, just say we're investigating and could use her expertise—something like that."

Nickson nodded and got to work, and the rest of the men in the room stared at the blank screen. "It's definitely a signal?" Adam asked. "We are receiving a signal through the wormhole, transmitting this image of nothing? Rather than just not getting a signal at all?"

"It's a signal," one of the aides said. His face was familiar, but Adam couldn't remember his name. "But, sir...." He was looking down at his comm, and it was clear that he wanted Adam to see whatever was on it.

"Put it on the big screen," Adam suggested. He wanted to see what the aide had found, but he also wanted to get rid of the image of vast, empty space.

The aide nervously complied, then said, "This is a graph showing the signal strength over the past twenty-four hours. It's natural for there to be some variation, but look at that dip, about two hours ago. There's no signal at all. Not for long; about five minutes. Normally, we'd say it was just a glitch; a system somewhere needed to reboot, or something like that. But this one... the fleet was inside the wormhole two hours ago."

Adam was still thinking about that when Nickson tentatively said, "Sir?" Adam looked at him and nodded acknowledgement. "Sir, I was just speaking to Dr. Abasi Pakhom at the University of Cairo. He's the head of the astrophysics department, and he confirmed that Dr. Holst was working with them, and that she came from Colony Four."

"*Was* working with them?" Adam asked.

"She returned to the colonies a little less than a year ago, sir." Nickson's eyes were wide as he added, "Dr. Pakhom said no one knew why she left. But prior to her departure, sir... she was working on a project involving wormhole manipulation and control."

Adam gave himself a moment to think, then said, "We need to contact the colonies. We were still negotiating with them; there was no declaration of hostilities. Hopefully they'll respond." He looked over at the general, then around the table to make sure everyone was paying attention. "If this is real—if the colonies have somehow found a way to control the wormhole—then military intervention is no longer an option. We've been half-assed with the negotiations because we knew we could always just take what we wanted if we had to. But if this is real...." He looked over at Sam Turay. "I want a briefing on the negotiations to date. And then I want to send my own message, as the leader of the council." He tried to rein himself in a little and remember that he was only the leader because he'd been the one to break the tie, but the same recklessness that had seized him in Baryman's office was on him again. "Have something ready for me in an hour, please." He turned to the general. "Please continue to assist the other nations in their rescue operations, but do *not* send any armed or manned crafts through that wormhole. And I'd like your scientists to look at whatever work Holst was doing before she left, and see if they can figure out what she's done. Assuming she's done it."

Before the general could argue, Adam turned to Desmond Chan and said, "I'd appreciate it if you could help me draft my message to the colonies. We need to get this right." He made himself turn to Morgan and add, "I'd like you in on that as well, if you have time."

"I have time," Morgan said neutrally. He was watching Adam with a strange, assessing expression, and Adam didn't want to think about what the man was trying to figure out.

"Wait a second," the general growled. "This is a council. You don't tell us what to do!"

"This is an emergency," Adam countered. "If anyone disagrees with the responsibilities as I've laid them out, I guess we can slow down and have another vote. But I think we need to move fast." He swiveled toward Morgan and Desmond. "You're okay with your jobs?" They both nodded, and Adam looked at Sam Turay. This was a bit riskier, given the man's vote that morning, but Sam was nodding before Adam even asked the question.

"I can get something put together. And I agree, a new voice will let them know we're serious."

Adam turned to the general. "Is there a reason you *don't* want your scientists to look into this? Or are you actually arguing that you think it's a good idea to risk our troops with manned crafts, or risk our relationship with our only food source with armed crafts? What exactly is it that you object to, General Mackie?"

"I don't like your tone," Mackie said.

"I'm sorry to hear that," Adam replied. "Is there anything more substantive you'd like to discuss?" Adam tried to forget that the general was the prime suspect in the assassination attempts, and tried to remember that they were all theoretically on the same team. He stepped a little closer to the general. "We can figure out the rest of it later," he said in what he hoped was a conciliatory tone. "For now... can you get your scientists working?"

The general's nod was jerky and reluctant, but he didn't argue anymore, so Adam took the victory. He looked over at Remy, and Remy looked back at him. There was no time for them to enjoy each other's bodies, not right then, and maybe not for a long while to come. But it was comforting just to have Remy in the same room. When Remy smiled sadly, Adam returned the expression. Team Challoner. The members seemed to be shifting a little, but it was still good to know that he wasn't alone.

CHAPTER EIGHTEEN

WORKING with Morgan wasn't as bad as Adam had expected. The man had a different perspective than Adam did, but that was valuable, he realized. There was no point in sharing ideas with someone who'd already had all the same ideas himself. And it was hard for either of them to be argumentative or uncooperative with Desmond Chan sitting there, watching them with his wise eyes. But just because they worked well together, it didn't mean the job was an easy one.

"Too weak," Morgan decided after the latest draft. "We need to go into this as equals or we're setting ourselves up for trouble."

"Their earlier demands—they were all political. All about independence and recognition and guarantees of safety. They weren't trying to gouge us on the prices of the food. They were acknowledging that we paid for the infrastructure they're using. And *we* haven't invaded their space, so there's no reason for them to be angry at us. *We* haven't lost our fleets, so there's no reason for us to be angry at them. I think we should completely ignore the events of the last couple days and just keep negotiating like we were before. Just, you know—we should do a better job of it now." Adam waited for Morgan's shrug of acquiescence, then turned to Desmond.

"*Completely* ignore it?" Desmond said. "Surely that will seem disingenuous. I think we need to acknowledge it...."

"Keep it separate, though," Morgan said. "We're concerned

about the lives of thousands of soldiers, not to mention the loss of billions of dollars worth of military hardware, and we'd like to know more about that. But that isn't a term of our deal. We're establishing diplomatic relations, and we're establishing trade: their raw materials for our manufactured goods and luxury items. Same stuff we always shipped, but now it's international trade instead of domestic. They aren't our colony anymore. We're *buying* grain from them and selling them manufactured goods, not *shipping* grain that we always owned and sending supplies in order to support them. Same materials, different names and technicalities."

They were repeating themselves. Adam looked over at Remy. He was sitting by the door, as he always did, seeing and hearing every detail, as he always did. He shrugged at Adam. In this room, with these men, Remy would know that his input would be welcome. He just didn't think he had anything to say.

Adam wasn't so sure. "You were born out there," he said. "That's a valuable perspective. What do they want? What do we need to give them?"

Remy frowned. "They're just people, Challoner. They want what everybody wants. Freedom. Fair treatment. A sense of security, for now and for the future." He looked at Adam as if frustrated by his cluelessness.

"The future," Adam echoed. He thought about Kara and remembered the panic he'd felt when she'd pushed her way into the revolution. "Their children." He wasn't sure, but he thought this might be something useful. "They did what they had to do to be sure their children would grow up free of oppression. If they've figured out the wormhole, they don't have to worry much about security. But they'll still want what's best for their kids. And that means they want good relations with Earth."

Adam smiled and saw a mirrored expression on Desmond's face, but it was Morgan who said, "That's it. We offer them... I don't know, not citizenship for the kids, but an exchange program, or automatic visas or preferred immigration status or something. We say that they're no longer our colonies, but we still want a close relationship with them. We want their kids to have the freedom to choose where to live, just like they've always had before this. Right?"

"I like it," Adam said firmly. "It doesn't cost us anything, and it absolutely demonstrates our good will. If we put that in instead of some of the weaker language... we're ready to go. Right?"

Their comm alarms sounded then, almost simultaneously, although Adam noticed that Morgan's was just a little bit ahead of his. The man certainly had connections, but that wasn't something Adam needed to worry about right then. He glanced at his screen. "Back to the council," he announced for Remy's benefit, and he shook his head. "What the hell has gone wrong now?"

For once, Morgan didn't have the answer, and they all trooped back into the chamber together. The councilors were gathering, and as they arrived, every eye was fixed on the large comm screen, which showed one of the huge intergalactic freighters used to transport food from the colonies.

"Where is it? Where is this image from?" Adam knew he sounded too intense, almost frenzied, but damn it, there was enough food on that freighter to feed the country for a month.

"It just came out of the wormhole, sir." Nickson seemed to be having the same sort of difficulty controlling his voice. "And we're receiving a signal from the ship. It's addressed to you. Should I send it to your private comm or to the large screen?"

Interesting question. Adam was tempted to watch it himself, first, but the tension in the room made it clear that no one would appreciate his discretion. "Large screen, please."

The screen flickered to an image of a simply dressed woman sitting in an office that would best be described as Spartan. She was mixed race, which should have marked her as a member of the lower classes, but she managed to look aristocratic all the same. Maybe it was her serenity that gave that impression, because it certainly wasn't her surroundings.

"Greetings, Mr. Challoner," she said in a well-modulated voice. "My name is Shana Waters. I have been chosen as the temporary leader of a group of people who have yearned for freedom for too long. Perhaps you can identify with my position, although at least I have the luxury of having been elected to my post." Her smile was calm, and Adam really couldn't be sure whether she'd just accused him of being a dictator or not. He put the thought away for another time and listened to the message as she said, "I *know* you can identify with the challenge of providing for the needs of our people while still maintaining our own morals and the ethical reputations of our governments. I'm contacting you now because of your government's decision not to join the invasion force that was sent to our young nation."

Her smile shifted and there was steel in her voice as she said, "By now you will have heard that the fleet did not arrive as expected. We can and *will* defend ourselves against attack. But we wish for peace." Back to the calm smile. "Our two nations were engaged in negotiations prior to the attack, and we wish to continue those negotiations now. As a gesture of good faith, and as a way to help you negotiate out of fairness rather than desperation, we have sent a freighter of food for you to unload and distribute as you wish. It is our expectation that the credit for this food will be applied against the debt we owe for all the infrastructure and equipment we have taken control of."

Another smile as Waters said, "I was told that you would behave honorably, Mr. Challoner, and I'm glad that your actions have confirmed it. You have shown your good intentions by not joining in the invasion force, and we have shown ours with this shipment of grain. I trust that our negotiations can now proceed in a more fruitful manner than they previously did." She nodded, and the picture cut out.

"Bullshit." The general's voice cut through the silence of the room. "Bullshit! There is no way those bastards have figured out how to manipulate the wormhole. It's impossible."

"Earth's ships are gone, and their ship just came through," Adam said as mildly as he could. "I think we have to assume that they arranged that." It probably wasn't the time, but he couldn't help musing a little. "In our revolution, we used the same technology that had oppressed us as a tool for our freedom. In theirs... maybe they've managed to do something similar. The wormhole is no longer a two-way street, not without their permission." He looked at the general and said, "Of course you'll have the wormhole closely monitored when the freighter goes back through. But don't attach any sensors to the ship, or do anything else too overt. We're getting somewhere with the colonies, and we can't afford to risk that, not now."

Adam turned to address the room as a whole. "The ship's still a week away from arriving here. Let's set a goal to have at least one more shipment through the wormhole and coming towards us before that one is unloaded. Our grain stores are low, and we need to build them back up." He clapped his hands in what he hoped was an invigorating, enthusiastic manner. "This is huge, people. Let's make it work for us. We need to make an address to the citizens. We need to stay in touch with the other nations and continue to offer our assistance with the recovery efforts. But let's get most of our fleet back here, General. If we've got food and no one else does, we'll try to share, but we can't be vulnerable if they get desperate. We need to be ready to defend ourselves—have the freighter escorted and guarded at all times." He turned to Morgan and Desmond. "We need to keep working on our reply, and work in some of what Waters said in her message." And then his gaze found Remy's beautiful, inscrutable face. "And I need to talk to you. In private."

THE late-afternoon sun didn't do much against the cool spring wind, and Remy hunkered down on the roof behind the shelter of the concrete parapet. He sat there, looking up at Adam, and waited.

Adam didn't want to say it. His mind was racing, trying to find a different explanation, but nothing came to him. "You were in contact with them. The colonies." It made sense, he was pretty sure. Things Remy had said, the knowing look in Shana Waters's eye as she'd said that they'd been told Adam could be trusted. "You were working for them? All along?"

"Working for them?" Remy frowned. "Working for you." He shrugged. "But, yeah, talking to them, sometimes."

"You were in contact with the people who were threatening to starve our planet into extinction, the people who just destroyed significant portions of three fleets of military vessels, and you're acting like it's not a big deal? Don't play that game, Remy! How did you even get the signal through? We were supposed to be monitoring and blocking all transmissions."

"I don't know the technical details," Remy admitted. "Dar had it set up. I just took over from him. We grew up out there; they were more willing to trust us. So we talked to them."

"You took over from Dar. Dar did it, so you had to do it too. Damn it, Remy, can you not make *any* of your own decisions?" Adam's mind was racing. Was this treason? They hadn't been at war, technically. Espionage, maybe? Would anyone else be able to figure it out? How could Adam protect Remy? And, damn it, how could he ever trust him again?

Especially when Remy didn't seem to even understand what he'd done wrong. "I make *all* of my own decisions," he retorted. "And I do it without the crutch of your ridiculous black and white 'morality'."

"*Black and white*? Jesus, Remy, this isn't exactly a subtle shade of gray! You were spying for a group of people who were threatening to starve our entire planet into submission. You don't see anything wrong with that?"

"Spying? I wasn't *spying*. I just told them they should trust you. The rest of it... they just wanted to establish a connection. They didn't ask for anything, and I didn't volunteer. I never told them anything that happened in the council chamber, or even anything you told me. I just said you were an honorable person."

"And they believed you?"

"I think they believed that I believed it. But, no, they weren't sure about you. I wasn't supposed to know about the wormhole trick, because they wanted to use it as a test."

"But you *did* know?" Adam stared at the innocent face in front of him, the calm visage of a man who'd allowed thousands of his planetmates to be destroyed.

"Not really. I suspected, I guess, but I didn't put it all together until today, with the bit about Celina Holst. I just figured they had an ace in the hole. I thought maybe it'd be the wormhole."

"You didn't say anything. You let all those men die." Adam was feeling queasy. He loved this man. Did he love a monster?

But Remy was shaking his head. "What the hell was I supposed to say? That I thought maybe the colonies had something planned? At this point, it's crystal clear that the colonies did it, and the general and his friends *still* won't believe it was possible. There's no way they'd have believed me before." He shrugged almost nonchalantly. "And I don't think the soldiers are dead. I don't think the ships are lost, not permanently." He raised his hands as if forestalling Adam's questions. "No, I don't have any proof of that. They didn't tell me anything about it. It's just a feeling. I think they were serious about wanting peace, and I think they're too smart to believe that they could destroy half the Earth's fleet and then cruise right into happy friendships."

"Why didn't you tell *me*?" Adam asked. The rest of it... he needed to think about the rest of it. But he needed to hear the answer to this question before his mind could go anywhere else.

"They asked me not to tell you about the communication," Remy said simply. "And there was no reason to. So I didn't."

"No reason to? You don't think it would have been helpful for me to know that they had some sort of super wormhole weapon at their disposal? You don't think that might have affected my judgment on these issues?"

"That was the whole point, Challoner. They wanted to know what you'd do when you thought you had the upper hand. They wanted to know how everyone would act, who'd try to negotiate and who'd go straight to military strength. They needed a test so they could trust you."

"So that's what it came down to." Adam couldn't make himself look at Remy. "After all the... after everything, you still don't trust me."

Adam wasn't expecting to hear laughter. "Don't be stupid, Challoner. *I* don't trust you? Trust *you*, to do the right thing? To be stupidly, annoyingly noble even when it would be a hell of a lot easier to be anything else? Of course I trust you. I didn't tell you because I wanted *them* to trust you." When Adam forced himself to look up, he found Remy smiling fondly at him. "I wanted *them* to know what *I* know, so it'd be clear that they could believe in you like I do."

"But...." It was getting hard to remember what he was objecting to. "What if I'd done the wrong thing? What if the general had won the vote?"

"If you'd done the wrong thing, that would mean that you weren't the man I thought you were, so it'd be fine that I hadn't told you. And if the general had won the vote, I'd have told. It wouldn't have done a damn bit of good, but I'd have tried. I was in the room the whole time, you know."

"Jesus, Remy...." Adam had no idea what to think. "How did you think I was going to feel about this? Were you planning to *ever* tell me?"

For the first time, Remy seemed uncertain. "I don't know. I guess... I didn't think about it, really. I mean, I didn't think it was a big deal." He paused as if thinking it over. "If the ships were really destroyed, if all those men are dead... obviously I'd... I don't know. I'd know that I'd made a terrible mistake." He seemed to realize how inadequate the words were, but he also seemed to know that there were no others that would be any better. "But I really don't think that's what happened."

"*You and me*, Remy." Maybe it was petty or immature for Adam to focus on this aspect of things, but he didn't seem to be able to get past it. "Were you planning to just keep this a secret from me? Forever?"

"Forever?" Remy looked confused by the word. "I don't... *forever*?" He heaved himself to his feet and stared at Adam. "Are you crazy? There's no *forever* for you and me. This is...." He waved his arms around as if trying to illustrate the temporary frenzy of their lives, then stilled. "I've met your wife, Challoner. I've seen the people you're friends with. You're the leader of the goddamned continent! You and I are not a real thing. You have to know that, don't you? I'm an ex-whore with no education, no family, no money... I'm nothing but a pretty face. I'm not the one you end up with, Challoner. Not a chance. Not *forever*."

"I don't understand. What do you think we've been doing? I...." Adam frowned. He hadn't wanted to say it, not at a time like this, but he couldn't think of any other words. "I love you, Remy."

Remy stared at him.

Adam tried again. "I do. I lo—"

"Stop it!" Remy's voice was quiet, but brittle. "You have no idea what you're talking about. Five minutes ago, I was a spy who'd betrayed you. Now you...." He stopped as if he couldn't bring himself to say the words, and shook his head as if to clear even the sound of them from his ears. "You need to think about what you're saying."

"I have thought about it," Adam said, but Remy wasn't listening. He was leaving.

He was halfway through the door and barely looked over his shoulder when he said, "I'm going to look at the stuff from Baryman. I'll let you know if I find anything. I'll stay out of the council room from now—"

It took a moment for Adam to understand what was happening. Remy stopped talking, staggered back onto the roof, half turned... and only then did Adam see the dark wetness on the blue fabric covering his chest. Remy's hand was inside his jacket, fumbling weakly, and when he managed to pull his handgun out, he didn't point it at the door but extended it—slowly, butt first—toward Adam. Adam stepped forward in time to half catch Remy as he crumbled to the cement rooftop, blood spreading out from the hole in his shirt, his gun pressed into Adam's hands like a final gift.

Adam functioned, somehow. He took the weapon and pointed it at the door as he desperately activated his comm. He had Remy cradled between his knees, and he squeezed tight as if the strength of his legs could somehow hold Remy's body together.

"I need security and medics to the roof—now!" he shouted as soon as the comm beeped. But that wouldn't be enough. "It's a small roof, not the main one." Jesus, he couldn't do this, couldn't stay calm while Remy bled to death and assassins made their way up the stairs and... "The stairway at the end of the main hall, up to the fourth floor. Then there's a jog, and another, narrower stairway with a door at the top." Surely that was enough. "Hurry! Remy's been shot."

He dropped the comm then and pressed his hand tight against the wound on Remy's chest. Blood was still pumping out of it, and Adam tried to think of it as a good thing, a sign that Remy's heart was still beating. He kept the gun aimed at the doorway and felt a savage rage, a fierce desire for revenge. He could almost picture the bastard's face peering through the open door, could see the way it would dissolve into red confetti when Adam's bullet smashed into it.

But the door didn't open, not until he heard a voice on the other side yelling, "Security forces! Can you unlock the door?"

It could be a trick, Adam knew. Could be the assassin just

claiming to be security, or it could be a real security guard who planned to kill Adam. He looked down at Remy's pale face and realized that it didn't matter. If Remy didn't get help, he would die. And if he died, Adam wouldn't want to live. So he shifted Remy to the side as gently as he could, then lurched over and opened the door.

CHAPTER NINETEEN

"IT'LL be some time before we know anything, Mr. Challoner."
The nurse seemed efficient, and too tired to be apprehensive
about Adam's position with the government. "He'll be in surgery
for several hours, and then recovery. That's if all goes well." She
fixed him with a firm look. "We're *hoping* for no news, at this
point. Do you understand that?"

Did he understand? He didn't think so. He didn't think he
understood anything, nothing but the warm gush of Remy's blood
between his fingers, the pallor in Remy's face as he'd been loaded
onto the stretcher and carried to the shuttle. He didn't understand
the bright lights of the hospital, or the way that everyone around
him seemed to be carrying on with their business as if they didn't
grasp the enormity of the moment, the terrible, terrifying future
that Adam was trying not to contemplate.

"You should sit down, Mr. Challoner. You have people to take
care of you, right?" She looked over Adam's shoulder, and then he
felt a warm, feminine hand slipping into his.

"Come sit down, Daddy." Kara looked frail and shocked by this
latest intrusion of violence into her previously civilized life, but
she smiled bravely. "They're taking good care of him."

Adam let himself be led to the chairs, and Antonia rose as he
approached. They were in a private waiting room on a floor that
had been emptied of all other patients. The guards at the door
scowled at everyone who walked by, and Adam wanted to scream

at them. Where the hell had they been when they were needed? What good was it for them to intimidate medical staff when they hadn't done a damn thing to protect Remy from an assassin? "Right in the Capitol," he murmured. "He should have been safe there."

"He should have been," Antonia agreed. "But he was prepared for this. He knew it was a risk."

And that made even less sense than all the rest of it. Why the hell would Remy have taken the chance? He thought there was no future for him and Adam, so why was he willing to risk himself to keep Adam safe? He'd been willing to die for the revolution, but that was over. He'd put himself in danger to help people in the city, but he'd given that up when Adam needed him. Even though he didn't believe he and Adam would be together for long. Not that they'd *ever* been together, Adam thought, but he caught himself. No. They'd been together. Just because they hadn't had sex didn't mean they hadn't had *something*. He thought of Remy's warm breath as he nestled in against Adam's chest, and he pushed himself to his feet and strode across to the window. He reached his hands out to brace against the cool metal frame and tried to collect himself. He felt tears welling in his eyes and tried to blink them away. The setting sun blurred, cleared, and blurred again. He took a deep breath and was almost back in control of himself, but then Antonia was beside him. Her familiar arm reached around his shoulders and the tenderness robbed him of his strength.

"I know, Adam. I know," she murmured, and she wrapped him in her arms and let his sobs shake both of their bodies.

He didn't allow himself the luxury of crying for long, and by the time Morgan appeared in the doorway, Adam was well under control. He stayed at the window as Morgan cautiously approached.

"They say it will be several hours," Morgan said.

Adam just nodded. He knew what they said.

"I'm sorry, Adam, but we need you at the Capitol." Morgan

clearly realized his words were unwelcome, but he continued anyway. "We've got drafts of the messages to the colonies and to the citizens. We need you to review them and present them." He interpreted Adam's silence correctly and said, "If there was anything for you to be doing here, we'd find a way around it. I have no idea what that would be, because, really, we need your credibility now more than ever. The colonists trust you, and the people trust you, and we need that."

"You really expect me to care about that right now?"

"Yeah, I do." Morgan's gentle tone was replaced by his more traditional bluntness. "And Remy would too. If you don't care about the well-being of this country, you should have quit the damned job months ago. Remy would still be healthy and Dar would still be alive. But they risked their lives to protect you so you could *do the job*. Don't make their sacrifices pointless now."

Adam had never hated Morgan more. His fists had never been so eager to smash into the bastard's pointy little face. Goddamnit, why did he have to be right?

Adam jerked away from Antonia's gentle touch and started for the door, with Morgan trailing behind him. "We can get you back here within ten minutes," Morgan promised, "if anything comes up. And if Remy makes it through the surgery, we can—"

Adam had no intentions, no conscious thoughts of it, but somehow he had Morgan shoved up against the wall, his forearm wedged against Morgan's throat to block off any further words. He couldn't hear it. Couldn't hear plans for what they'd do *if* Remy made it through the surgery, not when every "if" came with the unthinkable, unbearable acknowledgement that Remy might *not* make it. "Stop talking," Adam growled. He lurched away and started down the hall again.

For once, Morgan actually did as he was told, and they spent the trip to the Capitol in silence. As they prepared to land, Adam said, "Are they questioning the shooter? Has he said who he was working for?"

And now that Adam wanted Morgan to speak, he said nothing. Adam turned to stare at him. "They caught the shooter. I saw him, in handcuffs."

Morgan kept his eyes on the floor of the shuttle. "They caught him," he admitted. He finally looked up. "He was taken into custody. But he died before he could be questioned."

"Died? Of what? He wasn't injured, not that I could see."

"It's being investigated," Morgan said flatly.

"Investigated by whom?" The door slid open and Adam jerked to his feet. "This is bullshit, Morgan. This is complete...." He stopped and tried to regulate his voice. "The security footage? Will that tell us anything? Where he came from, how he got access?"

"The footage was compromised," Morgan said. "But that could be our best evidence. I need to talk to Remy about it. I know he was working with some people, trying to track the source of the video corruption. If he can put me in touch with them...."

Morgan trailed off, and Adam tried to ignore the "if."

"It has to end, Morgan," he said tiredly. "It can't go on like this."

"We'll figure it out," Morgan promised.

The council chamber was bustling, as usual, but it stilled when Adam and Morgan appeared. Adam couldn't deal with that, couldn't accept any sympathy without being weakened, so he turned to Morgan and said, "You have drafts for me to look at? Are the cameras set up in my office?"

"They will be," Morgan confirmed. "And we have a new shirt and jacket on the way."

Adam looked down at himself. Blood. Remy's blood, staining his white shirt and charcoal jacket. He couldn't think about it, couldn't let himself wonder how much blood Remy had lost, and how much damage the bullet had done. "The drafts," he ordered. "On my comm. Now."

He'd get through this, and then he'd get back to Remy. And Remy would be okay. Remy would be okay. Adam made himself read the messages, and he tried to concentrate on the subtleties of the words, but through it all, like the beating of his heart, Remy's name pounded and pulsed. Adam would get through this, and then he'd get back to Remy. And he'd *make* Remy be okay.

He couldn't find any changes to the wording of the messages. Maybe he'd have been more critical under other circumstances, but it seemed stupid to fight over details now. He shrugged out of his jacket and shirt when the aide supplied him with new ones, and then had to fight to control himself when he went into the bathroom to wash blood off his chest. Remy's blood, staining the washcloth, swirling down the drain, disappearing forever. He made himself take deep breaths, and he finished his cleaning with his eyes shut.

The general was speaking when Adam returned to the council chamber. "We cannot allow this to interfere with the progress we are making. We are on the verge of conquering the first major challenge of our leadership, and we cannot be distracted."

"The first major challenge?" Adam demanded. Every face in the room turned toward him. "You mean, the continued violent attacks on the leader of the nation, attacks that we seem unable to stop or even understand? Is that what you're referring to?"

The general's expression was patient and understanding. "I'm sure that's been upsetting to you personally, Adam. But, no, in a national sense, I think the food shortage is a bit more critical."

"General, is there any need to have this conversation right now?" Morgan asked. "Adam's about to go on the air, we have no issues that need to be discussed... the precise ranking of crises seems like a game for another time."

"A game? I'm sorry, Morgan, but I don't think the governance of our nation is a game. And I was about to suggest, before I was interrupted, that incidents like this make it crystal clear why we should *not* have made one man into a figurehead, the only identifiable figure in our government. I think we need to start diversifying the public face of this administration. Since the colonial message was directed to Adam, I understand having him return it, but I don't think it makes sense to have him speak to the populace as well."

"And you think *you* should do that?" As always, Desmond Chan seemed amused.

"This morning we had a vote in which fully half of this council expressed their confidence in me as their leader. So, yes, I think I am the logical choice as a second voice for the council."

"And you'll be the one to deliver the good news, while I was the one who gave all the bad?" Adam shook his head. "No. We're looking at rules and systems for the temporary council, and when the draft of those rules is ready, we can discuss changes. Until then, we need to stay the course. This isn't a time for power-brokering."

"Says the man who *has* the power," the general snarled. "You look like crap, Adam, and you're too emotional. We need a calm leader right now, not someone crying like a woman because his whore was damaged."

When Adam thought about it later, he realized that it wasn't "whore" that set him off. It was "damaged." The general was referring to Remy as if he were an inanimate object, not a human being. Adam started across the room before anyone knew what was going on, but by the time he arrived, the general had managed to scurry behind several of his supporters, and he leered at Adam over their shoulders.

It should have ended there, but Adam pushed someone aside with one hand and swung with the other, just as the general was leaning forward with another sneering comment. Adam's fist met the general's nose with an incredibly satisfying crunch, and the blood that sprayed out felt like a benediction.

"Goddamnit," Morgan growled, and he drove his body into the middle of the crowd and pushed Adam back. It was all over in a matter of seconds, all but the rush of adrenaline and rage that had thankfully replaced Adam's fear and sorrow. He let himself be shoved backward, but kept his eyes on the general, who was pinching the bridge of his nose and swearing gutturally.

Morgan dragged Adam to the far side of the room and then eased away far enough to get a better look. He kept one hand braced against Adam's shoulder, but he seemed to understand that it had been enough and Adam wouldn't be looking for more. "Goddamnit," he said again, and he looked at the scarlet spray on Adam's chest. He frowned as if debating the wisdom of any further words. Finally he sighed and turned tiredly to an aide. "We're going to need another shirt," he said, and, blessedly, that was all.

AFTER the messages were recorded, Adam went back to the hospital. Morgan went with him. It was annoying, like the man thought Adam couldn't be trusted to behave himself without a chaperone. But as the doctor approached them, his face serious, Adam took a deep breath to steady himself and realized that Morgan had done the exact same thing. They were both bracing for horrible news; they both cared about Remy. Antonia and Kara were hovering in the background, ready to support Adam as needed, but Morgan was right there, concerned about Remy himself, and it was strangely comforting to think that Adam wasn't alone.

"Mr. Stone came through the surgery fairly well," the doctor said without preamble. "We repaired most of the damage, and we left nanobots inside to tidy up a little. They'll automatically destroy any infection or cellular necrosis, and we can order them to repair any minor damage that we missed. We'll keep the patient sedated for the first twenty-four hours at least. That's mostly for pain management, but also to keep him still and give him a good start on his healing."

"But he's going to be okay?" Adam knew he sounded like a little kid, but he needed to know.

Unfortunately, the doctor wasn't going to give him the assurances he wanted. "We hope so. We're optimistic. But it was a serious injury. Frankly, I'm surprised he made it into surgery." He waited for any other questions, but Adam couldn't think of any, and the doctor nodded tiredly. "You can see him, if you want. As I said, he's sedated, so he won't know you're there, but it may help you feel better."

"Yes," Adam said simply. "I'd like to stay with him."

The doctor shrugged. "It won't hurt him. You'll have to get out of the way when we're working on him, but otherwise it should be fine. But you obviously have a lot of other commitments, a lot of demands on your time. And he won't know or care whether you're there, not for the first day or so. If you only have so much time, it would be better to spend it—"

"I'll stay with him," Adam said firmly. He turned to Morgan. "You'll just have to make that work. We can set up an office for me here, and I can deal with things on the comm. If that doesn't work, I'll quit. We've got food now. That crisis is resolved. I want the general arrested and charged, but if somebody else wants to take over the leadership, that's fine with me."

"The general?" Morgan looked puzzled. "What do you want the general charged with?"

"Attempted murder? Murder itself, in the case of Dar! Conspiracy, treason… whatever we can think of."

"The general?" Morgan frowned at Adam, then seemed to remember that they were in a fairly public situation. He turned to the doctor and said, "Can Mr. Challoner go in on his own, or does he need a nurse or something?"

"The nurses can show you the way the first time. After that, as long as you don't touch anything, you can go in on your own." The doctor seemed to realize that he was being dismissed, and he nodded politely, then left. Morgan turned to Adam, obviously ready to pick up where they'd left off, but Adam had lost interest in revenge, at least for the time being.

"I want to see Remy," he said. He *needed* to see Remy. Needed a new image to erase the one that was on replay in his mind, and even pale Remy in a hospital bed would be better than blood-covered Remy splayed across the gravel of the flat roof. Remy, who Adam had just accused of being a traitor. Remy, who hadn't understood Adam's hope for the future. Remy, who'd thought they could never last. Adam needed Remy to wake up so he could start proving to him just how wrong he was.

"We should talk," Morgan said, but Adam didn't think he was arguing, just penciling in a meeting for later. "I don't think the general's the one behind the attacks."

Adam would deal with Morgan's loyalty to his old ally later. "We'll talk. But I want to see Remy."

Apparently Morgan knew better than to argue. "Say 'hi' for me."

"Okay," Adam agreed. Better that than having Morgan trying to weasel his way in for a visit of his own.

He found his way to the nurses' station and followed a surprisingly young nurse down the hall to a glass-walled room. The blinds were drawn, but Adam could see a faint glow of light from inside.

"The patient is unconscious," the nurse said calmly. "If you want to hold his hand, that's okay, but don't move his arms, or any other part of his body. If you and the other visitor want to talk, that's fine, but keep your voices low. The patient is heavily sedated, but it's still best for the environment to be calm for him."

"The other visitor?" Adam asked. He looked behind him to see if Morgan had somehow followed along, but the hallway was empty.

"The other visitor," the nurse said. "I don't know his name, but security said he was fine."

Security. That meant nothing, of course. Adam thought about getting help, but he wasn't sure who he could trust, and the nurse had already pushed the door open and was standing back to let him go inside. "Let me know if you need anything," she said with a reassuring smile, and then she was gone, her soft-soled shoes not making a sound as she glided down the hallway.

Adam looked inside the room and let himself relax. It was odd for Ackerman to be visiting Remy, but not dangerous, at least.

"Come in, Adam," he said.

And that was when Adam saw the black barrel of the gun, held almost out of sight beneath Ackerman's arm. It was pointed straight at Remy's head. "This has gone on long enough. It's time for it to end."

It took a moment to process it all, and Ackerman waited patiently for Adam to figure it out. Ackerman. *Ackerman* was the obvious suspect, because he was in charge of the security services. Remy could see that, and so could Morgan, apparently. Anyone could have seen it, if they'd been looking at it rationally. But that wasn't Adam. Adam was ruled by emotion, and his "ridiculous, black and white morality." His propensity to be "stupidly, annoyingly noble." Remy's words echoed in his head, but Adam wouldn't let himself look at Remy's body lying motionless on the bed. Adam's naiveté had kept him from even considering that someone could be friendly on the surface but corrupted underneath, and Dar and Remy had paid the price for it.

Adam knew there was no one around, and he knew it was pointless to yell for security, since they all worked for Ackerman. He kept his eyes on the gun and stepped inside the sterile room. Maybe Ackerman was right. Maybe it *was* time for it to end.

CHAPTER TWENTY

"You shot Remy." It was an absurd opening; apparently Adam was still having some trouble catching up to events. "And Dar. You tried to shoot me. Jesus, Don, you tried to blow up the entire council with that shuttle attack! If Remy hadn't persuaded us to wait, we'd all be dead."

"Not *personally*. I didn't do any of that myself." Ackerman seemed to sincerely believe that this difference was important. "It was never personal, not any of it."

"Too bad we can't ask Dar how personal it was. When Remy gets better, ask *him*."

"The men in the shuttle from the Baryman Hotel, before the revolution." Ackerman looked closely at Adam. "Did you hate them? Did you want them dead, really, or just want them out of the way?" He raised a hand, the one *not* holding the gun, to forestall Adam's words. "And don't say that you were only indirectly involved in that. That's what I'm saying here. It was never me personally, and it was never personal."

"There was a larger goal then, Don! We were fighting to free an oppressed nation! What the hell are you fighting for? What's your goal here?"

Ackerman smiled softly and said, "Twenty dollars a day? Losing everything we had before, and then being expected to live on twenty dollars a day? I can't buy *lunch* for twenty dollars."

"But... that was the deal all along. That was our plan, from before the revolution. We'll open things up as soon as possible, let people start showing initiative, working to better their situations, but for now...."

"Who are you to decide when 'for now' is over?" Ackerman's voice was still quiet and reasonable. "I've decided that it's already over, and I've started to show initiative and better my situation. That's all."

"But why go through it all? Why support the revolution in the first place if you didn't want things to change?"

"Oh." Ackerman looked surprised. "You... you spoke to Baryman. He said he gave you the information."

"The information? Baryman's information? Wait, how do you know who we spoke to? Baryman's on your side?"

"Baryman isn't on anyone's side. Not anymore." Ackerman's calm was beginning to seem almost medicated, but it took a more sinister twist when he smiled and said, "I think people will *understand* why you and Remy killed him. It'll still be a crime, of course, and you'll be reviled. But you'll be understood."

"Killed him?" Jesus, Adam needed help, here. Remy, or even Morgan, someone more used to sinister machinations. Adam could philosophize about the theories behind these things, but trying to untwist the actual events was too damn much. "We didn't kill Baryman."

"I'm not sure if that's the approach to take, Adam. Denial makes it seem more sinister. I think you might be better off with a confession and throwing yourself on the mercy of the court. A crime of passion is different from something premeditated, after all."

"What crime? Jesus, is Baryman dead? Did *you* kill him?"

"He was killed with the gun you're holding in your hand right now, Adam." Adam looked down at his empty hands, then back up to the weapon Ackerman had lifted a little in demonstration.

Ackerman smiled patiently and prompted, "The gun you signed out of the shooting range when you took your lessons after the first attempt on your life. It was understandable, then, that you felt you needed protection, and taking revenge on the man who tortured your lover... that's understandable too. Some people, I think, will understand that, with all the stress you've been under, you snapped when you saw the man who had recently voted against your leadership in your lover's hospital room. They'll think it was tragic, but not unforeseeable that you attacked me."

Adam's mind raced. He'd taken the gun, but then left it locked in the drawer of his bedside table. He hadn't been able to think straight with its weight at his side, constantly reminding him of death and hatred. Had Ackerman retrieved it from the suite? Why? "You're recording all this. You'll edit out the parts that make you sound good, and play the parts that make me sound crazy. But they'll see through it, Don." Adam wasn't sure if he was trying to reason with a madman, or making a case to the reasonable man he'd been working with for months. "They can tell when a recording's been altered. You know that."

"It doesn't have to stand up to close scrutiny. And I'm the head of security—I can make sure it's trusted."

"I don't...." There was too much to absorb, and Adam was exhausted, and he couldn't keep his eyes away from the gun muzzle pointed at Remy's head. Would he even see the bullet, or would there just be a loud noise and then Remy's body jerking, his beautiful head dissolving.... "I still don't understand *why*. No, we haven't had a chance to look at Baryman's information yet. What would we have found?"

"*Why* isn't important, Adam. Just think about this. I'm about to kill your beautiful boy, and then I'll turn the gun on you. You're both about to die, if you don't do something about it."

"*Do something*? But what do you want?"

"Nothing. You just need to do something to stop me."

Adam stared at him blankly. "You mean... you want me to

attack you." Oh. "So you can record it. Edit out all the rest of it, all the things you said, and just play the part where I attack."

Ackerman was back to looking sinister, and starting to seem a bit impatient. "Do you have to analyze every single thing, every single time? Don't you ever just *do* something? Come on, Adam, be a man. Protect what's yours."

One way or another, this bastard was going to kill Remy. He was promising to do it if Adam didn't attack, and if Adam *did* attack, the bullet would be flying before Adam's first step was taken. "You did this now because of the information we got from Baryman. You need to make sure it didn't get out. But this is a rush job, Don. It's messy. It's a big gamble." He took a half step closer and tried to remember what he'd learned from Remy about telling convincing lies. "I've already sent the information to several different groups for analysis. They've probably already found whatever it is you're trying to hide. And I've got allies, people who aren't going to believe that I'd do something like this."

"Your beautiful wife and daughter," Ackerman said. For the first time, Adam noticed the gleam of sweat on the man's face. "I'll go find them next. After I'm done in here, I'll go find them, and I'll kill them too. Unless you stop me."

The words should have terrified Adam, but they didn't. "You're going to frame me for all this, kill me here, and then go and kill them? That doesn't make sense. It would be completely obvious that I didn't do it." He needed to think. He was a chess player; he needed to think in those terms, and plan several steps ahead. But he was good at chess because the pieces were clearly marked white or black, and because he could be cool and unemotional about it all. This... he looked at the man he had thought was his friend, pointing a deadly weapon at the man Adam loved. The same man Adam had accused of being a spy earlier that day. This was nothing like chess, and he was completely out of his depth.

"You need to *stop me*," Ackerman said. He was starting to sound impatient, and Adam didn't think that was a good thing.

But Ackerman was armed, and Adam wasn't. It was that simple. He was at least four paces away, which would be lots of time for Ackerman to pull the trigger to kill Remy and then turn the gun on Adam. Attacking would be suicide. And for whatever reason, it was what Ackerman wanted.

Adam's body tried to rebel. Every part of him wanted to rush toward Remy, but he forced himself to take a step backward instead. Ackerman stared at him. "What are you doing?" he asked, and Adam didn't think he was imagining the desperation in the man's voice.

"I'm thinking," he said, and he took another cautious, shuffling step backward. He reached behind him and felt the door handle. It was an old-fashioned door, not a modern slider, and Adam hoped he could use that to his advantage. Would the door stop a bullet, if Adam was able to open it quickly and duck behind it? Probably not, but maybe Ackerman wouldn't be thinking clearly enough to realize that.

"I'd like you to put that gun down," he tried. Of course it wouldn't work, but it might distract Ackerman a little, and it made Adam feel better to be using his words. "You know this won't work." As he spoke, he began to understand. "This is just desperation. Whatever Baryman told us, it's going to bring you down. You can't afford to wait around anymore, so you're making one last attempt. But it's too late, Don. It's over. I don't know the information, but it's out there. There's nothing that can happen in this room that will stop that."

"It won't matter." The desperation was still there, but Ackerman didn't sound crazed. "If you're out of the way, people will believe what they're told to believe."

"So why am I still alive? Why haven't you just killed me?" Adam shifted to the side. "Because you want to record me attacking you, sure. But you could fake that recording." Another half step, and Adam was ready. He mentally rehearsed the movements he'd make, warning his body that he was about to drive it against its instincts. Then it came to him. "You can't do it. Or at least, you don't want to. You don't want to murder an unarmed man, someone you called a friend. Every other attack was made by someone else. You could have come to my suite anytime. I would have let you in. You could have killed me, erased the surveillance recordings, and been all set. But you don't want to be a murderer. You want to tell yourself it was self-defense."

"I'll kill you both," Ackerman said raggedly. And there it was. The barrel of the gun moved away from Remy's head, started moving toward Adam, and that was the cue. Adam moved fast, jerking the door open, driving himself through it, and sprinting. He wasn't injured. He hadn't heard a shot. He still had a chance.

But Ackerman was sure to follow him. Ackerman *had* to follow him. If he stayed in that room, with Remy, and the gun... No. Adam let himself take a quick look over his shoulder, saw Ackerman coming through the doorway, and ran even faster.

It was a long hallway. There were doors all along it, but Adam couldn't take the chance of stopping to try one, in case it was locked. He had to keep moving, had to make it to the corner.

The first shot came when Adam was still a couple strides away from his salvation. He heard it, but didn't feel it. He was still moving, still running; he hadn't been hit. Another shot as Adam sprinted around the corner, his momentum carrying him several feet before he skidded to a stop. He could keep running, and probably get away. He could try to find Morgan, try to find guards that they could trust, and maybe they could catch Ackerman. But what would the man do in the meantime? Remy was still back there, defenseless. Adam wanted to believe he'd been right about Ackerman. Maybe the man really *couldn't* kill someone in cold blood. But maybe he could, and Adam wouldn't gamble with Remy's life. Besides, it was time for this to be over.

He spun around, searching for something he could use as a weapon, or a shield. He grabbed a plastic chair from a row lined up outside one of the rooms and hefted it thoughtfully. It was too light to do serious damage, but it had metal legs, and maybe that would be enough. Three large steps had him back to the corner and he had just lifted the chair over his head when Ackerman lumbered around the corner, gun outstretched.

It wasn't pretty. Adam swung without aiming and the chair caught Ackerman somewhere around his ear, then glanced down and hit his gun hand. There wasn't enough strength to knock the gun loose, but Adam had surprise on his side as he dropped the chair and grabbed Ackerman's wrist. Adam had never been much of a fighter, but he was desperate, and he kicked at Ackerman, threw an elbow when he got the chance, and kept his grip on the gun hand tight. "Morgan!" he yelled. "Help!"

Then Ackerman squirmed in a new direction, using his weight against Adam, and there was no breath left for any more yelling. They were both kicking now, both struggling to point the gun toward their opponent, and Adam was pretty sure it would have looked funny if it hadn't been so deadly serious.

"Drop the gun." The voice was firm and confident, but it wasn't the one Adam had wanted to hear. He and Ackerman turned their heads at the same time and saw Kara, posed in the stance she'd been taught at the range, her handgun pointed carefully toward Ackerman. "Drop it," she repeated, "or I'll shoot."

"You wouldn't—"

The roar of the handgun was deafening in the enclosed space, as was Ackerman's anguished scream. His knee was a bloody mess, and he dropped the gun as his body crumpled to the floor. Adam scrambled to retrieve it, making sure not to get between Kara and her target, and then father and daughter stood there together, both aiming guns at the man writhing on the floor.

Neither of them spoke for several moments. Then Kara said, "I shot him." Her voice was trembling.

"You saved me." But what was next? "You need to get out of here, I think. I'm not sure if we can trust the guards."

"Then somebody needs to have your back," she said, sounding stronger than she had moments before. "I'm staying."

There was a small crowd gathering at a careful distance, medical personnel drawn by Ackerman's screams. Adam carefully activated the safety on the gun, then tucked it into his waistband. Kara returned her weapon to the holster under her jacket.

"He needs help," Adam called to the hospital staff. "But wait until guards come. He should be searched for weapons as well." He pulled his comm out from his jacket pocket and hit a few buttons. It was absurd that there were no guards there yet. "Morgan?" he growled. "What's going on with hospital security? We need guards we can trust, down the hall from Remy's room."

A pause, then Morgan's voice said, "I'm on my way. But aren't there guards all over the place?"

"No." Adam looked around, then down at Ackerman. "Did you send them away?" he demanded. The tension in his chest began to relax, at least a little. If the guards were on Ackerman's side, he would have kept them around. Maybe this was a case of a rotten apple at the top, but not a diseased tree.

"Get me a doctor," Ackerman gasped.

Guards appeared at the end of the hallway, and Adam stepped back, keeping his hands carefully visible at his sides. "He attacked me," Adam said. "He needs to be searched for weapons."

"Mr. Ackerman?" one of the guards said doubtfully, but Ackerman seemed to have passed out, and the guards moved in and took over.

Adam reached down and found Kara's hand, cold and fragile in his grip. "Thank you," he said. Then he smiled tiredly. "I want to go sit with Remy. I'd like it if you came with me. I'd like it if you two could be friends."

She nestled in close to his chest. "Okay," she agreed quietly. "I'd like that too."

CHAPTER TWENTY-ONE

"HE WAS broke," Adam said. "That's all." He shifted a little in his chair, but kept his fingers wrapped firmly around Remy's. "That's what we got from Baryman's records. Ackerman was about to go under, before the revolution, so he wasn't risking anything, wasn't giving anything up by being part of it."

Remy nodded slowly. He still wasn't talking much, but that was just as well, Adam figured. It was nice to have a chance to say what he needed to without Remy interrupting all the time. Mostly, what he'd been saying lately was how sorry he was, for everything. But sometimes he took a break from that and gave Remy some news.

"He wanted me out of the way so he could steer the council away from full reforms. He was hoping to get his property back, property he'd been about to lose before the rebellion." Adam shook his head and ran his free hand gently over Remy's too pale forehead. "It was all just about money. Money and power."

There were wrinkles under Adam's fingers, and he realized that Remy was frowning. "He confessed?" Remy croaked.

"Yesterday morning. Once the hackers traced the manipulations of the security footage to him, and once the guards he'd recruited started talking, there was no point in denying any of it. We'll have a trial, of course, but it's just a formality." Adam took a deep breath and returned to his familiar litany. "I'm sorry, Remy. I should have seen it before. Before Dar. Before you." He shook his head. "I dragged you both into this mess, and you're the ones that got hurt. Not me."

"You can have some spiders," Remy offered, a pained pause between each word.

Adam smiled at the idea, not the delivery. "The nanobots are helping you heal. And the doctors say you *can't* actually feel them. They say you're just imagining it."

"Right there," Remy gestured with his chin. One hand was limited by the IV and the other was firmly locked in Adam's grip, so Remy was apparently making do by pointing with whatever he could manage. "They're scratching."

"Okay," Adam conceded. "I believe you. Do you want me to call the doctors and complain?"

"Bug spray," Remy managed.

"Probably not a good idea."

Adam's comm beeped and he tapped the screen to reveal Morgan's earnest face. "Sorry to bother you," he said, as he'd said each of the eight other times he'd messaged Adam so far that morning.

Adam sighed. The government was in turmoil, recovering from Ackerman's treachery, and Morgan was doing an excellent job of keeping things calm. Without him, there was no way Adam could have spent as much time by Remy's side as he was, so the interruptions shouldn't be resented. Besides, it wasn't like the nano-spider conversation had really been going anywhere. "What's up, Morgan?"

"Thought you'd like to know—the united fleet is back." Morgan sounded almost triumphant.

Remy leaned forward as if trying to sit up, and Adam gently pressed him back into the pillows. "Steady," he warned, "or I'll shut off the comm." He edged over so his head was near Remy's and they were both looking at the comm screen. "As promised," he said to Morgan. "The bastards have really done it. They've figured out how to manipulate the wormhole."

"They opened a passage to a different destination and sent the fleet there. Then opened the passage and called them home. Easy as that." Morgan shook his head. "They're still being pretty secretive about how they're doing it, understandably. But as long as they're controlling the wormhole, they're safe."

"And have they signed treaties with the other continents yet?"

"Almost there with Africa. Europe and Asia are still being picky, but they're going to get hungry soon enough." Morgan's voice had the confidence of a man whose national granaries were being restocked as he spoke.

"We need to set up elections." Adam had been thinking about it for a while, but hadn't known he was going to say it right then. He knew Remy was looking at him, but kept his attention turned toward Morgan.

Morgan nodded thoughtfully. "We seem to have found a little bit of stability. The Ackerman investigation is wrapping up, and we have food... there hasn't been any rioting since news of the shipment broke."

"And I want out," Adam said firmly. "I did my part, and other people paid a price for it. I don't want... I don't want a big life. I did my part."

Morgan frowned. "I assumed you'd be running for the presidency... I was already thinking up ideas for your campaign."

"Why don't you think up ideas for yours instead? You'd have my endorsement, if you wanted it."

"Of course I'd want it," Morgan retorted. "You're the man who brought food and freedom to the people. But I think you should reconsider. Even one term could be excellent for...."

"No." Adam's voice was firm, but he smiled. "I have a more important campaign in mind." He looked down at Remy, then back at Morgan. "I have *one* voter I need to convince."

"You're going to walk away from it all?" Morgan sounded as if he wasn't sure whether to be impressed or disgusted.

"I'm walking toward something else," Adam replied.

"Interesting. An election. And you wouldn't be running." Morgan was already thinking it through, already strategizing. It was the quality that would make him a strong leader, and Adam could admire it without being envious.

"But I'm still in charge for now, so keep me informed. Remy's going to sleep soon, so I'll be at the office in an hour or so."

"Will do," Morgan replied, and the comm screen went blank.

"I'll sleep when I want," Remy said slowly, with just a hint of petulance.

"Of course you will. And you'll want to pretty soon, 'cause you're already starting to fade. You've got to get your rest, Remy. Those spiders can't do *all* the healing on their own."

"You're sure?" Remy asked, and Adam knew he wasn't asking about the spiders.

"I never wanted the job. And now's as good a time as any to get out."

"So then what?"

"I have no idea," Adam admitted. "I don't think I care, really. Antonia's still got money, and she's offered her hospitality. Would you *finally* agree to go to Europe, if things were going smoothly here?"

"Me?"

"Yes. You." Adam leaned down and kissed Remy's temple. "Because you were wrong, on the roof. Wrong that we don't make sense, or that we can't last together. If you don't want to be with me, there's nothing I can do about that. But I love you. More than anything. More than my life, and absolutely more than your stupid hang-ups about being from different backgrounds or classes or anything else. I love you, Remy, and I want to be with you for as long as you'll let me, and I do not give a good goddamn what anybody else says about any of it." He took a breath and tried to calm down a little. "So if you want to go to Europe, I'll go there with you. If you want to stay here, I'll stay here. I'll follow you wherever you lead us, Remy. Forever."

Remy's eyes were wide before he squeezed them shut. He stayed like that for so long that Adam would have believed he'd fallen asleep if he hadn't seen the tension still wrinkling Remy's forehead. Finally, his eyes opened again, dark and impossibly deep, and he looked at Adam. "Not Europe," he said faintly.

Adam let himself breathe again. He wasn't being denied completely, at least. "Wherever you want," he vowed.

This time when Remy's eyes shut, it was in exhaustion, and Adam stayed with him a few minutes to be sure he was well settled, then stood to go. He stopped at the doorway and looked back toward the bed. Remy would survive, and be strong again, and if Adam was very, very lucky, he'd be there to see it all.

In the meantime, though, he had a country to run. One last look, then he turned and strode resolutely down the hall. The sooner he left, the sooner he could return. And the return to Remy was all that was important.

"So, you're 100 percent better, then?" Morgan was smiling, asking as a concerned friend, but Adam knew him too well to believe that there wasn't more to the questions, somehow.

Remy seemed cautious, as well. He squinted at Morgan, then said, "Ninety-nine percent." His gaze shifted to Adam as he added, "There's still a little problem they haven't resolved."

Adam groaned in amused exasperation. "They did *not* leave a nanobot in your chest, Remy."

"Yeah, they did." Remy pointed at a spot just below his collarbone and looked at Morgan. "Right there. I can feel him, still crawling around."

Morgan seemed unsure of how to respond. "I thought patients couldn't feel nanobots...."

"They *can't*." Adam wrapped his arm around Remy's shoulders and hugged him from behind. "Remy's hallucinating."

"And hallucinations are only enough to take 1 percent away from your health score?" Morgan asked. He'd loosened up a bit, since the election. Apparently the burden of being in charge of a continent made him realize that he wasn't able to control every aspect of every social conversation. And maybe Adam's enthusiastic endorsement of him had clarified the potential friendliness of their relationship.

But Adam needed to remember that this was Morgan, and that meant he always, *always* had a plan. "He's healthy. Is there a specific reason you're asking?"

Morgan nodded slowly. "There is." He walked further out onto the apartment balcony. The place was tiny compared to the presidential suite, but it had a good view of the river, and Adam and Remy couldn't afford much now that they were both unemployed. "Have you made plans for yourself? I know that Remy's health was your first priority, but now that he's better...." Morgan looked over with a grin. "Now that he's better, I'm trying to figure out how to best take advantage of your abilities. And I was wondering if you'd be up to a little travel."

"We're not going to Europe," Remy growled.

Morgan looked only a little surprised. "No. I was thinking of somewhere a little further away. Well, somewhere *much* further away." He smiled at their expressions. "The colonies are setting up a capital city. Well, more like a capital village, really, but the size of their population does *not* reflect their importance as our ally and trading partner. I need to send an ambassador, and I hoped you might consider the post."

"Me?" Adam stared at Morgan and tried to figure out the best response. "Me?" he asked again.

"You've already established a good relationship with them. They trust you. They trust Remy. You'd be great for the job. And it would be good for me too," he admitted with a grin. "I'd like to get you far enough away that people aren't always looking to you instead of accepting me as their leader, but I want you on my side so I can still rely on you for advice." He nodded in satisfaction. "This would be perfect."

It was an exciting idea. But Adam had a single priority in his life, and it had nothing to do with finding a governmental post for himself. "Let me get back to you," he said. "We'll talk."

Morgan nodded, and smiled at Remy. "Whatever's best for you," he agreed. His comm beeped, and he shook his head. "That was almost five minutes without interruption. I think it might be a new record." He glanced down at the screen and then stood up. "I'm needed." He extended his hand to both of them, smiled, and said, "I'll let myself out." Then he was gone.

Adam stayed where he was and wrapped both his arms around Remy. "The colonies," he mused, and he kissed Remy's neck right below his ear. There was a ticklish spot there, one that made Remy squirm delightfully.

"That's what you want?" Remy asked. He shoved gently and Adam loosened his arms enough that Remy could turn around and face him. "To be a diplomat?"

"I want you," Adam replied. "I could stay right here in this crappy apartment with you for the rest of my life, and I'd be perfectly content."

"You'd get bored."

"I wouldn't."

"I would. Maybe." Remy turned again and looked toward the water. "The colonies," he said thoughtfully. "But you can't be with a whore, not if you're a diplomat. That's a fancy job."

"Then I don't want it," Adam said firmly. "But Morgan knows

your history, and he knows I'm not going anywhere without you. If he suggested me for the job, it's because he thinks it'll be okay. I think things are more casual in the colonies. I think they're more willing to accept fresh starts."

"Hey, Challoner?" Remy turned around again. He edged his hands in between them, and braced them gently on Adam's chest. "I want you to be happy. It's more important than *me* being happy." He pinched a little when Adam opened his mouth to respond. "Wait. I know what you're going to say. You don't want that, because it's a leftover from me being a whore, and it's a sign that I don't value myself, and all that bullshit. But, Challoner... what if it just means I love you?" He grinned at Adam's expression. "Seriously. I want what's best for *you*, not for me. I respect you, and admire you, and trust you. I like being with you, and I miss you when you're not around. I think... I could be wrong, here, and of course I can't be trusted to know my own feelings, but I'm going to call it love." He tightened his fingers in the fabric of Adam's shirt, and the trace of shyness in his expression made it clear that he wasn't feeling nearly as casual about this as he seemed. "So, yeah. I love you. That's what I'm saying." He peered carefully at Adam. "Any thoughts about that?"

No. Adam had no thoughts. Nothing that finite. All he had was a warm, beautiful light burning in his chest, burbling through his brain, and surely extending through all the rest of his body and outward until it illuminated the universe. "You love me," he said quietly.

Remy nodded slowly, and then leaned as if he wanted to step away a little, but Adam's arms caught him firmly. "Is it okay?" Remy asked, and then he couldn't speak anymore because Adam's lips were crushing his.

It was as if Adam had been set free. The doubts, the restraint, the fear—all gone. Remy was his, and he was Remy's. He spun them around, leaned Remy against the wall and surged in to meet him, their bodies strong and hard against each other.

Adam pulled away for just a moment, just far enough to look and be sure that this was all real, and Remy stretched his hands up over his head in a languorous, catlike reach. His fingers found the wall sconce and locked around it, leaving his torso extended and vulnerable, his back arched in a perfect, graceful curve.

Adam forced himself to go slowly. He reached out with trembling fingers and undid the buttons on Remy's shirt. He slid the fabric to the sides and leaned down to gently kiss the twisted scars in the middle of Remy's otherwise flawless body, then let his hands stretch out to cover the rest of Remy's skin.

Adam had touched Remy before, but never like this. In the past, he'd explored and comforted. As Remy's recovery had progressed, he'd teased and tried, with some success, to arouse. Now, though, he was claiming. This was his. Adam had surrendered himself to Remy long ago, but had never been able to own Remy in return. Now, he did. He tasted his prize, chose a spot on Remy's chest and sucked hard, leaving his mark, and then looked up to see Remy watching him fondly. "I'm yours," Remy confirmed. "For as long as you want me."

"Forever, then." Adam straightened and kept his eyes on Remy as he peeled off his own shirt. He leaned forward and let their bodies meet skin to skin. The hair on the back of Remy's head was soft as Adam gripped it and gently turned Remy's head to whatever angle was best for Adam's kisses. He ran his other hand down, ghosting over his own hardness to find Remy... unaroused. Still completely soft.

Adam jerked away and found Remy watching him carefully. "Forever seeming like a long time, suddenly?" Remy asked. There was only a trace of bitterness in his tone.

"No." Adam tried to relax, and think. "I love you. You... love me. This is sex. It's separate."

Remy nodded slowly. "But important." He lowered his hands from the wall sconce, and shrugged. "I want you. Not exactly... not quite the same way you want me. I might not get hard, or come, or... whatever else it is you think makes sex 'count'." He looked at Adam with dark, serious eyes and said, "But it counts for me. Feeling close to you to, feeling safe with you... I've had sex with a lot of people, but I've never felt like that with anyone but you."

"You wanted me... in Baryman's elevator. And right afterward. You were hard, then." Adam had been clinging to that memory for quite a while, and he didn't want to give it up.

Remy nodded slowly. "Adrenaline, maybe? Or... or something else, I don't know. I'll look into it. I'll go to doctors, or whatever, and try to make it happen. But, Challoner, I'll be doing that for you, not for me. You know?"

"I feel like I'd just be taking. Like I'd just be one more of a long line of assholes using your body without giving you anything in return."

Remy exhaled sharply through his nose, almost a snort. "Challoner. I'm not going to Europe. I'm not eating any of that squid bullshit you were trying to feed me the other day. I don't care if I *have* eaten it before, I don't like it and I'm not eating it again. I'm not believing you *or* the doctors when they tell me they took all the spiders out of me." He grinned quickly. "See? I can say 'no'."

He pushed off the wall and steered Adam toward the door of their apartment, jabbing at his chest as he spoke, herding and controlling Adam's movements. "I want to talk about going to the colonies. If we go there, I want to raise chickens, and I probably won't let you eat any of them. Just eggs. Whether we're in the colonies or here, we'll have a cat, and if we aren't in an apartment, I want a dog. I want you to kiss me on my neck every single day, at least twice a day, from now on."

He raised an eyebrow. "See? I can say 'yes'. I know what I don't want, and I know what I want." Remy had guided them to the bedroom, and he stood in the middle of the floor, staring at Adam as if daring him to disagree. "I want you to fuck me, Challoner."

He grinned suddenly. "And I want you to fucking *enjoy* it, and spare me your guilty-rich-boy bullshit." He shrugged out of his shirt and let if fall to the floor, then stepped forward and fell to his knees in front of Adam, his hands on Adam's fly. "I want this. I want you."

Adam didn't say anything. He couldn't. But he didn't resist as Remy unzipped his fly and guided his pants and underwear down over his ass. He stood, unable to do anything but watch as Remy slid his lips over Adam's cock, the tight warmth so perfect it took his breath away. This was Remy, doing this for him, because he wanted to. "I love you, Remy."

Remy's hum of agreement sent vibrations to all the right places, and Adam knew he needed to get back in control or this would be over far too quickly. He ran his fingers through Remy's hair and tugged, and the man rose obediently. Fuck. Adam didn't want to be thinking of that word. Submissively? That was problematic too. Then Remy's face was in front of Adam's, his brows arched, his eyes calm and challenging. "Can I help you with something?" he asked mockingly.

Remy wasn't beaten. He wasn't defeated or oppressed. He was *Remy*. "You can get your damn pants off," Adam said. He gave himself a moment to think. "And then I want you on the bed, on your back, your legs hanging off this side."

Remy grinned. "I like the sound of this," he said, and he shed his remaining clothes with practiced ease. The artfulness of his pose on the bed stirred something in Adam, an awareness that Remy had done this before, countless times. He'd been trained, praised and punished based on his ability to seduce, and that was something that was always going to be part of him. Adam looked up suddenly and caught Remy watching him.

"I'm getting tired of your brain, Challoner. Turn it off and get your ass over here."

Adam smiled. "No, this time… this time my brain was being good." He walked over anyway, and he leaned forward enough for his hand to reach Remy's mouth. He slipped a single finger between Remy's soft lips and tried not to groan as Remy circled his tongue around it gently, then opened his mouth to release the spit-covered digit. "This time," Adam said as he guided his wet finger to Remy's ass, "I was thinking that everything you've gone through has made you who you are. And I love who you are." He slipped his finger gently inside. "I love all of you. I might wish things had been easier for you, but I don't want you to be any different than what you are." He wet one of his other fingers in his own mouth, then returned his hand to Remy's ass and slipped both fingers in. "Don't go to the doctors unless *you* want to. If you're happy this way, I'm happy too."

Remy nodded, then arched his back with a soft groan as Adam slipped another finger inside. This was almost certainly more preparation than someone with Remy's experience would ever need, but Adam was enjoying himself, and Remy wasn't complaining. Then Remy opened his eyes. "I have to talk to the doctor about the chest-spider anyway. I can ask for a referral then."

"I love you," Adam said, and he reached forward with one of his hands to lace his fingers with Remy's. The other hand guided his cock into position.

"I love you too," Remy said, the last word a little breathless as Adam eased inside. Remy used his free hand to lift his balls out of the way as he wrapped his legs around Adam's back, pulling him in deeper. "Now, get to it."

Adam couldn't have refused even if he'd wanted to. His body moved on its own, finding the primal rhythm it had been missing for too long. Remy moved in perfect harmony, enhancing every thrust and amplifying every sensation. There was no finesse to it, barely any technique, just Adam claiming one more part of Remy's body, a part that was shared freely and lovingly.

When Adam gasped and lost his rhythm, Remy took over and kept the motion rolling, encouraging and driving Adam to a deeper orgasm. And when the last wave of pleasure faded and Adam let himself collapse forward, Remy was there with warm arms and gentle kisses. "There, now, that wasn't so terrible, was it?" Remy whispered, and he nipped Adam's earlobe in punctuation.

"I survived," Adam managed. He found Remy's mouth for a long, deep kiss. "I might even be able to force myself to do it again someday."

"Well, don't get carried away," Remy said primly.

"Hey, Remy?" Adam kissed his way down Remy's jaw and found the tender spot beneath his ear. "Was this where you wanted to get kissed, twice a day?"

"Mmmm, yeah," Remy purred. "That's the spot."

"I was thinking that two times a day might not be quite enough. I was thinking more like... two *hundred* times. Any problem with that?"

"No complaints at all, Challoner," Remy said, and he arched his neck to give Adam more room. "No complaints at all."

EPILOGUE

On Earth, people called it the Colony Planet. Scientists referred to it as C-37L, and its residents had started trying to rebrand it as either Eden or Freedom. After living there for a little over a year, Adam Challoner thought of it as Home.

He shifted impatiently within the confines of his seat in the reentry shuttle. He'd been away for almost a month, half of that time spent in the cold sterility of an interplanetary cruiser, half on Earth. The trip had been important, a key step in reinforcing the hard-won relationships between the two planets, but damn it, he wanted to be home. He turned in his seat, craning his neck forward and trying to see out the front windshield of the shuttle.

"Not much longer, Ambassador." Celina Holst's voice was light and teasing. She was a brilliant astrophysicist with a keen sense of humor. While he'd been on Earth, Adam had introduced her to his newly ex-wife and wondered if he'd live to regret it; Antonia was a force to be reckoned with on her own, and probably didn't need the help of a sympathetic ally. "I'm sure he's just as excited as you are."

Adam didn't bother pretending not to understand. "Maybe not quite. He sent me messages every day, but they were almost all about the farm. He's got so many chickens he's starting to sell the eggs, and he wants to start raising alpacas, he says. Apparently their fiber is excellent for spinning, and he wants to start weaving...." Adam broke off. He was getting carried away, babbling about his favorite topic. "His father was a weaver," he finished lamely.

Celina just nodded. After a week on the cruiser with Adam, she was well aware of his enthusiasm for the topic of Remy Stone.

There was a lurch as the craft broke through a layer of the atmosphere, and then the calm voice of the pilot letting them know they'd be on the ground within minutes. Adam nervously gripped the small vial of orange pills in his right hand. It had been Remy's suggestion that Adam pick them up, and Adam hadn't argued, but there was going to have to be some discussion, at some point....

Then the shuttle lurched to a halt and Adam shoved the vial into his pocket so he'd have two hands free for unbuckling his restraints and grabbing his luggage. He knew he should wait for Celina, but she was openly laughing at him, now. "Go," she said as soon as the shuttle door began to open. "Go find him."

Adam went. He jogged down the walkway, scanned the small crowd waiting to greet arrivals or board the shuttle, and didn't see the face he was looking for. Where was he? Adam stepped back up the walkway for a better view. Still, nothing. Just as Adam was about to get alarmed, he saw movement in the shadow behind a concrete post, and he leaped off the gang plank and headed in that direction.

When he was close enough, he said, "Are you being shy, or being a ninja?"

Remy's diffident shrug made it clear that he wasn't being a ninja. But he stepped forward eagerly when Adam closed the distance between them and his kiss was as warm and open as Adam had come to expect. It was probably just as well that they weren't in the open, really, because Adam didn't want to restrain himself in order to conform to the standards of ambassadorial behavior.

When he finally needed to come up for breath, he pulled away just enough to see Remy's beautiful, smiling face. "We should get out of here," Adam said.

"Yeah," Remy agreed. He hooked his fingers through Adam's, then added, "You need to cook me some dinner. I've practically been starving to death without you here."

"You didn't feel inspired to cook anything yourself?"

Remy shook his head. "That's your job, Challoner. I'm the farmer, you're the cooker. And the cleaner."

"And the ambassador," Adam added mildly.

"We talked about this. It's fine for you to have a hobby, but you can't let it get in the way of your true responsibilities." Remy nodded sagely. "Looking after me is your top priority."

"Yeah. It is," Adam agreed, and that earned him another quick kiss before Remy tugged him out into the daylight and guided him toward their rover.

Remy drove, as usual, and Adam watched him. His movements were quick and confident, his expression open, so whatever had made him shy at the shuttle port was clearly resolved. Remy had moods, sometimes, and Adam didn't mind at all.

Remy pulled over to the side of the dirt track when they reached Carralina's cottage, and she looked up from the garden she was pulling weeds out of. Livia called out a greeting and swung down from her perch in the apple tree, and Breanne came out on the porch long enough to wave.

"You made it back safely, then," Carralina said, and she tweaked a dial on the side of her visual apparatus, probably to compensate for the shade cast by the roof of the rover. "It's good to see you. We'll miss Remy at the dinner table, though."

Remy grinned quickly in Challoner's direction, no trace of guilt on his face. "I said I'd been *practically* starving to death. Not completely."

"Was he eating all your food, Livia? Did Uncle Remy come over and eat everything in the house?" Adam smiled at the little girl, then burrowed around in his luggage until he pulled out the stuffed giraffe he'd bought for her. "See this, Livia? It's a real animal that used to live down on Earth. They'd be twenty feet tall, or maybe more. There aren't any alive anymore, but we still have some of their DNA. We're thinking about setting up some land up here and seeing if we can get them growing again. Do you think that would be a good idea?"

Livia squinted skeptically at the stuffed animal, then looked back up at Adam. "Do we eat them? Or milk them?"

"Not really, no. I guess we could, but that wouldn't be the idea."

"Ride them?"

She was Dar's daughter, all right. "No, I don't think we'd ride them."

"It'd be a just 'cause." Remy said. He and the little girl seemed to have a shared understanding, an unwritten code that Adam could never quite break. "Just 'cause they're giraffes, and we like them, and they'd make things more interesting."

She looked at the stuffed animal again, then nodded solemnly at Adam. "Yeah. Okay. I think it's a good idea." She smiled at Remy as she added, "Just 'cause!"

She had turned to take her toy back up the tree when Carralina coughed ostentatiously. Livia whirled like a top and said, "Thanks for the graffe!" before spinning off again and running for the trunk.

"They're really thinking of doing that?" Carralina asked.

"They are. There's people who are worried about taking land out of production, worried that we'll end up with a food shortage, but those are the Earthside politicians. The leaders up here seem more open to the idea, and it'll be their call, ultimately." Adam thought of the heated meetings he'd been in on Earth, and the cool intelligence with which Shana Waters had stood her ground. Toni's campaign for women's rights couldn't have found two better examples of powerful, wise women than Shana Waters and

Celina Holst. If Shana wanted giraffes, she'd have them, especially if Celina's wormhole explorations led to the discovery of other planets where food could be produced. It was an exciting time, all of Earth buzzing with potential and curiosity. Adam was happy to be back home, far away from it all.

"I'll be over tomorrow to help with that solar panel," Remy said as he shifted the rover back into gear. "And you should all come by for dinner sometime soon. Adam needs to thank you for filling in for him while he was away."

"I do," Adam agreed. "Words for now, but I'll absolutely try to return the favor. Thanks for looking after him."

Carralina smiled and went back to her garden, and Remy drove the rest of the way down the dirt track until it dead-ended at their homestead. The house and the barn were both constructed of wood; an absolute luxury on Earth was a standard building material on a planet with so much remaining forest. They had solar panels on their roofs, supplying all the electricity needed for the buildings, vehicles, and tools of the farm. There was a sizable vegetable garden fenced off against the rabbits that some fool had allowed to escape from captivity a few decades ago, and.... "What is that? A new building?"

Remy glanced over in the direction Adam was pointing, then shrugged. "No, I don't think so."

"It is," Adam insisted. "It's... Remy, is that a dog house?"

"Oh, that," Remy said. "Yeah, it's the dog house. But they only use it when I have to go out and I lock them in the pen... otherwise they like to be inside."

"We have dogs now?"

Remy raised an eyebrow. "Rose and Daisy. We've always had them." He swung out of the rover, hooked Adam's bags out of the back, and started for the house.

"We haven't always had dogs, Remy." Adam wasn't sure whether to be alarmed or amused by this situation.

Remy dropped the bags on the ground and headed over to the dog pen. "Girls!" he said as he approached, and there was an excited yipping followed by a squirming jumble of brown fur. Remy unhooked the latch and the dogs rolled out through the gate, almost knocking him over with their enthusiastic greeting. He looked up as Adam approached. "Come on, Adam. You remember Rose and Daisy." He captured one of the pups and pointed her muzzle in Adam's direction. "Look who's back, Daisy!"

The dog obediently scrambled over to greet Adam, and he bent to pet her. "These are puppies, Remy. Are they even old enough to leave their mother? There's no way they were here before I left."

"They're orphans," Remy said seriously. "I've been bottle-feeding them, but they're on solid food now." He shook his head. "You should start writing stuff down, if your memory is this bad."

Adam let it go. Remy was playing a game. It was a strange game, and there was no point to it since Adam would never have even tried to get in the way of Remy adopting new pets, but if it entertained Remy, that was reason enough for it. "Should we go find some food?" he suggested.

"You don't want to say 'hi' to the other animals first?" And there it was, the tiny gleam of light in Remy's eye that made it clear that Adam's surprises weren't quite over.

"How many other animals are there?" Adam grinned. "I guess I forget."

"Well, the chickens, of course," Remy said, waving an arm in the direction of the field where the birds were roaming. Without predators, the chickens were able to go where they wanted, even if it made egg-collecting a bit more difficult. Remy was apparently willing to suffer through the inconvenience in the name of chicken freedom. The man had a strange bond with the hens. But now he was walking away, the pups frolicking around his feet as he looked over his shoulder and said, "And the ducks."

"Ducks?" Ducks were new.

"By the pond," Remy prompted.

"The pond? I... I forgot we had a pond."

"We do," Remy confirmed, and he led the way to a little hollow in the ground where, it was true, he and Adam had discussed installing a pond. The expanse of water was a clear indication that Remy had gone a little beyond just discussing the idea.

"It's very nice," Adam said carefully.

"It's deep enough for swimming. You like to swim in it."

"Even with the ducks?"

"It's a big pond, and they're small ducks. You don't mind sharing."

"Okay. And what are we doing with the ducks? They aren't for meat, are they?"

"No. Eggs."

"Excellent. We can never have too many eggs...."

"I've got a market for them. Everything's under control."

"Any other animals I should meet? I mean, greet, after having seen them the last time I was here?"

"Well, there's the trout, in the pond, but there's not much 'meeting' to do with them. We can eat them, though. I've thought about it, and I'm okay with eating the fish." He waited for Adam's nod of agreement, then added, "And of course there's the five cats."

"Five? Not three?"

"No. Five. You remember."

"I guess I do."

They started back up the path and were just passing the barn when Adam heard an unfamiliar snuffling sound from behind the shed. He looked at Remy. The whinny made Remy grin. "Oh, the horse! The horse... yeah, the horse is new."

"And is he going to give eggs too?"

"Of course not. He's a retiree."

"A retiree?"

"Harold Dean used him to haul logs out of the forest. But he's old now and Harold has a new horse. So he was looking for a home for Boxer."

"And is he paying you for boarding his retired horse for him?"

"He's not charging me," Remy said. "So that's something. And Boxer isn't a big eater." He shrugged casually. "Besides, I'm rich. Some crazy guy down on Earth set up a trust fund for me, and I could keep fifty retired horses just on the income from the capital. So I'm not too worried."

"Okay," Adam said. And it was. Remy could keep fifty retired horses if he wanted to. He could raise chickens and ducks and swans and eagles, right in the house. He could dig a pond, and if he decided to fill it in tomorrow, that would be okay too. "I'm not worried, either."

He reached for Remy's hand and they walked together up to the house. Where they met the parrot.

It turned out that Remy wasn't quite as hopeless in the kitchen as he'd led Adam to believe. There was a vegetable stew simmering in the slow cooker and a loaf of fresh bread waiting to be sliced. "I bought it all," Remy confessed. "Premade. Tomorrow, you're back on kitchen duty. But for your first night back...." His smile grew a little wicked as he eased forward. "For your first night back, I thought there might be other priorities."

Kissing Remy would never get old, but it had grown wonderfully familiar. Remy was, as always, submissive and compliant in the face of Adam's demands, playful when Adam backed away, and more than anything else, just Remy. Adam could have stood there in the kitchen all day, pinning Remy against the pantry door, the counter, the kitchen table, any surface that would allow Adam to push into full contact with Remy's perfect body. But eventually Remy pulled his head away, and after a quick parting kiss to the special spot on Adam's neck, he asked, "Did you get them? The pills?"

Adam didn't want to think about that. It was too confusing, and he had no idea whether he was doing the right thing or not. But Remy was waiting for an answer. "Yeah," Adam said. "Sasha gave them to me."

Remy nodded in satisfaction. "Okay, then. Where are they?"

Adam reached into his pocket and reluctantly pulled out the vial. He didn't hand it to Remy, though. Instead, he wrapped his fingers around the plastic and said, "This is because you want it? All that stuff about orgasms not being all that matters... you don't think that way anymore? You're sure you want this? Because if you're doing it for me, don't. Okay?"

"Dr. Rosen says lots of men use them. He says they might lead to a dependency, but he says that after a year without them, my body's as clean as it's going to get. If I can't get hard now, it's not because my body's tweaking for the pills. It's just because... because that's the way I work, now. So taking the pills won't do any harm."

"Lots of men use them to deal with physical impotence. You've had the tests. There's nothing interfering with your arousal, not physically. I don't know if it's a good idea to take a pill that's designed to deal with a physical issue when you've got a psychological issue." And that didn't sound quite right. "Or no issue at all. I mean, if your brain is telling you that you've spent enough time having sex and it would like to focus on some other stuff... I think that's a reasonable message. I don't have a problem with that."

Remy looked down at Adam's clenched fingers and brought his own hands up to slowly, gently uncurl Adam's. "I want to try them," he said. "Nothing's written in stone. But I want to try."

"I love you, Remy," Adam said. It wasn't directly on topic, but it seemed like an important reminder.

"I love you too." Remy expertly flipped the lid open and fished out an orange caplet, dry-swallowing it with calm determination. "So, do you want to take this party to the bedroom?"

It felt wrong, or at least strange. Adam had found his own ways of dealing with Remy's impotence; he'd made sure that their sex was always lovemaking, had focused on finding ways to make Remy feel good that didn't involve arousal or climax. But Adam had always gotten off, and now it was clear that his fumbling efforts hadn't been satisfying Remy after all. Remy wanted more than Adam had been giving him, and now Remy was taking steps to make sure he got it. Adam felt guilty for having taken without giving, but if he was being honest, maybe there was a little hurt pride too. He'd done his best, and it hadn't been enough. But how petty was that, for him to be upset about Remy taking steps to deal with the trauma he'd suffered through? So, really, Adam was just giving himself one more thing to feel guilty about. Fantastic.

"Challoner?" Remy raised an eyebrow at him. "You too tired? Do you want to just hang out? Maybe play some cards?" He slowly undid the top button of his work shirt, his eyes as hot as his voice was cool. "I know, you're not as young as you used to be...."

And there went the guilt. "You are a piece of work, Remy." Adam crowded forward again and caught Remy's wrists, pulling them up over his head and then pinning them there. Adam pulled the pill bottle out of Remy's unresisting grip, tossed it somewhere in the direction of the counter, and then let himself go. Remy wanted something more than Adam had been giving him? Well, that was just fine, because Adam had more to give.

He kissed, licked, and nipped his way down Remy's neck and across his collarbone, then held Remy's wrists with one hand so he could use the other to start tugging on their clothes. The trip down the short hallway took a quarter of an hour, Adam stopping them whenever there was a new surface to press Remy against, and for once, he let himself think about himself. Instead of trying to make this good for Remy, he let himself take what he wanted. He'd always been so careful to control his desire, but it had been too long, and he wanted Remy too much. Remy had taken his pill, and if that worked, it worked. If it didn't, they'd find something else, but Adam would worry about all that later.

He'd felt Remy growing hard as they made their way down the hallway, and now in the bedroom, both of them wearing only pants, no shirts or shoes or socks, now it was time for Adam to enjoy Remy's cock with all of his senses. As always, Adam watched Remy closely as he stripped him out of his clothes, but this time it was for Adam's pleasure, not because he wanted to be sure Remy was okay. Remy was fine. He was more than fine, he was perfect, his eyes wide as Adam kissed his way down his chest and finally pulled far enough away to see Remy's dark, hard cock curving up toward his stomach. It was as beautiful as Adam had known it would be, and he pressed a kiss to the head, then opened his mouth to let himself taste Remy's arousal. He felt like a member of some primitive religion, worshipping the mighty phallus, and then he turned his brain off and let himself just enjoy. This was Remy's blood-hardened flesh, his arousal. His rapid, shallow breathing....

Adam straightened quickly and took another look at Remy's face. "You're not just hard. You're excited. You're turned on."

"Yeah," Remy said. He let Adam see his amazement for just a moment, then brought back the teasing arrogance as he said, "So? What are you going to do about it?"

"A lot," Adam vowed. He surged forward and drove Remy back until his knees hit the bed and he let himself fall. He watched as Adam shucked off his own clothes, then opened his legs to welcome him onto the mattress. "You're beautiful," Adam said, and he returned his mouth to Remy's cock. Remy's gasp was the sweetest music Adam could imagine and he was tempted to keep going, to suck Remy over the edge and take the victory. But he wanted more. He watched Remy's eyes track his hand to the bedside to pick up the lube, and watched them widen as Adam squeezed a generous amount onto Remy's own cock. "Okay?" Adam asked. "I've been thinking about this. I want you inside me. Okay?"

Remy nodded wordlessly and stared down to where Adam's fingers were wrapped around him, jacking him slow and easy. Adam had been thinking about this, and had spent some of the endless hours of travel in his bunk using his fingers to prepare his ass for an intrusion it hadn't felt in a couple of decades. But he was still nervous as he shifted into place, hovering over Remy's cock. "You're a bit bigger than I expected," he admitted, then he grinned. "You're always surprising me."

"I'm going to roll you over and surprise you hard if you don't get on with it," Remy said through a tightened jaw, and Adam realized that he'd been rubbing himself against the head of Remy's cock, teasing the sensitized flesh.

"Sorry," he said, and he lowered himself. The angle was wrong. Or something... something wasn't working. There was blunt pressure, but no penetration, and it was beginning to really hurt.

Remy rolled his eyes. "Fucking rookie," he grunted, and he brought his hand between their bodies, shifting his cock a little and guiding it to a better position. He tickled Adam's hole with his finger, eased it inside, pulled it out, and shook his head. "You need some prep, Challoner, otherwise it's going to hurt."

"I want it to hurt," Adam growled, and this time when he lowered his body, Remy guided himself into place.

Adam tilted his head back and breathed in hard through his nose. Damn it. He'd forgotten the feeling. There was pain, yes, and maybe Remy was right that a little more prep would have been a good idea, but there was also an intensity, a vulnerability, that no amount of stretching would have lessened. This was Remy, gritting his teeth to hold still while Adam allowed himself to be invaded. "Ohhh," Adam groaned, and then he felt Remy's hands on his thighs, reaching around to the muscles of his ass, kneading and soothing.

"Take it slow," Remy said softly. "You're okay. You're doing great." He squirmed a little, actually easing his cock partway out as he sat up and pulled Adam further onto his lap. "You're good," he said, and then he kissed Adam, soft and sweet. "You think you've proved your point? You want to switch it up, now?"

Adam moved cautiously, a gentle experiment that made Remy moan in appreciation. "No. I don't want to switch." He set up a slow rhythm, not even trying to be as graceful and sinuous as Remy always was in this position. "I'm good."

"You're great," Remy said, and he wrapped his hand around Adam's half-softened cock. "You're beautiful. I love you."

And then Remy couldn't say anymore because Adam was kissing him, their tongues dancing more delicately but no less intimately than their bodies. Remy's cock was hard and insistent inside Adam, and as the flush spread from Remy's neck down his chest and up onto his face, Remy began to move his hips, tiny, gentle thrusts in time with Adam's more vigorous movements. Adam was so enchanted he almost forgot about his own climax. This was what Remy looked like when he was truly excited. This was what he looked like just before he came. This was how his breathing hitched, how he lost the coordination to even kiss properly, how his eyes unfocused... and finally, how he arched his whole body, his head falling backward just before the cords in his neck tightened, how he gasped and thrust and lost the control that he'd clung to as long as Adam had known him.

By the time Remy's body had finally relaxed, Adam had stopped moving. He'd just witnessed something more beautiful than he'd ever imagined, and it seemed silly to worry about something as petty as his own orgasm.

But Remy apparently had different ideas. "Roll over," he ordered, and after a moment's pause Adam obediently lifted himself off Remy's softening cock and rolled onto his back. Remy snuggled in to his side, his head on Adam's shoulder, and it was so close to their usual sleep position that Adam wondered if Remy was forgetting about Adam's orgasm after all. But then Remy propped himself up on one elbow and leaned over to kiss Adam while he wrapped his free hand around Adam's cock. "Thank you," he murmured. "I enjoyed that."

"You came," Adam replied. There wasn't much that would make him pull away from Remy's kisses, but that statement needed to be repeated. "You came!"

"And no pill, for that," Remy said proudly. "I did it all by myself."

"Well, I'd like to think you had a little help."

Remy tightened his fingers around Adam's cock, bringing him just to the edge of pain, just the way he liked it. "A lot of help," he agreed, and then they were kissing again. It wasn't long before it was Remy's turn to watch Adam's climax. A more usual sight, to be sure, but still one that Remy seemed to enjoy.

"So," Adam said, just before he drifted off to sleep. "Little orange pills. Maybe not such a bad thing."

"Maybe not," Remy agreed, and he nestled in against Adam's shoulder and said no more.

THE pills were a success, and over the next few days just the sight of the little vial became enough to get Adam's blood pounding. But on the evening of the third day after his return to the planet, Adam returned home to find Remy sitting at the kitchen table, the bottle of pills in his hand and a confused frown on his face. Somehow, Adam didn't think the vial was a precursor to sex, not this time.

"What?" he asked, although he wasn't sure he wanted to know. "What's wrong?"

"Nothing," Remy said slowly. "Not wrong."

Adam pulled out the chair next to Remy and sank into it. Close enough to provide support if needed, far enough to give Remy some space. "So... what's up? What's got you looking like that?"

"I got a comm message from Sasha. About the pills."

It was Adam's turn to frown. "They're not dangerous, are they? You swore to me that they were fine, and Dr. Rosen said they were safe...."

"They're safe." Remy snorted in disbelief. "They're completely safe." He shook his head, then lifted the comm tablet off the table and shoved it in Adam's direction. "Watch the message."

Adam took a deep breath before he hit the play button. Everything had been going so smoothly.... Sasha's smooth face filled the screen, but instead of his usual professional smile, his grin was almost nervous.

"Remy, baby. Hi." Sasha looked down, then back up, and made a face. "I have no idea if you're going to be thanking me for this or if you're going to be really, really angry." Another twisted expression before he took a deep breath and said, "Baby, I meant well. I hope you believe that. The thing is... you don't need those pills, Remy! There's nothing wrong with you. You've got a good man, and a good body, and there's no reason in the world you should need chemicals in order to put those two good things together and make something great. So I think... Remy, I really, really hope... that you've just gotten yourself tied up in knots about all this, believing you can't do something that really you can. You know sex is all in the mind, baby." The next words came out so quickly they took a moment to register in Adam's brain. "So, Remy, I gave your man some sugar pills instead of the real drugs. A placebo. I have a friend who works in a pharmacy and I took the regular pills down and showed him the casings, and he found some that match, and... he filled them up with some sort of mineral oil or something. I don't know what, but the thing is, Remy, there wasn't any medicine in them." He paused long enough for Adam to take a quick look at Remy, but then Sasha spoke again and Adam returned his gaze to the screen. "I was going to try to get in touch with you and see how they worked, but let's face it, Remy... you're a pretty good liar when you want to be. So I wasn't sure you'd tell me the truth if the pills didn't work, and then you'd be walking around thinking they'd lost their effect when really they hadn't been real medicine to begin with. I didn't want that, baby, so I decided I'd better come clean. Your man's been home for a few days so I'm sure you've had a chance to use them by now. Look, Remy, if they didn't work, I will send a new batch out on the next mail cruiser, I promise. No tricks, no placebos. I hope you'll trust me with that. And I really, really hope you'll believe that I had good intentions with all this." Sasha reached out as if he were going to turn off the comm recorder, then grinned and waggled his eyebrows. "And I really, really hope you've been having great sex with your fine man with no chemical assistance, because, damn, Remy, wouldn't that be excellent?" His smile was more restrained as he said, "So, I hope you get in touch with me and let me know how it went. Sorry, baby." And then the screen went blank.

Adam stared at it for a little longer, then raised his face cautiously. "This... it's surprising, obviously, but it's good news, isn't it?"

Remy didn't look too sure. "Without the pills...."

"You can still take the pills," Adam said quickly. "Some people like a glass of wine, others like a hot bath. You like to take a pill filled with inert liquid. That's fine. Whatever."

"I feel crazy," Remy said. "I mean... that's all it was? Just a placebo?"

"Well, it sounds like it," Adam agreed. "I don't know. Did it feel the same as it used to?"

"Not really," Remy said slowly. "It felt... it's been more of a whole body thing. And I never used to be able to come without taking the other pill. But I've been doing fine with that."

"You have." Adam set the comm carefully down on the table. "Look, Remy, if you're upset with Sasha, I guess I can understand that. He tricked you, even if his intentions were good. But, come on... you're getting turned on naturally. Just my fine self, that's all you need! That's good news!" He tried to ease off a little. "For me, at least, it's really good news."

"I don't know," Remy said, but his shoulders were relaxing. "I guess." He paused, then looked up quickly and the light in his eye made it clear that everything was going to be okay. "But, damn, what's all this about wine and hot baths? Have you been holding out on me? I think you'd better pour me a nice vintage and then trot off to the bathroom to get that bath running." He leaned forward as if about to tell a secret, and whispered, "I like bubbles."

Adam took advantage of the proximity, leaning forward for a kiss. Remy held back for only a moment, then let it deepen, and when Adam tugged him to his feet, there was no resistance. Of course, there never had been. It wasn't compliance Adam wanted to see, it was excitement. He forced himself to take it slow, easing Remy around until his back was to the wall, running his hands all over Remy's tight body, everywhere but the one place that would let Adam know whether any of this was working. Slow, sensuous, clothes being stripped off, skin rubbing against skin, and absolutely no contact with Remy's groin.

When Remy's shoulders started to shake, it was alarming—until Adam realized the man was laughing. "What?" he demanded.

Remy grinned at him. "Hey, Challoner?" he said, and he laced his fingers through Adam's, then jerked their joined hands down to wrap around Remy's hard cock. "Got any questions?"

"Just one," Adam said, and he didn't even try to keep himself from grinning like a lunatic. "Now that you've got it, what do you want to do with it?"

"I've got a few ideas," Remy said. He pressed a quick kiss to the side of Adam's mouth and said, "I wasn't kidding about that bath, buddy. Let's go."

Remy started down the hallway, and Adam followed. He'd

follow Remy anywhere. And he was looking forward to the bubbles.

About the Author

Kate Sherwood, Cate Cameron, Catherine Dale... and probably a few new names, eventually. They're all one person.

One person who's lucky enough to get to live a bunch of extra lives through all the characters in her books, and who's trying desperately to keep all the lives organized into some sort of categories... so each name writes a different type of story.

But really, beneath the genre categories? All the stories will have some kind of humour, even in the darkest times. They'll all show characters who are far from perfect, but who are trying to be better.

Basic bio stuff? Kate/Cate/Catherine lives in Cottage Country, the water-filled world north of Toronto, Canada, the land where summers are sunny and crowded with visitors and winters are snowy and isolated. She loves it there. Not that she doesn't sometimes miss the city, especially when her internet is acting up or she wants something delivered!

She works full-time at a non-writing job but would love to shift into a more writing-centred life. There's a five-year plan. It might work....

OTHER BOOKS BY KATE SHERWOOD

For details, see www.booklives.com

Writing as Kate Sherwood (m/m)

All That Glitters – contemporary romance

Long Shadows, Embers, Darkness, Home Fires – four book contemporary action

Feral, Lap Dog, Twice Shy, Pure Bred – four book NA contemporary romance

Sacrati – fantasy/alt history

In Too Deep – NA contemporary romance

Chasing the Dragon – angst and adventure!

Mark of Cain – contemporary romance

The Fall, Riding Tall – two book contemporary romance

The Shift – contemporary fantasy novella – monster hunters!

Room to Grow – contemporary romance novella

The Pawn, The Knight – two book futuristic romance with plenty of angst

Poor Little Rich Boy – contemporary romance

More than Chemistry – light contemporary novella

Dark Horse, Out of the Darkness, Of Dark and Bright – three book contemporary romance with extras

Shying Away – NA romance

Lost Treasure – contemporary romance

Writing as Cate Cameron (m/f, YA)

The Billionaire's Forever Family – contemporary romance

Center Ice, Playing Defense, Winging It, Breakaway – contemporary YA hockey romance

Just a Summer Fling, Hometown Hero – contemporary small town romance

Shining Armor – contemporary romance (originally published under "Kate Sherwood")

Writing as Catherine Dale (YA, contemporary fantasy, general fiction—everything but romance!)

Dark Houses – Speculative YA